MOTHER
OF ALL
SECRETS

HER
OF ALL
SECRETS

A NOVEL

KATHLEEN M. WILLETT

LAKE UNION
PUBLISHING

Published by Lake Union Publishing, Seattle

www.apub.com

Amazon, the Amazon logo, and Lake Union Publishing are trademarks of Amazon.com, Inc., or its affiliates.

ISBN-13: 9781542038959
ISBN-10: 1542038952

Cover design by Eileen Carey

Printed in the United States of America

How do you like Mother's friends? Do you think they're pretty?

—*Daisy Buchanan, The Great Gatsby*

Prologue

I'm running, or trying to, at least—staggering along, wheezing, fighting to get as far away from that house as quickly as possible.

I used to love running, but I haven't even considered trying since having Clara. And I certainly didn't expect circumstances like these, in which I would *need* to.

But here I am.

There are a few people on the street; it's late, but it's New York, so there are always people. I hope I just seem like a jogger exercising at a slightly odd time and not someone fleeing a horrific scene that I won't ever be able to erase or unsee. I pray the people I pass can't see the blood, that the darkness of both the night and my clothing will protect me and my secrets. All of them.

I have no idea where to go. I'm only a few blocks from my own apartment, but going home isn't an option. I can't see my husband and baby right now. Can't risk catching a glimpse of myself in the mirror, either. I'm scared of the woman who would be looking back at me.

I just need to keep moving until I figure out what the hell to do.

The problem is that the me who agreed to do what we've done isn't really me. Not that I could tell you who that is. I haven't been me for months. I've been an exhausted, overwhelmed, depressed woman I don't even recognize. And this woman agreed to commit a violent crime. But she isn't me.

There were so many holes in the plan. Why couldn't I see them?

And now I'm going to lose everything. Clara. My sweet girl. What will you do without your mommy? What will I do without you? A life without you is no life at all. No matter how hard the past few months have been, I have never once doubted that I love you more than anything.

And even if we somehow get away with it—somehow, by some miracle—I'll never really be *me* again, because I will always be able to truthfully say: *we killed someone.*

We killed someone.

We killed someone.

Chapter One

Screams woke me, as they had every night (and morning, and afternoon) for the past eighty-six days. Immediately, my heart started pounding. Despite eighty-six days of practice, I still wasn't used to being yanked from sleep by shrieks. There was something so violent, so merciless about it, like it was some kind of military training drill I was being forced to undergo. Except this wasn't a drill—it was my life, and there was no end to it in sight. I felt fairly certain I would never sleep again.

I looked to my left and could just make out the slow rise and fall of Tim's shoulder blade. *Could he honestly be sleeping through this?* I wondered with an anger that surprised even me a little bit. *Seriously?* I checked my phone for the time, hoping it was at least 2:00 a.m. That would mean that I had been sleeping for nearly three hours. That maybe I'd feel okay tomorrow, even if the rest of the night was a disaster. Three hours was pretty good. But, predictably, I had no such luck. It was 11:53 p.m. Great. I had been sleeping for a glorious, blissful forty-five minutes.

I sighed as loudly as possible and made no effort to quiet my movements as I rose from tangled sheets, inadvertently kicking off a dirty towel as I did. I couldn't remember the last time I'd changed our sheets and properly made our bed. There was a distinct sour breast milk odor clinging to our room.

Tim stirred—*finally*—and mumbled, "You need anything?"

What I needed was to go somewhere remote and sleep for a week straight. To shower more than twice a week. To look in the mirror and actually recognize my reflection, to see me, Jenn, rather than the swollen, grumpy, leaky ghost of who I once was. To think about something other than this now eleven-pound alien who had taken over our home and lives. Better yet, for my husband to miraculously start lactating.

What I said instead of all these things, huffily, was "No. I got her."

I walked over to Clara's nook. She slept in our bedroom—our tiny apartment only had one bedroom—but we had her partitioned off to maintain some semblance of separation. Apparently, a little distance between the baby and the mom was important for longer sleep stretches. I'd read on a lactation website that "babies can smell the milk" and she would never stop crying if she knew I was near. "Jenn, get that baby out of your room as quickly as possible," my sister-in-law, too, had advised me enthusiastically. "As soon as we moved Tyler to his crib in his own room, he started sleeping through the night immediately!" But she wasn't exactly in the trenches with me: they lived in Connecticut in a huge house, and her kids were in middle school now. I didn't remind her that we didn't really have anywhere to move Clara, but I did order collapsible room dividers from Amazon that same afternoon, recharged with hope that this would be a game changer. So far, providing her with a makeshift cubicle had made no difference. At three months old, Clara had not slept more than three hours straight, and even three-hour stretches were a rare treat. Of course, that meant I hadn't slept more than three hours, either.

I stood over Clara's bassinet for a minute, watching her face contort as she vacillated between a shuddering whimper and an all-out wail. I'd read in *Bringing Up Bébé* that I should pause for a moment before picking her up and give her a minute to settle herself. She probably wasn't actually hungry, the book had advised, and the sooner babies started "doing their nights," the better for everyone. Well, obviously. But as much as I wanted to be a cool French parent, with a chill, self-soothing baby, her cry set off every alarm in my body, and the only way to turn off the alarms was to pick her up. And *pardonnez-moi*, but she *always* seemed hungry to me.

I picked her up, and she stopped crying as if I had flipped a switch. I nestled her cheek into my neck and padded back to bed, whispering, "Hi, sweet girl. Shh shh shh, you're okay, you're with Mama now." Sometimes it amazed me that as blind tired as I was, a part of me was still so relieved to see her. Sure, it wasn't ideal that she was awake throughout the night, but her being awake meant that she hadn't choked on her own spit-up or suffocated on her crib sheet, which was something I spent admittedly way too much time thinking about (and googling).

I flopped back down on the bed, holding Clara with one arm as I rearranged pillows behind me with my other, again not bothering to attempt to spare Tim from the commotion. If I was awake, Tim should be, too, although he didn't seem to be anymore, with his back still to me, steadily rising and falling. Our pediatrician had recently given us the green light to start phasing out night feeds, since Clara was growing well, but I knew I could return to sleep sooner if I just stuck her on a boob. It was pretty much the only thing that soothed her; I'd end up being awake even longer if I tried to get her back to sleep without feeding her, engaging in an exhaustive and most often fruitless routine of rocking and shh-ing and deliriously singing weird songs that I made up.

As Clara latched, I vaguely considered with guilt the large glass of wine—had I topped it off?—I had consumed just a few hours before. But the challenge of getting up and walking to the fridge and preparing a bottle of pumped milk right now felt insurmountable. Clara nursed contentedly, her eyelids drooping and fluttering as she did so, falling back to sleep within seconds. I closed my eyes and willed myself to stay awake through her feed. I was constantly dozing off while holding her, and I knew it wasn't safe; I could roll onto her, or she could roll off the bed. *Stay awake, stay awake,* was the last thing I remembered thinking when I opened my eyes to the clock showing 2:30 a.m., my neck a solid block from sleeping in such a contorted position, Clara stirring in my arms, crying out softly, ready to be fed once again.

Chapter Two

Later that morning, I was awoken not by Clara, whom I was still holding, but by Tim, who was sitting at the foot of the bed, already dressed for work and pulling up his stupid socks. They weren't really that stupid—in fact, I was pretty sure I'd bought them for him a couple of Christmases ago. That was just how I felt toward him and everything about him lately, especially when he woke me up, even though I could tell he was trying really hard not to. I couldn't help but resent the fact that he was actually sleeping at night and then getting dressed up to interact with other adults all day. From what I could see, his life hadn't really changed all that much since Clara was born, but mine had been turned upside down by this little person. I hadn't anticipated feeling so much hostility toward my husband when I envisioned our blissful first few months at home with our bundle of joy, but the truth was that his very presence made me livid sometimes. I still loved him, of course. I was just finding it remarkably difficult to be nice to him.

We'd been together for six years now and had met in the bathroom line at a Stephan Jenkins concert at City Winery. I was feeling high on the wine and the music, and I'd smiled at him when we made eye contact; he smiled his crooked smile back, unabashedly, and it was as if we already knew each other somehow. When I came out of the bathroom, he wasn't there anymore. I was relieved beyond measure when he found me upstairs a few minutes later and asked for my number.

It was just easy between us, from day one. I met him and didn't want to meet anyone else, and unlike before, with other guys, that feeling lasted. Our lives and even our friend groups merged seamlessly. When we moved in together, we barely argued about what to keep and what to get rid of, or who got which parts of the closet. He parted ways with his heinous and inexplicable cowboy boot collection without putting up a fight, and I willingly conceded that his pots and pans were much nicer than mine. It was all so straightforward. Prior to Clara, Tim and I had been one of those couples who pretty much never fought. Then again, what did we have to fight about back then? What to eat for dinner? Where to go for a weekend getaway? Whether to watch another episode of whatever show we were bingeing? Our lives were so blissfully uncomplicated. We'd arrogantly told ourselves—and even, embarrassingly, other people—that having a baby wouldn't change our dynamic. That this next chapter, starting our family, would only make us closer, an even stronger team. Cringeworthy stuff, in retrospect. And so far, very incorrect.

Of course, compounding the challenges we were facing as brand-new parents was the fact that I'd also lost my mom to cancer when I was six months pregnant. She had been an integral part of what I'd imagined when I pictured life as a new mom—that she'd be around, helping me with the baby, showing me how to bathe it, making lasagnas for me and Tim. Instead, she was buried in a cemetery in New Jersey, her breast cancer from ten years ago having returned with no warning or mercy. I missed her so much it made my insides howl. I thought of her constantly; every Clara-related question that popped into my head was a brutal reminder that I couldn't ask it of the one person I most wanted to. Tim had been a rock since her death, of course, supportive and loving, but I knew that my newfound resentment of him also stemmed from the fact that, through no fault of his own, he was not able to fully understand the depths of my loss and pain, having two healthy and eager parents.

And eager they were—Tim's mom often offered to drive up from Delaware to help out. But as I'd explained to Tim, the last thing I wanted was to give my mother-in-law a front-row seat to my 24-7 half-nude bodily fluid show. He'd gently asked her to hold off. They'd so far limited themselves to a single visit, when Clara was first born, but kind and well meaning as she was, his mom's presence only called attention to the absence of the one person I really needed.

On this particular autumn morning, Tim was freshly showered and looking dapper in a crisp white shirt, dark-blue blazer, and khakis, with the perfect intentional clean scruff on his inexplicably tan face. And the stupid socks, of course. *Why the hell was he tan?* Tim was an architect and met with clients most days, so he always left the apartment looking handsome and polished, which only made me feel worse about how unkempt I was. I sat up in bed, gingerly for still-sleeping Clara's benefit, and put on my glasses, which was a mistake, because then I could see myself clearly in the mirror above our dresser. I looked like I was wearing a mask, but it really was me: pale face, dark circles under my eyes, knotty nest on top of my head, the sides of my hair darkened with grease. My breasts were rocks under my T-shirt, ready for Clara to drain them at the moment of her waking.

"How was your night last night?" Tim asked in a whisper, trying not to wake Clara, though it was a wonder she'd been spared by his sock acrobatics. *God, I was mean.*

But come on—*how was my night?* Great. Just great. After I took her out for sushi, Clara and I went to a club and ended the night with a movie and late-night pancakes on the couch. *How was my night?* What did that even mean?

"Not the best," I said instead, trying hard to extinguish the inexplicable rage fire I felt burning within me. Clara's eyelids were fluttering.

"Kind of just dozed holding her for most of the night between feeds. Did you manage to sleep through?"

"Yeah. I guess I really needed it." I didn't have the words to respond to that one. "Babe, I really don't think it's safe to sleep holding her. What if one of us rolls over onto her? Plus, how will she ever learn to sleep on her own if she gets used to being held all the time?"

"I know, I know," I said guiltily. Of course he was right, but in the middle of the night, the distance from our bed to her bassinet felt like a marathon. "It's just that I'm so tired, I can't help but doze off. And she wakes up half the time when I try to put her down, even if it's just on the DockATot right next to me. It's like the only way she'll stay asleep is if I'm holding her."

"I know. Can't blame her, though—she loves being close to you." When his flattery bounced off me, he continued: "Hey, I'm more than happy to try bottle-feeding her at night again, if you want. You just have to promise not to tell me that I'm doing it wrong." He was try-ing to be funny, but he was also right; I was certainly guilty of some maternal gatekeeping, and we had decided after several unsuccessful attempts at Tim taking a night feed that there was no way I was going to sleep through it, and there was no point in both of us being exhausted. Which meant that our solution was that only I was exhausted. "Let me know if you want me to do it tonight. And if sleeping while holding her is better for you, that's fine. Forget I brought it up, please. Anyway," he said, changing the subject after surveying the cloud of frustration form-ing on my face, "what are my two favorite ladies getting up to today?"

I thought about it. It was Friday, which I supposed was good, since that meant we had made it through another week, and my moms' group was meeting, so I'd have a reason to force myself to leave the house, which, while difficult, always made me feel better. "We've got the moms' group at two. Otherwise, maybe a walk in the park? And I have some laundry to do." That part went without saying. There was *always* laundry to do. Whether I would actually find the time, energy, and will to do it was another story. "Not sure what else."

"Sounds fun." *Does it?* "Well, I'll miss you guys. Have a good day. See you tonight."

"What time do you think you'll be home?"

"I'm hoping for seven," he said, as if he weren't the one who chose when he walked out of his office. And even if he was home by seven, it would be too late to help me during the critical witching hours of extra fussiness, an always-harrowing bath, and finally getting Clara dressed, fed, settled, and into her first leg of sleep. Of course I understood that he had to work. Obviously, he was doing it for us, to support our family. I just wished that his support of our family could somehow involve a little less time at his office and a little more time at home elbow deep in dirty diapers.

He gave me a quick peck on the cheek, grazed Clara's head with his lips, and walked out the door with what unmistakably sounded like a sigh of relief.

Chapter Three

Clara and I muddled through the morning; after she woke and I fed her, I got her dressed and into her Ergobaby carrier, strapping her to my body so that I could free up my hands long enough to unload the dishwasher. She fell asleep immediately, face smooshed up against my floppy, emptied breasts. I was too scared to take her out of the carrier and transfer her to her bassinet because I didn't want to wake her up. Things were more manageable when she was asleep, though I would have preferred for it to not be on me, so that I could shower, get dressed, or even pee. I couldn't really sit very well when she was in the carrier because the sudden stop in motion usually woke her, so I just puttered around the apartment, thinking about the chores and reorganization projects I could be doing with my time at home but wasn't managing to even attempt. "Babies just sleep all day! You'll feel like you're on vacation!" one of my coworkers had told me before I started my maternity leave. I vowed I would never speak to this woman again. Or maybe I'd find an opportunity to secretly spit in her coffee.

Bravo was on in the background as I aimlessly skulked about, and not even something halfway decent like *Real Housewives of NYC*, but instead a show about people who were supposed to be working on a cruise ship but spent most of their time hooking up with each other and getting in fights. It was borderline unwatchable, but the thought of trying to find something better just felt pointless.

Perching gingerly on our trusty sports ball—which I used not for exercise (God no), but for bouncing Clara—and retrieving my phone carefully so as not to wake her, I opened Instagram. It seemed that I inevitably, and unfortunately, spent most of Clara's sleeping hours scrolling mindlessly through my phone.

Only two new posts since I'd last checked: a celebrity had posted something political, and a food account had shared a recipe for butternut squash soup that sounded delicious but that I knew I would never, ever make. Also, my dad's wife had responded with heart-eye emojis to a photo of Clara I'd put in my Instagram story (where she's sleeping peacefully, like an angel—talk about Instagram versus reality). My parents had been divorced since I was little, and my dad lived in Arizona, so I hadn't seen much of him growing up, though our relationship was perfectly cordial, and his wife was nice enough. But it was just my mom and me for a lot of my childhood, which of course only made losing her even more painful. She was honestly my best friend, and the only person I'd have been brave enough to ask: Is it normal to be this miserable with a newborn? Are these sad and scary thoughts that I'm having common? Am I an awful mother?

I closed Instagram and opened Facebook. The first post in my feed was something from the Upper West Side Moms Facebook group, which I had recently joined to learn about things like day cares, schools, and playgrounds in the neighborhood. There was plenty of non-neighborhood-specific content, too, just baby and kid advice in general. It was strangely addicting to read about what other moms were doing with their children.

Kyla Trevor: Hi mommas! I'm wondering what your favorite baby carriers are? I have the Ergo

360, but I find it really bulky and cumbersome.
Thanks in advance for your recs!

57 replies

I clicked on the replies. I also had the Ergo 360 (was wearing it now, in fact) and thought it was fine, but maybe there were better options. I made a mental note to check out a few brands that kept getting mentioned or "liked," like Baby K'tan, and also saw some other comments that I knew would be nagging me for the rest of the day, such as:

> **Rachel Brandon:** Be really careful with baby carriers tho. Even though brands say they can be used for newborns, they really aren't safe for smaller babies and can be suffocation hazards.

And another that went so far as:

> **Cleo Patra:** TRIGGER WARNING: My sister-in-law's friend's baby died in a carrier. The mom fell asleep wearing it and rolled over and that was it. Ladies, please be so careful. We only get one chance with these precious babies.

I was deeply disturbed by this, but also strangely jealous that this woman had been able to figure out how to lie down wearing the baby carrier. Then I felt terrible for thinking that. And terrible that I was wearing a death trap and also frequently committing the crime of sleeping while holding. Basically, I felt terrible for being so terrible at this.

There were several more replies to the tune of:

Amelia Conners: Don't overdo it with the carriers—babies need to stretch their bodies, build their muscles, and of course, need to learn to sleep independently in their cribs too. If they get too used to sleeping on you in the carrier, they'll never sleep on their own!

Never? As in, not ever? Like, I'd have to go to college with Clara so that she could sleep on me? My head had started to hurt. I couldn't bring myself to read any more of the baby carrier comments, but against my better judgment, I scrolled ahead to other posts. Maybe I'd find something useful that didn't make me feel like crap, or at least something salacious or funny: sometimes there were fun matchmaker posts, or gripes about a snoring husband, and those were always pretty entertaining.

Jess Norton: Best brownies on the UWS? This pregnancy craving won't leave me alone and ya know what I'm just gonna lean in lol

Nikki Friedman: Try the Viand, their brownies slay! Enjoy!

Amy McGuire: I love the brownies at By the Way Bakery! Kind of pricey though since everything is gluten free.

Kate Younger: Dietitian here. I agree that it's good to listen to your body, but what is it really telling you? Sometimes these sugar cravings can be satisfied with a piece of fruit or even a glass of water. Your body, and your baby, will thank you!

Kirsten Gemma: @Kate Younger why are you trying to kill her buzz, girl's just trying to get her brownie on! Let her live, geez!

Jess Norton: @Kate Younger Yeah I'm gonna stick with brownies but thanx, enjoy your kale. @Kirsten Gemma THANK YOU.

This brownie exchange already made me feel a bit better about the Ergobaby carrier nightmare. I scrolled on.

Stephanie Ring: Hi ladies!! Looking for some mommy and me classes for me and my 6 wk princess! Preferably music but open to anything, doesn't have to be in person either, would do virtual. Lmk what you've taken and loved! Thanks!

30 replies

Virtual infant music classes? Was this a thing that we were supposed to be doing? I pretty much had *Grey's Anatomy* season one playing on a loop while I was home with Clara (when it wasn't the god-awful yacht show on Bravo). Was Clara going to be trailing behind her peer group as a result of my selfish incompetence? Or worse, was it possible that I was traumatizing her with these bloody surgery scenes on *Grey's*? I honestly hadn't thought about it. So while the other babies were learning to play instruments and sing songs in Mandarin, Clara was watching Ellen Pompeo make out with Patrick Dempsey in an on-call room. Great. Typical Jenn. Another day, another mom fail. I couldn't bring myself to read through these replies now, though; my head was really starting to hurt. So I quickly wrote a note in my phone: *look up music classes for Clara and turn off Grey's, you jerk.*

I put down my phone and took a deep breath. I needed to get outside. Then I immediately picked up my phone again to check the time. Clara had been sleeping in her carrier for an hour; I could probably squeeze in a short walk before she woke up. I walked to the door and clumsily wedged my feet into hideous slip-ons that a few years ago I would never have believed I'd be wearing every day. My hand was on the doorknob when Clara let out a wail. The walk would have to wait.

"Hi, my little lady," I murmured as I took her out of the carrier, unclipping it eagerly from my sore hips. She glared at me, her face contorting as she cried, ready to be fed. Again.

She quieted down as soon as she was on my breast, like always. She stayed awake during this feed, but when she was done eating, she spat up all over herself and me. It was so much, I wasn't really sure if it was spit-up or vomit, which worried me. A quick Google search told me it was definitely vomit and that she would probably die. Thanks, Google. I texted Tim a picture and said, *do you think this looks like spit-up or vomit?* To his credit, he wrote back right away, but only with, *what's the difference?* I assured myself it was spit-up and tried to move on.

While I was changing Clara's bodysuit, I heard that unmistakable thunderous rumble from below, accompanied by her signature mid-poop blank stare, telling me she would also need a new diaper—and in this case, new pants, too.

It was 1:10 p.m. now and I honestly couldn't name a single tangible thing I'd done that day. Well, no: I'd made coffee and unloaded the dishwasher. And I hadn't cried yet today. Did those count as accomplishments? These days, they sort of did, sadly. I put Clara on her play mat and walked to the fridge and ate a plain hamburger bun. Thank God it was almost time for me to leave for my moms' group meeting— it was clear that I pretty much needed to be forced out of my apartment in order to make it to the outside world.

In my room, I tried wrestling my legs into jeans and made it only about halfway up my legs before peeling them back off in favor of the same Old Navy leggings I wore literally every day. This was a fun little game I played. *Do the jeans fit yet? Nope, not yet.* And why would they? It wasn't as though I had exercised or eaten particularly healthfully in the past year. Who was I kidding? I was definitely not ready for jeans (except my maternity jeans, which, wouldn't you know, still fit perfectly). Finding a top to wear was actually pretty easy, because I could only wear a nursing top, and there were only two in my dresser, as most were in the overflowing heap of laundry that was practically leaping, accusingly, out of our hamper.

In the bathroom, I laid Clara on the bath mat and put on some blush and mascara despite not having washed my face yet. I didn't even attempt to tackle the huge dark circles under my eyes. It was obvious that they were beyond the help of makeup, and I was already running late. At the door, I put Clara in the stroller and took one last look in the entryway mirror before walking out—the news wasn't good. It wasn't actually *that* long ago that I had considered myself fairly attractive and could leave the apartment feeling confident. I didn't have to scroll that far back in my phone to find pictures of myself in a cute outfit, blow-dried hair, and a wide lipsticked smile. A *real* smile, too. But it felt like a lifetime had passed. I barely recognized that girl when I looked at those pictures.

I hadn't thought I was the type of person to be in a new moms' support group. The idea of sitting around talking about breast pumps and swaddles didn't exactly appeal to me. But Tim suggested I try to find some "mom friends," undoubtedly after one of my bigger "I can't do this anymore" meltdowns, so I wrote an embarrassingly pathetic post on Upper West Side Moms—*Are any new moms' groups meeting this summer? Clara is looking for some friends!*—with a hilarious picture of Clara making a squinty face, as if she's searching for her friends. I thought it was pretty clever, but for weeks, it earned only a single response, asking me if I'd be in the Hamptons, and if so, then we should meet up! (But sadly, no, I would not be summering in a Hamptons mansion.) Then, randomly, after I'd all but forgotten about my post, this woman named Isabel reached out and invited me to join a group of moms, all with babies around Clara's age, who had been meeting for a couple of weeks.

I had been in the group for a little over a month, and I thought it was helping me. A little. I liked the other women—they were smart and kind, and a couple of them were funny. Often I couldn't help but feel like they were doing a much better job at all this than I was—they just seemed to know so much more than I did, about everything—but for the most part, everyone in the group was pretty honest about how hard this all was, which was refreshing and reassuring. It felt good opening up to them about the various challenges of swaddling, sleeping, and clinging to some semblance of LBB (life before baby). I hadn't told them about my mom, though; I wasn't yet capable of gracefully accepting sympathy. At my mom's funeral, everyone had some version of *Look on the bright side, it could be worse* to share with me—*she had ten good years after her original diagnosis, she was nearly in her seventies,* and so forth. But I wasn't at all ready to concede that her death was anything but shitty, shitty, shitty. And so, because I didn't want to make my new friends uncomfortable, I avoided the subject entirely. Which was a little challenging, especially when they talked about having their own moms around to help out, causing a lump the size of a peach pit to rise in my throat.

The five of us met weekly at the West Side Women's Center (WSWC), a rather swanky private women's collaborative work space on Eighty-Ninth and Central Park West. One of the women in our group, Selena, was a member, luckily for us (especially me, because I never could have afforded a membership there, though maybe the other women in our group could have). Because it was a work space, every week I walked into a sea of polished, energized, impressive women dominating their workdays, clicking away at laptops with manicured fingers, laughing in groups over lattes, legs crossed in skinny black pants. It was inspiring and demoralizing all at once. I always felt a little self-conscious about how disheveled I must have looked, but they also had a gym there, so I hoped that I looked like I was coming to work out. Though that was probably wishful thinking, as my body didn't exactly look like it belonged to a gym enthusiast.

Just as the doorman at WSWC had asked me "What are you here for?" I heard "Jenn! Wait up!"

It was Kira, so far the mom I felt closest to—maybe because she sort of made me feel like I had my shit together, by comparison. Last week she actually had dryer sheets stuck to her sweatpants—the kind of thing I thought only happened on TV shows, like slipping on a banana peel. (Then again, who was I to judge—the dryer sheets meant that, unlike mine, Kira's pants were at least clean.) Kira might've been a hot mess, but she was also refreshingly authentic and open. No "Isn't having a baby a miraculous joy?" rhapsodies, but a generous helping of "Why in God's name is my hair falling out?" and "Is anyone else still wearing the mesh underwear, or is that just me?" It was a relief that I didn't have to be the one to say some of the things that she said, because I probably wouldn't have had the courage.

"What's up? How was the week? How's this one treating you?" She gestured to Clara with her head, precariously clutching a half-full Starbucks cup labeled "Kerri" with her non-stroller-pushing hand.

"Meh. She's cute and all, but she still doesn't understand how great sleep can be. How's Caleb?" Kira's son was ten weeks old, a couple of weeks younger than Clara. Notably, Kira was mostly dressing Caleb in hand-me-downs from her sister's daughter, which meant Caleb wore a lot of flower prints and pinks. Kira seemed completely unconcerned that people would think he was a girl, which made me like her even more.

"Ugh! Don't these babies *want* to sleep? Sleep is so great. I don't get it. What is their problem? Also, Caleb's poops are green. Like, bright green. That can't be right, can it?" I hoped the question was rhetorical, because I had no idea what color baby poops were supposed to be.

Clara's were yellowish but I had never thought to verify whether that was an appropriate shade. I'd google it later, and probably come away convinced that her poop color signified her imminent demise.

We walked into the room where we met each week, which was spacious with comfy lounge chairs, a huge window facing the park, and a big, plush play mat for the babies. One of us was in charge of bringing snacks each week, and as we parked our strollers, I could see Selena arranging croissants and cookies from Kirsh Bakery, making today one that would unfortunately bring me no closer to fitting into my jeans again.

"Hey, ladies! How are you two?" Selena greeted us with a wide, warm smile and blew kisses toward us as she continued working on the pastries. Like Kira and me, Selena was also in "athleisure," but unlike us, she looked like she had stepped off the cover of a yoga magazine in her high-waisted crimson leggings and matching crimson crop top (yes, a freaking *crop top*), with white sneakers and an oversize denim jacket. Her long black braids were pulled back into a low ponytail, held there by a velvet scrunchie. Selena's seemingly effortless look was one that would have, for me, required unfathomable effort, and even with that effort, I could never have pulled it off. Especially the crop top. My God. But Selena rocked it. "Vanessa is in the bathroom, so we're just waiting on Isabel," she told us.

Selena's son, Miles, was on the play mat, reaching for a stuffed duck toy. "This man right here is driving me crazy!" she exclaimed. "He decided to start rolling over *already*, so now we have to ditch the moon suit thing, which had been working wonders. Just when I got used to sleeping again! This is really early to be rolling, right? Come on over here for some carbs. Are we having wine after this?" Selena made motherhood look easy, and even when she chimed in to add to or corroborate the litany of challenges that we all described, it almost seemed like she was just doing it to be congenial. Motherhood wasn't dominating her. She was dominating it. Even if she was too gracious to admit it.

Vanessa entered breezily, her daughter, Phoebe, asleep on her chest, snugly attached to her in a charcoal-gray Boba wrap.

Vanessa.

To be honest, it made no sense to me that Vanessa was even part of this group. It was a new moms' *support* group, after all, and while I know you can never know someone until you walk in their shoes, it simply did not seem like she needed support. Vanessa was "dressed down" in skinny jeans, ankle boots, and a *tucked-in* white button-down—and the reason she was so "casual" was because this was her *day off.* From *work.* And not just any work: she was a plastic surgeon at a posh dermatology practice in the neighborhood. Vanessa had already returned to her practice (albeit part time), and was apparently balancing new motherhood and her professional commitments with grace and ease, judging from the lack of dark circles under her eyes and her stress-free, freshly glossed smile. Her face was unlined and she looked younger than the rest of us, though it was hard to know if that's because she was or if she just regularly partook of the Botox that she could undoubtedly access at work. Her Phoebe seemed a contented, peaceful baby who, according to Vanessa, had slept through the night at five weeks. I genuinely didn't know what kind of "support" she felt she was getting from any of us, unless it was to simply confirm that she was superior. But, to be fair, Vanessa had only recently moved to New York City, so she was probably just looking to meet new friends, too.

"Hi, girls!" she exclaimed cheerily. "Oh my God, Jenn! Clara is so much bigger than last week, even! She's twelve weeks now, right?"

"She *is.* You have such a good memory." As if her pristine appearance weren't demoralizing enough, she was always so considerate. "Twelve weeks. So I should be out of the fourth trimester, right? Things should be nice and easy soon."

She laughed politely. "Totally! In the clear from here on out!"

"Anyway, how are you?" I asked.

"We're good!" she responded, nodding vigorously. New moms tended to answer in "we" form, even when it made no sense to do so. *We* need a sweater. *We* keep breaking out of *our* swaddle. *We* go to day care. Or even, as a woman in the park with a newborn once said to me, *we* had a blowout poop this morning. "Work is already so busy," Vanessa continued. "So much for easing back in. I have back-to-back patients. Still, being in a private practice is so much better than being in a hospital, which is what I was doing before. Also, I basically live next door to the office, so I can sneak in some visits and feeding sessions during the day, which is amazing."

Yes: *amazing*. It honestly did astound me that Vanessa was already back to work and surviving—not just surviving, but apparently thriving. The idea of returning to the classroom made me feel physically ill. I couldn't imagine facing a room full of expectant twelfth-grade English students feeling as exhausted as I felt—and yet, I was due to return to school next month, so I would have to figure it out. I loved teaching and had always planned to return as quickly as possible—but lately, I couldn't read a sentence in a book without wondering if I had remembered to take Clara's lovie out of her bassinet before putting her down for her nap, or thinking that I might've heard her spit up in her sleep, or feeling guilty about every undone chore. It was going to be kind of hard to lead a discussion on freaking *Gatsby* if I couldn't actually reread the damn thing. It would also be quite challenging to run class effectively while breast milk inevitably bled through my shirt—high schoolers didn't really roll too well with that kind of thing, in my experience. They'd probably start calling me some mean nickname like Ms. Donnelleaky instead of Ms. Donnelly. But maybe life would feel more stable by next month. It would have to.

"Has anyone heard from Isabel?" Selena asked. It was 2:15 p.m., and it was unlike Isabel to be late, especially since she was technically the facilitator of the group, though the role was casual and didn't entail anything other than that she'd been the one to organize our meeting schedule and snack responsibilities. Where Kira wore her "hot mess" persona with transparency, Isabel seemed rather humorless about her new role as a mother—like being a mom was now her number-one job, and she was determined to execute it to perfection even if it killed her. Unlike Kira's Caleb, who was always in mismatched socks and stained pink onesies, Isabel usually dressed Naomi in stiff, doll-like dresses, as if they were shooting their Christmas card photo later that day. Isabel herself always arrived looking chic, too, in cute linen jumpsuits with a white sweater over her shoulders, giving off Charlotte from *Sex and the City* vibes. She was a petite, reserved blonde who, like Selena and Vanessa, showed little evidence on her body of having recently given birth, though she shared my dark undereye circles—so much so that once I even wondered if her face was bruised, though I quickly dismissed the thought—and nodded vigorously when someone lamented about how difficult all this was. I really didn't know Isabel all that well, mainly because she didn't usually hang around for wine afterward, like the rest of us; she always seemed in a bit of a rush to get home, checking her watch and putting her dark sunglasses back on hurriedly at the end of every meeting before heading outside. To me, on the other hand, probably the best thing about being in this group was that somehow it made drinking wine with my baby at 3:00 p.m. on a weekday totally acceptable. I wouldn't have bailed before happy hour for anything.

I'd seen Isabel in the park a week or so ago with Naomi and was about to say hi before realizing that they were having a moment I wouldn't have wanted to interrupt. She was sitting on a bench near the Ninetieth Street entrance to Central Park, holding Naomi up before her. It was sunny. Naomi was smiling, and I was close enough to hear Isabel saying, "Thank you for letting me be your mom. It's very nice of you. I really appreciate it. Yes I do. You're very kind. Thank you very much indeed." It was a funny mix of an adult-sounding conversation in a baby voice, and both of them appeared delighted by it. It warmed me, too.

No one had heard from her. "That's weird. I'll shoot her a quick text," Vanessa offered. "I hope she's okay. But in the meantime, let's just start without her, I guess. How's everyone's week going? I've got a question, actually: Does anyone have any tips on bottles? Phoebe's nanny is reporting that she's suddenly resisting the bottle a bit; it's making her gassy, apparently. Which is very inconvenient timing, given that I've just returned to work, so she's mostly getting bottles now!" Vanessa took a sip of her coffee, which I then noticed was labeled with a *D*. Decaf. Was she seriously drinking *decaf*? Ugh.

"Have you tried Comotomo?" Kira asked. "It's the only bottle that Caleb will take."

"Agreed! It's the best." Selena picked at a croissant while lightly jiggling Miles, who was lying on his stomach on the floor between her legs.

And here I'd been using the generic Medela bottles that had been included with my pump. Wrong move, apparently. *Sorry, Clara.*

"Caleb's poop is green," Kira announced, having gotten no help from me on the subject. "Anyone else seeing green poops? Or know why that would be?"

"Hindmilk," Vanessa and Selena said in unison.

Huh? Kira shared my quizzical look.

"He may have a foremilk/hindmilk imbalance," Vanessa explained patiently. "There's different milk that comes out in the beginning of the feed versus later in the feed. If you keep him on your breast until he's drained it before switching him, it might help. Or give him more pumped milk to even things out, maybe."

"Totally," Selena agreed. "I had this problem for about a week, and it almost scared me into switching to formula. Thank God my pediatrician helped me figure out what was going on."

Yes, thank God—since formula is basically poison, right? I dreamed of using formula. I had a tub of it in my kitchen, "just in case," that I literally looked at like I was an addict and the white powder was cocaine. But every time I thought about shaking up a bottle, it was as if

I got zinged by an electrical fence, and an alarm went off that screamed "Breast is best! Breast is best!"—even though sometimes, like in the middle of the night when my nipples were red and raw after a feed, it felt anything but best to me.

"Okay, now, for the most important question," Selena said. "How's everyone doing with sleep? Getting any? Ha ha, that sounded dirty—which is pretty much how I think of sleep now. Sexier than sex. The forbidden fruit!"

I did my best to join the group's laughter but had to lip-synch it. Sleep deprivation was a pretty humor-resistant topic for me at the moment.

Kira went first. "Caleb is finally, *finally* giving me a break and doing like, five, six hours pretty regularly. Last night I only fed him once during the night, which felt pretty manageable compared to what we've been doing. I've honestly got no problem waking up once a night. I even told my mom she didn't have to come over yesterday to help with the baby so I could nap." Kira laughed, but I bristled reflexively at the mention of a mom who could come over and babysit, feeling my mom's absence so profoundly. I hoped no one noticed. "If he keeps this up, I feel like I'll start slowly approaching 'I can function like a real human' territory. Almost. I mean, I'm still not gonna put on real clothes or anything," she added, completely serious.

"That's awesome, Kira," Selena said. "Likewise, I'm happy to report that Miles has joined the ranks of his friend Phoebe over there and has decided to sleep through the night—twelve hours, for the past three nights, in fact. I don't want to jinx it—and I know, with the four-month mark coming up, we're soon headed into sleep-regression territory—plus now we're rolling, who knows what will happen, but man, I hope this lasts. I could really get used to this."

There it was: the explanation for Selena's glow. She'd been *sleeping*. Lucky bitch.

"That's amazing!" Vanessa said. "Ha, now I know why you asked the question: just to brag. Jenn, how are Clara's nights going?"

I couldn't help it: I winced. I knew Vanessa genuinely cared, but I hated the inevitable comparing game that we played at least a few times during each meeting. I was embarrassed to tell them that Clara was still only sleeping two to three hours—and doing that almost only while being held. I knew they'd have helpful suggestions about schedules and timing the feeds differently, giving her more bottles, or whatever, but I also knew that behind the upbeat, supportive advice, there would be judgment, condescending sympathy, and relief that it wasn't them, that their babies were easier, more impressive, more content—and perhaps, that they weren't as inept at caring for them as I was.

I took a deep breath, as if preparing to down a foul-tasting shot. *Here we go.*

"Um, not great. Could be worse, I guess. About the same as Kira," I lied. "I'm still pretty tired but I know it'll get better soon. She's still so little." I wasn't sure why I felt so defensive, not just of myself, but of Clara, too.

"It definitely will," Vanessa assured me. "Totally normal for babies not to be sleeping through the night when they're this young." *Thanks, woman whose baby is sleeping through the night.*

After thirty more minutes of commiserating mixed in with a bit of poorly disguised boasting *(enough about the rolling, already, Selena)*, I was ready for wine and hoped I wasn't the only one.

As though I'd said this aloud, Selena piped up with, "Where are we taking these children for happy hour today? Who's in? Also," she added as she wrestled Miles into her stroller and covered him with a fleece elephant blanket against the October chill, "I hope Isabel is okay—really strange she never showed. Text the group if anyone hears from her, okay?"

We all murmured our assent and concern. It *was* odd that we hadn't at least heard from Isabel.

Vanessa couldn't make happy hour because she had some errands to do on her day off, so it was just me, Kira, and Selena: the athleisure crew (though there was no doubt that Selena could have definitely rocked jeans if she'd wanted to).

Our meetings had two phases: phase one, at the WSWC, where we talked about the babies, and phase two, at the bar, where our conversation tended to shift more toward the husbands.

Chapter Four

"'Cause, like, God forbid he empty a freaking dishwasher!" Kira lifted a finger into the air to hold her place in the conversation while she took a healthy slug of wine. "I am literally one handed at all times while holding Caleb, so it takes me like forty-five minutes to empty the damn thing. Not to mention the fact that I've seen him use a fork, put it in the dishwasher, and then three and a half minutes later *take out another fork.* So he is producing *more* than his fair share of dirty dishes. How does he think the clean dishes make their way back into the cupboards? Magic?"

We'd only been at the Viand, an upscale diner on Eighty-Fifth and Columbus, for about fifteen minutes, but we were already on our second glass, and by some miracle, all three babies were sleeping in their strollers. We'd chosen the Viand (the same Viand of the epic brownies) because we figured it would be relatively quiet at this time and there was a little alcove perfect for the strollers by the bar. Also, they had a generous pour and a very respectable wine selection.

"I swear, when I was working," Kira went on, "Jack was actually way better about making an effort to divide household labor. Now that I'm on maternity leave, he thinks that I have all this time to pick up his dry cleaning or whatever. He actually referred to me being 'off work' the other day. Um, not quite! If this is supposed to feel like a vacation,

I want my money back." Kira worked in book publishing, in the kind of job that had her not only reading hundreds of manuscripts a year, but also constantly entertaining booksellers, going out to dinners with authors, and attending book launch events. She'd confided in me that, though she absolutely loved her job, she couldn't imagine doing it now that she had a baby, and wasn't sure when—or if—she would return.

Selena took a sip of her Chablis. "It sure as hell isn't vacation. Cameron really does 'try' to pitch in, but he's always like, 'What can I do to help?' and I'm like, ugh, why do *I* have to be task manager? Look around, dude! Do you see something that's messy? That'd be a good place to start! But at the same time, I don't want to be too snarky when he asks, because I do want him to help. So basically, I treat him like a child and explain things ever so patiently. And this"—she held up her glass with a smile—"is why I drink."

I nodded with genuine understanding. Both of their grievances sounded way too familiar. "Tim is convinced that Clara doesn't like him, which is of course ridiculous, and his solution is to basically just politely give her space until she changes her mind. But this strategy doesn't exactly help me when I want to do stuff like, I don't know— shower?" I was nearly done with my second glass. I knew I needed to slow it down, as Clara would need to feed again before too long. But I suddenly felt so much better, so energized.

"Jack does a lot of that, too," Kira said. "He's like, 'You're just better at this stuff than I am.' And I guess I am. Maybe women are in general. Just more equipped to care for these tiny humans." She shrugged and glanced down at Caleb, who was still sleeping, sucking his paci rhythmically.

"We're *not*, though," Selena said, suddenly serious. "Or, if we are, it's only because we don't have a safety net. The doctor puts the baby into our arms when it's born, and from that moment on, we're the first line. We rise to it because we have to. Not because it's intrinsically eas- ier for us. I hate this idea that we're in charge and the dads are just the assistants. Oh my God, the other day in the park, Cameron was holding Miles in the baby carrier, and I swear, every person we passed was giving him congratulatory 'What a great dad' looks. Like, it's his kid, too! Of course he should be holding him! No one hands me a freaking medal when I tote him around all day, that's for sure."

Kira and I both nodded quietly. Selena's words sat heavy for me. Every day for the last three months, I had heard this little voice in my head saying, *You're responsible for this human, so don't screw it up. Also, you chose this, and it's a freaking blessing, so stop feeling sorry for yourself. You're a woman—you're supposed to be* good *at this. This is your job. Your job. Your job.* It wasn't a kind voice. But I didn't know how to make her shut up.

"Okay, I have another one." Kira broke the brief, weighty silence, then paused to drain her glass with gusto. "Anyone else's husband *so damn loud*? How did I never notice this before? He stomps around the apartment like he's auditioning for freaking *Riverdance*!" Selena and I both burst out laughing. "Honestly," she said, "I'm shocked the neighbors have never complained."

"*So* true," I said. "Even the way Tim turns on a light switch is enough to wake the baby. He literally slams it with his fist. Like it's a jukebox and he's John Travolta in *Grease*. It drives me crazy! I never even noticed it before we had Clara." But as I joked, a blaze of guilt lit up my stomach, because I knew that, for all my husband's noisy light switch usage, or the fact that he'd been a bit slow to warm up to his new role as a father, he was a much better person than me. Much. For reasons I tried hard not to let myself think about.

In the midst of our laughter, all three of our phones buzzed with a text from Vanessa to our group chain. The text read simply Hey all, but there were three little dots to indicate that she was still typing.

"I'm assuming Vanessa's husband is perfect and super helpful," Kira noted as we waited. Her tone was joking, but her eyes flashed with something a bit more serious.

"And good looking," I offered.

Selena laughed. "And light on his feet."

"And gentle on the light switches." Kira giggled.

So I wasn't the only one who had registered how off-puttingly per-fect Vanessa was.

The next chunk of text that came in from her was extremely long. We each read it simultaneously, silently, to ourselves.

> I walked past Isabel's on my way home and there were police there. Her husband was outside so I stopped and introduced myself and asked if everything was okay. He said that Isabel had gone missing sometime last night, and they were trying to figure out where she was. Naomi is fine, she was on the steps with a lady who looked like she may have been a grandma. Anyway, I'm just updating you guys and I'll let you know if there's anything we can do to help or if I find out anything else. My convo with him was super short so that's really all I know. Really alarming and concerning news. Take care, ladies.

"Holy shit," Kira murmured.

"What the hell," I added uselessly.

Selena said nothing. Her hand was on her mouth.

"What do you think happened to her?" I asked.

Kira looked down before bringing her eyes back up to meet ours. "I hate to even say this, but . . . do you guys think maybe . . . suicide? She seemed . . . stressed. I can barely remember seeing her smile."

I didn't want to admit it, but that's the first thing I had wondered, too. There was something about her that just seemed a bit sad. Actually: very sad. And very anxious. The pristine way she dressed both herself and Naomi, the way she was always looking at her watch toward the end of our meetings. When someone is that wound up, there's always a breaking point. Maybe she reached hers. Plus, there was what Vanessa had said about the police presence—maybe her husband knew she was a risk to herself, and that's why the police were engaged, even though she'd only been missing for less than a day.

Of course, I was completely speculating. Unkindly so. And who was I to judge? People probably thought I was on the verge of a mental breakdown myself. I may very well have been.

And then I remembered what I had seen Isabel doing with Naomi in the park, their adorable little "conversation," and suddenly I didn't think there was any chance she had taken her own life.

"Does anyone know where she lives?" Kira asked. "We could . . . I don't know, just walk by. See what's going on? And I mean, I guess tomorrow, we should bring food or something? Or is that just when someone dies?" She pursed her lips with uncertainty.

"I know where she lives," Selena said. "We had a playdate once, a couple of weeks ago. Eighty-Eighth between Columbus and the park, I think." She scrolled hurriedly through her phone. "Yeah. Forty-three West Eighty-Eighth Street." She signaled for the check and cleared her throat, glancing anxiously down at Miles, who was still sleeping peacefully. "But I can't go. I really need to get home. Will you guys let me know if you find out anything else?"

We nodded solemnly, settled up—and hugged goodbye, which we'd never done.

Chapter Five

Friday, October 2

We'd been having drinks just a few blocks away from Isabel's apartment, so Kira and I were there in a matter of minutes, though there was a slight delay when Kira had to transfer Caleb from his stroller to her carrier when he woke up screaming. "Take your pacifier, please," she shushed him, pleading. "I promise you'll be eating soon." Mercifully, and shockingly, Clara was still sleeping.

There were a few police cars outside Isabel's apartment, which, as it turned out, wasn't an apartment at all, but a gorgeous, recently renovated town house. Unlike Selena, I had never been there. To be honest, I wondered how and when she'd had Selena over. It seemed a little random—or maybe I was just hurt that I hadn't been invited. Then again, she'd known Selena a bit longer; Selena had told us she'd met Isabel in the park across from her building's entrance, and that's when Isabel had invited her to join the moms' group. This was a few weeks before Isabel reached out to me on Facebook. Kira had been connected to Isabel through Vanessa, who she'd met at Mommy+Baby Barre. I wasn't sure how Vanessa and Isabel had met.

"Do you think this whole building is theirs?" Kira asked quietly.

It seemed like it was, because there were no unit numbers listed at the door. A couple of police officers were at the top of the stairs talking to a man I assumed was Isabel's husband. *He's hot,* I immediately thought, which was a terrible thing to think in the moment, but he was. Tall, brown hair flecked slightly at the sides with gray, muscular chest discernible through his tight, blue collared shirt.

In the small courtyard below the stairs, the grandma that Vanessa had mentioned was sitting at a table with her head in her hands. She glanced up occasionally, looking toward Isabel's husband and the police officers he was speaking to. Her face was stoic, but her shoulders were hunched with stress. A baby monitor emitted static on the stone table in front of her; Naomi must have been napping inside.

The town house stood out among its neighbors as it was white brick, rather than brown. It was stunning. The windows were enormous, sparkling clean, and trimmed with clean, dark steel. I didn't have much of an eye for design—and as the wife of an architect, I didn't need to, fortunately—but every aspect of this town house made passersby aware of its beauty, its brightness, its modernness. I was sure that I'd never admired a door before until this one, with its midnight-blue hue and long, slender silver handle. Now that I had seen where she lived, I was relieved that Isabel had never been to my unkempt, charmless one bedroom.

"Is that . . . Isabel's husband?" Kira asked, looking up toward him, her voice a bit unsteady.

"I assume so," I whispered back.

"Let's keep walking. I don't want to stop." She was speaking very quickly. "I feel really weird about being here. It's like we're spying. I mean, we really don't even know her that well. We don't belong here." She was right, but the urgency in her voice caught me off guard.

As we walked past, we had to maneuver our strollers around some police tape. At first, it looked like it was just blocking off a patch of uneven sidewalk. But the square of sidewalk wasn't only uneven in texture: it was also discolored, spattered liberally with rust-colored stains.

I saw Kira take it in at the same time, and knew we were both likely moving along the same progression: *Blood. This could be blood. This was probably blood. This was probably Isabel's blood.*

This time, it was me hustling us away. "Let's go," I said. "Keep walking."

I felt like I was going to be sick. I wondered if my pounding heart would wake Clara up. She was stirring now as we bumped our way off the sidewalk, past the police tape.

I looked back toward the house just one more time as we were walking away, and saw Isabel's husband looking in our direction. He seemed to be staring straight at us. His expression was unreadable, especially from this distance. But his eyes lingered for several seconds.

Kira was at least ten paces ahead of me, practically running as she turned the corner onto Columbus, finally out of view of the house.

"Wait up! Kira, are you okay?"

I found her just around the corner.

"I'm just so freaked out," she said. "I'm sorry. But, dude: that was blood. Do you think she was murdered?"

"I don't know. I don't want to think about it. But it might not have been—it could have been anything. It's New York, after all."

"Please. It's the Upper West Side. There aren't blood-soaked sidewalks everywhere." She sighed and pulled me in for another hug. "Be in touch if you hear anything, or if you talk to the other girls. I don't think I'm going to be able to sleep tonight—and not for the usual reason," she said, nodding toward Caleb with a gentle eye roll.

Clara woke up as soon as Kira and I parted ways, but she seemed surprisingly pleased to find herself in her stroller, able to look at trees and sky as we walked home, oblivious to what I had just seen while she'd been asleep. Even though she was just a baby, I was grateful to have Clara for company as I digested the shock of whatever may have happened to Isabel. I wouldn't have wanted to be alone at the moment.

March 15

Dear Baby,

Where to begin? In a few months, you'll be here with me in this crazy world. I can't wait to hold you, to see you, to smell you. I know that's weird, but I've heard babies smell amazing.

I got the idea to start writing you letters from a mommy Pinterest board—it pains me to even have to say that. Gag. *Really, Allison? You're this person now?* But the idea resonated with me. I have a lot to say to you already, and I haven't even met you yet. So I'm going to write to you, now and throughout your childhood, and give you these letters when you leave for college—or on tour with your band, or Barcelona, or culinary school, or a dance academy, or the army, or my basement, or wherever. Wherever you want.

I suppose the first thing I want to acknowledge is that the circumstances by which you came to exist were not at all as I'd imagined they would be. To the degree that I'd imagined them at all. To be honest: I was on the pill when you were conceived. Yes, it can happen. But look, even if it was the last thing I was planning for—how thrilled I am that you'll be with me soon. Life is never what you expect.

Sure, in vague corners of my mind I'd assumed I'd have a baby one day, when I was more established at work, when I met a partner worth staying with. When I had a bigger apartment, lived in a neighborhood in DC with better schools. If I stayed in DC at all. I like it, but there are other places I'd like to live, too. Like New York. Anyway, I wasn't thinking of a baby. I'm only twenty-eight, after all—by today's standards, that's practically a teen pregnancy.

But after a couple of months of unusually light periods and a strong aversion to eating anything before noon, I knew I had to take a test, even though I was on birth control and hadn't had sex with anyone except . . . well.

Suffice it to say that I never expected to see that second blue line. But there you were. A doctor confirmed it days later.

And what can I say? It was like a line from *Gatsby* (which was actually one of my least favorite novels in high school, and yet, this part came back to me the night I saw you in those blue lines): "I can't describe to you how surprised I was to find out I loved her, old sport." That's how I felt about you. I loved you, and nothing has ever surprised me more. I couldn't quite believe it myself. But I loved you already. And I wanted you, unequivocally.

I knew I had options. Of course I did. And please understand: I'm as pro-choice as they come. You'll become well acquainted with my collection of pink hats. It was never about feeling guilty about taking a different path.

But I wanted you. I did and I do. And that's the thing I hope you'll take most from these letters: that despite how you came to me, you were, and are, wanted. You are cherished. You are loved, and always will be.

Also, please don't hurt me too much when you come out. Please? K, thanks.

Love you forever,

Mommy

Chapter Six

Like any normal person, I immediately took to Google to find out as much about Isabel as I could. And her husband. Connor. Connor and Isabel Harris. There weren't any missing persons bulletins or news items on her yet, which wasn't surprising given it had barely been a day, but I set up an alert on my phone to notify me as soon as that changed. Once I got started on my Google rabbit hole, I immediately realized how little I actually knew Isabel, which was strange—from our meetings, we knew intimate details of each other's schedules and daily struggles. She had seen me cry, I had seen her breasts, she had kissed Clara's head once, we'd talked about how many weeks our vaginas had bled after giving birth, and yet I didn't know where she was from. We weren't even friends on social media.

I quickly discovered that that was because she wasn't *on* social media.

Strange, because she had been at one point—after all, she'd been the one to respond to my Facebook post about looking for a moms' group. I pulled up her message: Hey! We have a group that started meeting a few weeks ago. Send me your email and I'll send you the details. Now, that message just appeared to be from "Facebook User." Maybe she was taking a social media hiatus. I could hardly fault anyone for that—I would have probably benefited from one of those myself. Still, it was odd for someone my age to be so disconnected. She wasn't on LinkedIn, either; then again, if she didn't work, which I was pretty sure she didn't, why would she be?

I did manage to find that she was from Tarrytown (ancient field hockey stats still available online) and had gone to Williams College (acting major). I also found their wedding announcement in the *Times* and learned her maiden name was Wahrer. It was from 2010, which meant that she and Connor had been married practically forever. In 2010, I was in grad school and could barely handle the responsibility of buying groceries, opting instead to just grab a bagel, or nuts at whatever bar I was at, for dinner most nights. While I was still living like a suddenly unsupervised teenager, Isabel was getting *married*. She was the same age as me, though; we'd graduated the same year. Connor had a beard and looked totally different in their wedding picture—still gorgeous, just a lot younger and a bit more rugged looking than the polished man I'd seen on the steps in front of their house.

My search on Connor provided an explanation for their incredible town house. He was a partner at Zomar Capital, a boutique hedge fund in Manhattan that was wildly successful, having invested early in several hugely popular social apps. I was a teacher who had no interest in or knowledge of the world of investments, but even I could understand how much money investments like theirs would have yielded. He was probably worth tens, maybe hundreds, of millions. I found out that he'd gone to Williams, too; I assumed that's where they'd met, which explained, to some degree at least, why they'd gotten married so young.

Other than a few articles that mentioned his company and their deals, Connor's internet footprint was as small as Isabel's, which must have been by design. He wasn't on social media, either, and perhaps he was the one to encourage her not to use it; after all, maintaining investor relations surely required discretion. And with a sizable fortune to safeguard, it was little surprise that they seemed to value their privacy.

From Friday afternoon until Saturday morning, our text chain was radio silent, which made me feel antsy and unsettled. Clara woke up at 5:00 a.m., and I tried and failed to get her back to sleep. I considered waking Tim to take her for a while, but I knew there was no chance I'd be able to fall back to sleep anyway, so I used our early morning as a chance to take a walk with her and go scope out Isabel's house again. The police tape was still up by the bloody sidewalk, which appeared to have been scrubbed, because the blood was barely discernible. There was one police car parked outside their house, but I didn't see any officers, or Connor, or the grandma. They were likely sleeping; it was barely light outside.

Finally, late Saturday morning, Vanessa sent a text to the group.

Nothing to report. She's still missing. I reached out to her husband and asked him to keep me updated if they found out anything, or if there is anything we can do. I'm planning to bring some food over there this afternoon, around 3:00 p.m. Anyone want to join me?

Moms are notoriously slow at texting back, so even though I read the text about thirty minutes after it came in, no one had responded yet when I saw it. Since it was a Saturday and Tim was home to help with Clara, I had been taking one of my weekly "real showers"—actually washing my hair, shaving, and, well, getting clean, instead of just standing under a stream of water for two minutes.

I heard Clara start crying a minute after I stepped out of the shower, and a minute after that, Tim came into the bathroom holding her while I was naked and generously applying desperately needed serum to my face. I picked up my towel off the floor and wrapped it around myself tightly. I knew I didn't look disgusting per se, but I was definitely hyperaware of the stubborn stretch mark–streaked eight-pound tire around my midsection. Compounding my self-consciousness around my husband seeing me naked was the fact that, despite having been "cleared" for sex several weeks before, Tim and I hadn't done it since before Clara was born. It was pretty much the last thing I wanted to do, and he hadn't tried, either, which was both offensive and a total relief. I wasn't sure if he hadn't tried because he could tell I didn't want to, or because he didn't want to, either. I hoped the former, but talking it through would require me to muster energy I simply didn't have. It would also force me to acknowledge that the baby wasn't the only reason I didn't want to have sex with him yet, that there was something else going on with me, something I hadn't told anyone and vowed to myself that I never would. I was trying to avoid at all costs opening that particular locked box inside me, which I intended to keep locked forever and throw away its key.

"She wants you." He sighed, sounding spent, as if his fifteen minutes alone with our baby had done him in.

"Okay, well, I need a few more minutes."

"Well, what am I supposed to do with her? I have no idea how to make her stop crying. I really think she might hate me."

This again. "She doesn't hate you," I assured him.

I was trying to be kind. I wanted us to have a good weekend together, and I genuinely did feel bad that Tim, like me, was not having the experience with new parenthood that he'd hoped for. I also knew that I was at least partially to blame for that; my anxiety around Clara had made me possessive and controlling, and my anger around my mom's death pervaded every second of my day, including those spent with Tim.

"She's just getting used to you still," I told him. "It takes time." I kept applying lotion. "What have you tried so far? Have you tried bouncing on the sports ball and giving her a paci? At the same time? You have to pretty much hold it in her mouth for her for at least ten minutes before she'll take it herself. Have you tried reading her a book? She loves *Brown Bear, Brown Bear.*" I was using my "nice voice," but I was also getting tired of always being the teacher. I was new to this, too, after all. I had no idea what I was doing, either.

"I didn't think you'd want me to bounce her, because I didn't think you'd want her to fall asleep yet." This was a fair point. She'd only been awake for about forty-five minutes and needed to eat soon. I'd been reading all about "wake windows" online and had just given Tim a lecture about their importance. Apparently he'd been paying attention, and he was right: the ball did tend to put her to sleep right away.

"I'll be there in literally two seconds. Can you just . . . ?" An exasperated wave of my hand replaced the end of my sentence.

He shut the door and the crying commenced with heightened intensity.

When I looked at my phone again, Selena and Kira had both responded to Vanessa's text that they couldn't make it today.

Hey hey—busy day with family in town, wrote Selena. I'll likely pop over there sometime this week.

Brutal night with Caleb, read Kira's reply. We don't really have it together over here today. Trying to catch some naps. Please keep us posted, though. Haven't stopped thinking about her.

I didn't want to make Vanessa go over there on her own. Also, I had to admit to myself that, in addition to being genuinely and deeply worried about Isabel, and sickened by the thought of being separated from my baby, as Isabel was from hers, I was also curious—about Isabel's house, her husband, and Naomi's grandma, if that's who Kira and I had seen the day before. When I was still actually able to read a page before falling asleep or succumbing to anxious thoughts about my daughter, I had been addicted to thrillers—I used to spend hours perusing the shelves at the Strand Book Store, picking out the perfect suspense novel to keep me up well into the night. Isabel's disappearance had awakened whatever part of myself craved mystery. Or perhaps just distraction from my own insular little life. Either way, I wanted to scope things out a bit for myself. See what her life may have been like at home.

Besides, I figured Tim would be grateful for a little break. From Clara and me both.

I'm in, I wrote. Text me when you're on your way and I'll meet you outside my apartment—86th and Amsterdam. I had never been to Vanessa's apartment, but I knew she lived on West End Avenue in the high Seventies, making my apartment on Eighty-Sixth Street on her way to Isabel's.

Vanessa texted me at exactly 2:50 p.m. Hi! We're outside. Right on time—surprise, surprise. (Also, we were going to our missing friend's apartment, but still, if you don't start a text with Hi! you're a bitch, right?)

I had ducked out earlier while Clara was napping to pick up some Levain scones and muffins to bring over to Isabel's family. The solo time on this errand had rejuvenated me somewhat, though leaving the house without Clara was so rare that I'd felt like I had left a limb behind or was walking down the street naked.

As predicted, Tim was supportive about my going to Isabel's—though he had been oddly aloof the night before when I'd told him about Isabel's disappearance, swiftly delivering wisdom akin to "I'm sure there's a logical explanation." When I looked at him sideways, he realized that wasn't a big enough reaction, and he recovered: "Crazy, though. How are you doing with it? Are you okay?"

I grabbed my Levain bag and gave Tim a peck goodbye before darting into the elevator, deciding to leave the stroller behind, Clara happy in her carrier, awake and sucking her thumb. Hopefully she would stay that way, but I didn't exactly want to stay at Isabel's all afternoon anyway, so if she did get fussy, it would give me an excuse to dart out. I also knew that there would be plenty of places for her to sit once we were there, since their house was obviously set up for Naomi and would have plenty of baby gear. My heart hurt when I thought of Naomi—if she was wondering where her mom was, when she would nurse again. While I (mostly) relished my occasional moments away from Clara, the idea of actually being separated from her in any real sense or for a long period made me nauseated and dizzy—especially thinking about whether it had happened against my will, which could be the case with Isabel. She could be kidnapped. Murdered. Lost. Anything.

Vanessa looked as polished as she usually did, in black high-waisted jeans (had she really given birth just three months ago?), a long-sleeved white T-shirt, and white sneakers. Even her stroller was sleeker and more stylish than mine, beige instead of black, narrow and light for the New York City sidewalks it was navigating. Mine felt like I was pushing a minivan.

She pulled me in for a quick hug. "Ready?" she asked. I saw that she had two massive quiches from Kirsch in her stroller storage. The perfect choice. Classy as always. I was suddenly self-conscious of my scones. Did anyone even like scones, really? I suddenly remembered a *Curb Your Enthusiasm* episode about this very conundrum. I wished I had recalled it before choosing this as my offering.

I shook off my scone anxiety. "So, what did Connor say when you reached out to him yesterday?" I asked.

"I think he was surprised. I messaged his work email, since I didn't have his number or anything. He definitely didn't know who I was. I guess she didn't talk about our group much at home. Which is totally fine, I don't care or anything—our exchange was just a bit awkward. Isabel mentioned before that he travels for work a lot, so maybe he's just out of the loop."

"That's kind of weird, though." I took a breath, unsure how candidly I could talk to Vanessa about my theories. "Listen. I have to ask—usually they always look at the husband first, right? Is he . . . being investigated, do you think? Do you think there's any way he could have . . . ?"

"I mean, I don't know. I'm sure the detectives are looking into him—like you said, they always look to the husband first. But the fact that he's home means he probably isn't really a suspect, or he'd be at the station, I assume. In any case, we'll be safe going there, if that's what you're worried about. There will be people around, I'm sure."

It struck me then that, even though Selena, Kira, and I had joked about how perfect Vanessa's husband probably was, I had never actually heard Vanessa mention a partner before. She usually didn't come to the husband-talk second act of our mom meetings, over wine. Now seemed the wrong time to ask, but I made a vague mental note to casually revisit this sometime soon.

We walked up the stairs of the town house and knocked quietly on the door, as if we secretly hoped there would be no answer. As interested as I was in getting some firsthand knowledge of who Isabel's people were, seeing her house, and diving into this crime as if it were a novel I was cracking open, I also felt like I was invading Isabel's privacy by doing so. How would I have felt if these women, whom I'd only known a few months, showed up at my cluttered apartment? Then again, if Isabel were dead—and I prayed she wasn't, but it seemed possible—perhaps the issue of her privacy was no longer relevant. I didn't have too long to mull it over, though, because suddenly the long silver door handle I'd admired from afar turned, and the door slid open.

Chapter Seven

Saturday, October 3

The same older woman we'd seen yesterday answered the door, Naomi cradled in her arms. "Hi!" Her cheeriness didn't quite match the situation. It was as if she realized the same thing I was thinking, because she said, again, "Hi," this time in a much more muted, somber manner. She was more beautiful than I had realized yesterday—her white hair had made her look old from a distance, but up close, it gave her kind of a Meryl Streep vibe. She was elegantly dressed, too, in black pants and flats and a white wrap sweater, and tortoiseshell glasses. She also had, rather adorably, a leopard fanny pack at her hip, an extra paci dangling from it. A very prepared grandma.

Vanessa spoke first, which was what I had hoped would happen. "Hi—we're in a new moms' group with Isabel. I'm Vanessa, and this is Jenn. We are so sorry to hear about what happened. We're all praying she's okay. You must be so worried."

"We are, of course. It's very distressing. I'm Isabel's mother. Naomi's grandma. Though I'm trying to get her to call me *Lollie* instead of *Grandma*—short for Louise, which is my name. I think it sounds a bit younger than *Grandma*. And having a young nickname is certainly cheaper than a face-lift. Ha. Anyway. I'm sorry. I babble when I'm stressed. And make jokes. And of course, I'm stressed beyond belief. But trying to keep my cool for Naomi. She's a much-needed distraction for me. Would you like to come in?" Louise was immediately endeared to me; I appreciated her utter lack of filter.

"Just for a minute, if you're sure it's okay. We don't want to intrude." Vanessa started unclipping Phoebe from her stroller. "We brought some food—it can be hard to remember to eat at times like these, plus you're so busy with the baby. We all know it isn't easy caring for a newborn." *Though Vanessa made it look so,* I thought with a mental eye roll.

"That was very sweet of you to bring food. Naomi's been an angel, but she definitely misses Mama. Can I get you two a cup of coffee?" She placed Naomi in her bouncer, so we followed her lead and put Clara and Phoebe on the play mat next to her. They seemed calm enough, apparently pleased with the new gear selection and the flashing lights from Naomi's bouncer. Louise whizzed around the kitchen, taking out oversize white mugs from the crisp white cupboards and organic oat milk from the massive fridge. The fridge door was glass. I couldn't imagine having a glass fridge. My disorganization would be on display for anyone to see. But this fridge was meticulously organized, with lush fruits in one section, several blocks of cheese in another, rows of neatly labeled bottled breast milk on the top. Everything was in clear glass bins. There was nothing shameful about its contents or the way it was set up.

Louise whistled softly, clearly an old habit, as she moved and chatted, but her hands shook slightly, and she kept clearing her throat, possibly as a way to fight off tears. Still, she was keeping it together remarkably well, given the circumstances. If I were missing, I don't think that my mom would have been able to even get dressed for the day, let alone make small talk with guests. Of course, I'd never know.

Vanessa broke the silence and pulled me back from my wallowing drift into thoughts of my mom. "So, if you don't mind me asking, do the detectives have any leads?"

"Well. I know they're working hard. The first step is always to look at the husband, so they've been talking to Connor quite a bit. Fortunately, I think they've more or less ruled him out, which is a relief for all of us. Not that we'd ever suspect him, but . . . you know." Louise raised her eyebrows and took a sip of her coffee.

"That's . . . great," I said, feeling a bizarre sense of disappointment. "How were they able to rule him out so quickly?" I was aware that this may have been pushing too far, but I had never been in the situation of having a missing friend and so had little sense of what was appropriate and what wasn't. Louise's anxiety about the situation seemed to be loosening her lips, and while I hated to take advantage of that, it was hard to resist.

"Well, it's lucky that your generation is so obsessed with watching your babies at all moments of the day! Isabel and Connor have a—is it called a Nest?—set up in their bedroom, since Naomi still sleeps in there some of the time. The camera was able to confirm to the police that Connor was in bed sleeping when Isabel disappeared. He was the one to discover she was missing in the morning when Naomi's cries woke him up. Usually, Isabel would have been the one to get her"—*of course*—"but she wasn't there. I'll tell you, when I was a young mother, we definitely did not have the surveillance capabilities that you all do. I'd be in the yard gardening or something and Isabel would be up from a nap screaming her head off and I'd have no idea. Especially since I was on my own—sometimes things fell through the cracks. My husband died when she was a baby, and I never remarried."

So Isabel was raised by a single mom, too. I wish we'd talked about this. I hoped we would still have a chance to.

"I'm babbling again," Louise continued, her frenetic energy making her appear bizarrely chipper. "But my point is, even without these snazzy Nest cams, our babies still survived!" She started to laugh, then seemed to realize the weight of her comment and stopped laughing abruptly: her baby had survived her camera-free childhood, yes, but may not have survived whatever had recently happened to her.

Connor's whole Nest camera alibi sounded flimsy to me. Couldn't the camera have shown, like, a body-shaped pillow under the covers? Or, more realistically, Connor easily could have hired someone to abduct or kill Isabel, if he'd wanted to. Him being in the bed when she actually went missing didn't clear him of anything, in my opinion.

"And did the camera pick up any clues about her disappearance?" Again, I knew I was probably crossing a line of nosiness at this point, but Louise seemed perfectly willing to discuss it. Vanessa was tending to Phoebe on the floor, but I could tell she was listening intently.

"Unfortunately, nothing helpful. She left the house at around ten to walk Murphy"—I'd totally forgotten that Isabel had a dog—"and then Murphy came back to the house by himself and apparently stayed outside all night. He's still very spooked, poor thing. There are no street cameras until the next block, but they're reviewing the footage. None of the people at nearby bodegas remember seeing her. She just truly disappeared. But something must have happened. I know she wouldn't leave Naomi. Besides, if she *had* wanted to leave, which she didn't, she wouldn't have brought the damn dog with her." This rang true. No one who's planning to run away, or hurt herself, brings along the dog.

I was considering whether it'd be completely over the top for me to ask about the bloodstained sidewalk when Connor entered the kitchen. He was even taller and more handsome than he'd seemed from afar. He appeared to be freshly showered, and there was gel in his perfectly coiffed hair, which irked me. I knew I was being too judgmental about the way other people dealt with stress (especially given that I didn't have the best coping mechanisms myself), and I shouldn't be comparing, anyway, but I did not think Tim would be primping and fixing his hair up if I were a missing person. Connor was cut and lean and looked as if he probably kept up with an intense workout regimen.

The inconvenient kind, like six-hour bike rides, or triathlons in remote places or something.

"Hi," he said quietly, his lips flashing the briefest closed-mouth smile, which was not reflected in his brown eyes.

Vanessa covered us again. I guess we had established that she was in charge of social niceties, and I was in charge of gracelessly asking invasive questions about the investigation. "Hi . . . I'm Vanessa," she said to Connor, putting her hand on her chest. "I spoke to you here yesterday, briefly? We are so sorry for what you're going through. We're all praying that Isabel turns up soon. It's just awful."

"Thanks," he said shortly, barely looking at her, instead turning to his mother-in-law. "Louise, just remember you aren't supposed to discuss the case." He took out a mug and poured himself a cup of coffee, not acknowledging Naomi in her bouncer.

"Of course. Of course," Louise said, flashing us an ever-so-brief "oops" look. "I hope I haven't said too much. But talking about it with friends helps me. It makes me feel like everything will be okay. That there's an explanation. Of course, the bloodstains are most concerning . . ." She crossed the room and started rubbing Connor's back. He looked visibly uncomfortable, and I could understand why. Tim and my mom had been close, but it had never gotten further than a very brief, friendly hug. This back rub was on a whole other level.

"Bloodstains?" I played dumb, pretending that Kira and I hadn't seen the stains for ourselves.

Louise nodded and drew and released a deep breath. "Yes. Unfortunately, they found six large bloodstains between the house and the river—a few on the sidewalk, a few in Riverside Park. It's Isabel's blood type, A positive. They're running more tests to see if it's actually hers. It's a common blood type, A positive. It's easy for me to remember, too, because I always told her that it made sense that she had A positive blood because she was such an A-plus girl! Always trying her hardest, always looking on the bright side. She never gives up. She always finds a way." She looked at Connor and smiled proudly, expecting him to share in her admiring reflection on Isabel's character.

Instead, Connor said only, "Louise, please." He shot her a scathing look, which she either didn't register or completely ignored. I was liking her more and more, and him less and less.

"Could she have, like, cut herself?" I asked lamely.

"The stains aren't consistent with a minor injury," she explained. We looked at her. "Too much blood," she elaborated, in case we weren't following, choking a bit on the word "blood."

"Louise," Connor warned once again. He was trying to keep his cool, probably since we were there, but it was clear he was becoming exasperated.

"I know, Connor—sorry. But these ladies are her friends, and they're worried about her. And besides, maybe they know something that could help." She looked at us and opened her palms to us, as if prompting us to go ahead and offer up what we knew.

"If that's the case," Connor broke in, "I'm sure the detectives will talk to them. And, I'm sorry—you're going to have to remind me who you are, exactly. I know she's in a yoga class for moms—is that you?" He was looking at us with an even combination of suspicion and annoyance.

"No, that's not us," Vanessa said. "This is more like a support group for new moms. To talk about issues with feedings, naps, whatever. We meet once a week at the West Side Women's Center." She was looking at Connor carefully, to see if any of these clues raised any recollection whatsoever on his part.

But Connor was looking at me now. "Have we met before?"

This brought me up short. "No, we haven't. I don't think so. I live a couple of blocks away, though, so it's possible we've passed each other on the street." He did seem familiar to me, too, but it was hard to say why or where from, especially now that I had googled him.

"Right." He didn't take his eyes off me, which was disconcerting.

Vanessa was looking at me now, too. "Anyway, we should get going," she interjected. "We don't want to impose any further during such a sensitive time."

Right on cue, both Phoebe and Clara started fussing a bit on the floor. The perfect wingwomen. I couldn't recall ever being grateful to Clara for fussing, but I was getting uncomfortable and was glad to have an excuse to hurry out.

"Please," Vanessa went on as she bent down and scooped up Phoebe, "let us know if there is anything at all we can do for your family while you search for Isabel. Or anything we can do to help in the search efforts." I started wrestling my carrier back on.

"Thank you so much for coming by," Louise said. "Come back anytime. I'm going to be staying here, helping with Naomi. For as long as Connor needs me." She nodded firmly, punctuating her renewed commitment to him. Connor's facial expression remained blank, but I thought I saw irritation flash in his eyes.

We said goodbye in the kitchen, insisting that they not take the trouble of walking us to the door. I had a feeling Louise was in for a lecture as soon as we left.

On our way to the door, a framed eight-by-ten of a late-term ultrasound picture of Naomi caught my eye. It was such a beautiful idea—the very first picture of mom and baby together, really. I made a mental note to frame one of Clara's ultrasound pictures, too. It made me sad, though, because all I could think was, *Will Naomi get her mom back?* I glanced at Vanessa, who was also registering the ultrasound picture, emotion visible on her face; she must have been feeling the same way I did.

I took a huge gulp of air as soon as we got outside. I felt like I hadn't really breathed the whole time we'd been in there. I wanted to debrief with Vanessa, but I had to tread a bit carefully, since we weren't that close. I didn't want to seem gossipy or insensitive, but at the same time, I was curious to get her take on Connor and Louise.

"Louise seems very nice," I offered as we walked away. Nice and way too forthcoming and jumpy and really pretty for an older lady and a little weird with her son-in-law? And also I dug her fanny pack? But I couldn't say all these things. I also couldn't deny that I liked her immensely. She reminded me a little bit of my own mom—quirky and honest and somehow perfect in her imperfections.

"She does. I feel so sorry for her. Her only daughter. Though she seems to be managing." Ever diplomatic, so far Vanessa was giving me nothing.

I waded a bit further into gossip territory. "Any idea what Connor does for work? That house is insane." Of course, I already knew where he worked. But maybe she knew more than I did.

"I'm not really sure. Finance, I think. That world is kind of foreign to me. Isabel had mentioned his job involved demanding clients, a lot of travel. Seems like he does pretty well for himself." Another understatement. The idea that someone my age could own that house astounded me.

We both paused at a crosswalk. When the signal changed and we stepped off the curb, she finally spoke. "I think it's a little strange that Connor didn't know she was in a new moms' group."

Finally. "Totally! I thought the same thing. Like, I'm not sure if Tim would be able to name every single woman and baby in the group, but he at least knows I'm in one."

"Right. Of course, it doesn't mean anything—he seems like a nice enough guy. It just bothered me a little bit."

"Yeah. And oh my God, remember he was like, 'Are you the yoga group?' Kind of douchey." It was a relief to be communicating openly with Vanessa, at last.

"Right. It seems certain that she would have mentioned us, no? And it's sad to think that he couldn't be bothered to care what she was up to, how she was spending her days with their new baby." She spoke with a slight bitterness that made it seem like this was personal to her.

"I definitely wouldn't like it if Tim treated my friends that way. I'm sure you feel the same way about your—I'm sorry, are you . . . with anyone? I can't believe I've never really asked!" It seemed the right time to ask, since we were on the topic of partners. I hoped my tone sounded open and casual.

She took a deep breath.

"I'm actually not. Phoebe's father . . . didn't want anything to do with this. That's part of the reason that we moved here, actually. It's just me and her, and I wanted a fresh start."

"Wow, I'm so sorry. That's—"

She cut me off, shaking her head, refusing the sympathy I'd been about to offer. "It's okay. So far, it's going well this way. I don't want anyone around her who doesn't love her the way she deserves to be loved. And to be honest, I didn't even know if I'd ever have a baby . . . this was all a pretty big surprise." She looked over and held my gaze as we walked. "Listen. I felt a little weird telling the group, since you guys talk about your husbands so much. I didn't want to be the odd woman out, or make you feel reticent talking about your own husbands, because you totally shouldn't."

I felt guilty that we had made her feel uncomfortable with what was admittedly, at times, excessive husband chatter. "I totally get why you didn't want to say anything, but it only makes me think you're even more amazing than I did before! You're a badass single mom." *Like mine,* I almost added, but I still didn't want to talk about her. I also didn't want to change the subject. "I give you so much credit. Plus, you're a catch . . . You'll probably meet someone very soon who loves both you and Phoebe. If you want to, of course." I was rambling but actually meant every word.

"That's sweet of you to say. Of course, I have help—my nanny, Cynthia, is amazing. She does so much for us." Leave it to Vanessa to be unfailingly gracious. "I thought it would be hard to find help on such short notice, since my move happened kind of suddenly, but I really lucked out."

"Another question I can't believe I haven't asked yet, but where did you move from again?"

"DC. I was here in the city for med school, though, so it's familiar to me . . . and it's good to be back. It was time for a change."

We were approaching my apartment on Eighty-Sixth Street. "Okay, well . . . this is me." I couldn't even think about inviting her in because my apartment was a sty. Plus, it was time for me to feed Clara, who was fidgeting and groaning, though not actually crying, in her carrier. "Thanks for today. I'm so glad we went together. God, I hope she's okay. What Louise said about the bloodstains sounded really bleak. Too much blood for a minor injury?" I shuddered.

"Yeah, very much so. Well, I'm sure we'll learn more in the days to come." We hugged. I started to walk toward the door. "Oh, and Jenn?"

I turned around.

"Do you mind not saying anything to the rest of the girls about me being a single mom? I don't know, I just still feel a little self-conscious. I'll probably tell them at some point, but I'm not sure when."

"Of course. I won't say anything. I promise." I could certainly understand where she was coming from, having not yet told them about my mom. Some things were easier to compartmentalize.

"Thanks. See you next week. Enjoy the rest of your weekend."

I doubted how much I could enjoy it, with thoughts of Isabel trailing blood down West Eighty-Eighth Street. But I wished Vanessa the same before heading inside.

Chapter Eight

Sunday, October 4

I continued to obsessively search for news hits on Isabel, and remained disappointed to find very little. I didn't understand why her family wasn't offering a big reward, plastering her face all over every local news source they could access. With Connor's big job, I was sure that he had the connections and resources to make that happen. But maybe his job was the exact reason they were trying to keep it quiet. He had seemed very concerned with privacy when we were at their house.

And maybe a young missing mom wasn't even a big news item. Especially since it had only been a couple of days. Still, the lack of publicity concerned me. How would they ever find Isabel if no one, save for a few detectives who'd already ruled out *my* prime suspect, was looking for her?

But while the story of Isabel's disappearance wasn't making national news, Upper West Side Moms on Facebook did catch wind of it. I was mindlessly scrolling through it early in the morning while nursing Clara when I saw:

> **Hope Grutman:** I heard a mom in this neighbor-
> hood was abducted, or attacked, or something
> like that. My nanny heard the grandma talking to

someone about it at the grocery store. Does anyone know anything about this? So worried for her, and so scared this could happen in our neighborhood.

14 replies

Cece Asher: Yes. She's my neighbor. She's been missing since Friday, apparently. She has a three month old. I feel so terrible for her family. But I don't know about abducted. I heard she just bailed. My girlfriend has seen her with the baby and said she seems like a total space cadet.

Andrea Sweeney: I heard about this. I heard that she committed suicide but the family is trying to keep it a secret. It's so sad but thank god she didn't hurt the baby. Moms, if you're struggling, get some help. Don't suffer in silence.

Sarah O: Does the family need anything? Food? Is there anything we can do? Where do they live?

Tina Butler: They're like millionaires based on his linkedin title and the fact they apparently live in a town house by themselves so I really doubt they need anything from us. It's always rich people involved in shit like this. Just wait—dirty little secrets will start to come out.

Marni Becker: Isn't it always the husband in these situations . . . googled her husband and he's a big shot . . . probably the kind of guy who thinks he can get away with murder, if that's what he wanted. Poor woman and poor baby.

Annie Schwartz: Disgusted with the above comments. What do you mean "shit like this"? This is a tragedy, not gossip. This is none of our business. Respect the privacy of the family. Does anyone in this group even know her?

Katherine Rodksy: She goes to my yoga studio. She wasn't very friendly, though. Also way too thin for someone who just had a baby. Prayers that she's okay.

Angela Hunter: Stuff like this never used to happen in this neighborhood. This is EXACTLY why they shouldn't have moved the homeless men to the Two Parks Hotel. It's ridiculous to have these CRIMINALS living as our neighbors. And now one of us is dead. When will our council people come to their senses and get those men relocated?

Laurie Balick: @Angela Hunter Think before you type, please. You can't just blame innocent people for murder, and we don't even know that there WAS a murder. If it were a hotel filled with white people, would you make that assumption?

Natasha Glaze: @Angela Hunter Ew. Good to know racism is alive and well on the UWS. Not that I ever doubted it.

Eric Weinstock: @Natasha Glaze To come to @ Angela Hunter's defense, the fact is that there is a hotel filled with criminals and drug addicts a few blocks away from the scene of the crime. You can call it racism, but a healthy dose of suspicion is valid here. Crime has gone up since they moved here. It's a fact. It's not a race issue.

Natasha Glaze: @Eric Weinstock Nothing is a race issue for you because you're white. You don't get it. They are human beings who need a place to live, and because of their race, they're presumed guilty about anything and everything, and always have been. So yes, it's a race issue to accuse them of something based on no evidence whatsoever. Btw dude why are you even in this group? It's for MOMS.

Eric Weinstock: @Natasha Glaze Excuse me for wanting to be part of our local parenting community. Based on the hostility I see here regularly, it might not be the right resource for our family after all.

Natasha Glaze: @Eric Weinstock Calling out someone for blatant racism isn't hostile, but I'm not surprised you'd see it that way. Have a nice day.

The chain continued to veer further away from Isabel's disappearance. I was familiar with the conflict they were referring to: a couple of months ago, Project Renewal had partnered with the Two Parks Hotel on Seventy-Ninth Street, using it as a temporary shelter for eighty homeless men in treatment for addiction. The neighborhood seemed divided on this: some people were outraged by their newfound proximity to recovering addicts, some of whom did have criminal records, and others thought it was a great use of the space and the neighborhood resources, an example of effective housing justice that we should all be proud to be participating in. I personally hadn't noticed any concerning behavior near the hotel, or sensed any decline in safety in the neighborhood whatsoever, but for a while, you couldn't walk a block without a NIMBY approaching you asking you to sign a petition to remove them, insisting that there were too many families and schools in this neighborhood to safely host these men. Which made me wonder: Where in New York, or the world, *weren't* there families and schools?

I wasted time scrolling through other, more trivial, posts, trying to take my mind off Isabel:

> **Valerie Baker:** Hi moms! Where can I find XXXXL (lol) sleep sacks?! My 3 y/o does NOT like sleeping with a loose blanket. It *hurts* his legs. Yes. Hurts. But it's hard to find a sack that fits because the kid weighs 40 pounds. Lolol. Help please.

> *27 replies*

> **Melissa Gross:** Moms of kids in gifted and talented programs—when did you start practicing for the test? Are you happy with the programs at PS 9 and PS 166? My girl is 2.5 but it's never too soon to think ahead right! Also interested in music programs for her if anyone has any recs.

> *53 replies*

Allie Brennan: If you have a vista stroller with a yellow cup holder, and a roughly 4 y/o son with a Paw Patrol raincoat, please PM me. I want to talk to you about your nanny. I have some rather serious concerns and if I were you I'd want to know what I saw her doing.

107 replies

Anika Ayub: Planning my mom's surprise 75th birthday! Does anyone know which restaurants in the neighborhood have private rooms?

9 replies

Finally, I put my phone down, exhausted. Clara was dozing noisily, no longer latched to my right boob, but using it as a pillow instead. Reading Upper West Side Moms almost always left me with a headache, and yet, I continued to do it regularly.

I had just managed to successfully transfer Clara to her bassinet—a rare feat for me—and was tiptoeing out of her room (actually, my room, though it certainly didn't feel that way anymore) when loud knocking on my apartment door made me jump.

I hadn't heard the buzzer downstairs and I had no idea who this could be. Even though it was Sunday, Tim had to be at work most of the day, since he had a big pitch coming up midweek. I was annoyed that he had to work on a weekend, but I believed him when he said it was unavoidable. And I knew he'd been trying to be home as much as possible; he'd managed to dial back his travel significantly, having taken only a couple of day trips to DC and Boston since Clara had been born. Maybe it was him knocking if he'd forgotten his key, but I wasn't expecting him back until close to dinnertime. I hadn't ordered food, either;

I actually hadn't eaten at all yet that day—just coffee—and I couldn't remember any significant meals yesterday, either. A lot of string cheeses and peanut butter spoonfuls. Tim and I had ordered Thai for dinner last night, but it took so long to arrive that I was passed out on the couch by the time it did, and he hadn't wanted to wake me. I'd shoved a spring roll down my throat following a 1:00 a.m. feed.

I hustled to the door to avoid more loud knocking, thinking, *Whoever this is, if you wake my baby, you can get her back to sleep yourself.*

My heart leaped into my throat: two police officers stood at my door. They weren't wearing uniforms, but they were each holding their badges for me to see. They were a man and a woman: he in his late forties, she just a little older than me, maybe.

"Are you Jennifer Donnelly?" the male officer asked.

"Yes?" It squeaked out as a question.

"Hi. I'm Detective Sherer," he said, "and this is Detective Blaylock." She smiled faintly and nodded, looking past me and seeming to briefly take in the hurricane of baby gear that was my apartment. "Okay if we come in?" her partner went on. "We have a few questions for you about Isabel Harris. We're investigating her disappearance."

"Oh, um, sure. Of course. My baby is sleeping in the next room, so can we talk quietly?"

"Absolutely. Been there." He smiled with pursed lips. "Mine are grown now, of course."

I felt like I couldn't breathe. I knew they were probably just covering their bases, checking in with all Isabel's friends and acquaintances, but regardless, my face was burning, and I knew my neck and chest were suddenly blotchy. It was like being pulled over: even if I knew it was only for a minor speed infraction or a broken taillight, I suddenly and inexplicably felt as if I had drugs and guns in my car.

"Do you guys want something to drink?" I had no idea how I was supposed to act in this situation. I probably wasn't supposed to call them "you guys," though.

"No, that's okay," Sherer said. "Thank you." They each perched gingerly on the breast milk–stained, well-worn sofa. I sat directly across from them in the glider that we had bought a few weeks after Clara was born, when we realized how necessary it was for soothing, even though we'd initially resisted it since it didn't go with anything else in our living room.

Detective Blaylock, the woman, spoke up this time. "So we'll start with the basics. When was the last time you saw Isabel before she disappeared?"

I tried to think. What day was it today? Sunday. How long had it been since she disappeared? Three days—two and a half? To my foggy, sleep-deprived brain, this felt like a very difficult question.

"Well, let me think," I said, trying to sound competent. "I learned of her disappearance this past Friday afternoon. Our moms' group met, and she wasn't there. After the meeting we all got a text from Vanessa, that's a woman in our group, saying she found out that Isabel was missing. So I guess the last time I saw her before that was at our meeting the previous Friday." I took out my phone and pulled up the calendar. "Friday, September twenty-fifth, looks like."

"Are you sure?" Blaylock's response was immediate.

"Yes, I am. Pretty sure."

"Hmm. That's a little perplexing," Sherer said. He was like a caricature of a cop—a little paunchy, with a Brooklyn accent. I wouldn't have been surprised if he'd taken a doughnut out of his pocket. "The thing is that one of the reasons we're here is that we thought—we *hoped*, actually—that you were one of the last people to see Isabel. That maybe you'd have more information for us."

"No. Like I said, I haven't seen her since two Fridays ago. Honestly, I've only met her a handful of times and really didn't know her well." I could hear that I sounded sketchy, like I was trying to distance myself from her and her disappearance, though I myself had no idea why. I had nothing to hide.

"You can use present tense, Ms. Donnelly. We don't know that she's dead." This felt like a line that Detective Sherer had used before and enjoyed deploying.

"Oh, I know. I just mean before she disappeared." I tried to recover, though I realized my use of past tense there really was a bad look. "Anyway, I don't really understand. I'm sure her husband saw her shortly before she disappeared, right? Like, that night? So it's not like I would have been the last one to see her, even if I had seen her another time between Friday the twenty-fifth and when she disappeared."

"But you didn't."

"Right."

"Her husband was traveling for work and was just back that night. He did see her, but their interaction was brief. So we need you to help us figure something out."

"Sure, of course. I mean, I'll try."

"Isabel's Google Calendar had 'drinks with Jenn D.' slotted for Thursday at seven p.m., Thursday the first, that is. Ultimately, this was the night she disappeared, at around ten thirty p.m. Did you have plans and she didn't show up? Or did she cancel? Knowing this is very important for establishing our timeline."

"No. No. I mean, that's so weird. We never had plans. Like I said, I really didn't know her well." Man, I could *not* speak in the present tense to save my life. "We've never hung out outside of the moms' group meetings. Definitely never just the two of us." *What the hell?* was flying through my head on repeat.

Blaylock tipped closer to the edge of the couch. "Then, do you have any idea why she would have these plans logged in her phone? Is it possible that you had plans and you simply forgot? It would be totally understandable. You've got a lot going on." She smiled and gestured gently to my bomb site of an apartment. She genuinely seemed like she was trying to be helpful. I wondered if she was a mom, too, and could empathize with my messy home and malfunctioning brain.

My brow was furrowed. Lately when I was aware that I was doing that, I quickly reminded myself to unfurrow because I could see the wrinkles taking up a permanent home on my face. In this case, I couldn't maintain a relaxed expression for anything. *Did* I have plans with Isabel the night she disappeared? I really and truly didn't think so. But my mind also did not feel like my own these days. Between the lack of sleep, thinking only about the baby, and admittedly drinking too much wine as my only method of relaxing, forgetting plans with a friend didn't seem too far outside the realm of possibility. I had actually just stood up my best friend from college, Jules, a few weeks ago, thinking our plans were for Friday when they were actually for Thursday. I was in a near-constant cycle of receiving Amazon packages that I had little recollection of having ordered. But it seemed crazy that I wouldn't remember making plans with Isabel, since it would have been our first "date," so to speak.

"Could it have been a different Jenn D.?" I offered hopefully. "Like a Jen with one *n*?"

"Well, you're the only Jennifer in her contacts," Blaylock said. "And it was your spelling. Two *n*'s. And, given that your friendship is what we call 'active,' it seems most plausible that she was talking about you."

"Right. Well, I don't know. I mean, that's really weird." I knew I sounded like a broken record. "I don't think I had plans with her. But in any event, I definitely didn't see her that Thursday."

"And you're sure." Sherer looked dubious.

"Yes. I am."

I heard Clara whimper from the bedroom. Great. She'd been sleeping for roughly fifteen minutes.

"One more question," Sherer said. "In your moms' group meetings, did Isabel seem well? Did she seem to be managing okay?"

"Definitely," I said, my voice sounding anything but definite. "I mean, she seemed overwhelmed at times, but, well, we all do. She was handling everything very well, I think. She seemed very organized. She seemed a little . . . intense? But like, she was on top of it. If that makes sense." It was the best I could do to describe Isabel. Some kind of ineffable sadness clung to her, but it wasn't like she ever forgot diapers.

Clings to her. *Clings.* Present tense, Jenn.

"Okay." Sherer looked disappointed and skeptical at the same time.

Clara let out another cry.

"Well," he said, "it sounds like you're about to have your hands full here. Glad we could catch you during a free minute." Yeah. I was thrilled to have spent my few free minutes of Clara's nap being rattled by detectives, too. "By the way, what happened to your hand?" With his head, Sherer gestured toward my right hand, which had about a dozen tiny scratches covering my knuckles and fingers. I hadn't even noticed them until he'd pointed it out.

"Um . . . I have no idea, actually. Weird. It doesn't hurt or anything, though."

"Well, that's good," Blaylock said kindly. "Might be from the baby's fingernails. Sometimes they can be sharper than you realize!"

I silently added that to the list of things I was doing incorrectly: not keeping Clara's nails short enough. If that's even where the scratches were from. I truly didn't know.

Sherer hoisted himself to his feet, Blaylock rising lightly with him. "If you think of anything," he said, "anything that might help us reconcile this . . . misunderstanding about the drinks date, please give us a call. Either of us." He handed me a card, and she did the same.

"You guys don't think she did this to herself, do you? Is that why you were asking about how she seemed? Do you think she . . . hurt herself?"

"We're investigating every possibility right now. But the evidence that we have points to a crime. Not self-harm. We're just trying to get a sense of the state she was in at the time of her disappearance."

I followed them to the door. "Well, do you guys have any leads? Any idea what might have happened to her?" Just as when I was at her house, I was aware that I was probably pushing too far. But I couldn't help myself.

Blaylock cocked her head slightly. "We're not really at liberty to discuss where we're at with the case, Ms. Donnelly. But I'll say this: no body is a blessing and a curse for investigators. It leaves us with hope that she's alive, but without the clues we would have if there was a body."

"I heard you found blood." I swear, I used to have some kind of a filter back when I actually slept.

"Yes, we did find some of her blood." She gave nothing further.

"Wait, one more question. Her husband—you know, he didn't even know she was in a new moms' group." I realized it wasn't a question at all after the words had finished tumbling out.

"And?"

"Don't you think that's kind of . . . like, inconsiderate? Neglectful? A red flag about their marriage?"

Sherer stepped in. "With respect, I have no idea what my wife does all day, and I'm pretty sure she prefers it that way," he said, again sounding like this was a line he delivered often and that never failed to please him with its cleverness. I thought I caught an almost imperceptible eye roll from Blaylock at this, as though she were thinking the same thing I was, which was *What a bunch of misogynistic bullshit.* But it may have been wishful thinking on my part. "Besides, as you may know, he's been cleared already." Sherer seemed too smug delivering this news.

"Right. Why was he cleared, again?"

"Conveniently, the couple have a Nest camera. It clearly shows Connor sleeping in their bed all night. A trip to the bathroom at two a.m. confirms his identity."

So what Louise had said was true. And the bathroom trip debunked my theory that Connor was trying to pull some kind of *Weekend at Bernie's* stunt by putting a dummy in the bed.

"But wasn't *he* the last person to see her? When was that, again?"

Sherer sighed as if explaining all this to me were a huge chore, but really, I could tell he was the type of person who enjoyed delineating information to others (especially women, in all likelihood) as if they were children and he was the teacher. I wondered how Blaylock dealt with being his partner. He was sort of insufferable. "Yes, he was the last person to see her that we know of, but she left to walk her dog after they said good night. And then the dog returned to the front steps alone. So she could have seen other people. We just don't know. Yet." He looked at me pointedly, as if to say, *We think it was you.* I shuddered involuntarily.

Sherer checked his watch. "If you think of anything alarming that you witnessed concerning Isabel in the days or weeks leading up to her disappearance—or anything regarding the plans that you may or may not have had the night she disappeared—you'll give us a call right away, please." It was a statement, not a question. They only wanted to ask me about how she seemed and the drinks date that never happened—they clearly weren't interested in my hot take on the case beyond that, which I could hardly blame them for.

"But couldn't he have hired someone?" It just popped out.

Sherer looked at me sideways yet again. "Do you have reason to suspect him, ma'am? Other than the fact that he didn't know about your group?" The sudden interjection of the word "ma'am" and the slight disdain with which he said "your group" let me know that this conversation was no longer a particularly friendly one and needed to come to an end.

"No, I don't. I guess I just read too many thrillers. It's always the husband." I laughed a little to try to get myself out of the hole I had dug. *Why* am *I so suspicious of Connor?* I truly wasn't sure. There was just something about him that irked the hell out of me.

Blaylock smiled reassuringly but was silent. Sherer said curtly, "Right. Well, you probably know this from all those thrillers you read, but if you *did* happen to see Isabel on that Thursday night, we'll find out. And soon. So if anything occurs to you that would make you want to edit your story, you know where to find us. It would be much better coming from you than—than not. You have yourself a good rest of the day." He nodded at me. "It's beautiful out there, you know," he added, condescendingly. Apparently it was obvious that I hadn't been outside yet that day. I felt a fresh flush of shame over how filthy my apartment was, with piles of clothes everywhere and a faint milky odor. Even the cops were judging me for my maternal incompetence and slovenly apartment.

But I couldn't muster too much concern for that, because all I could think about was *Why would Isabel's calendar declare plans with me the night of her disappearance?*

Chapter Nine

Sunday, October 4

The second they left, I grabbed my phone to check my own calendar. Thursday, October 1: nothing. I searched the surrounding days, too, to be thorough. Aside from moms' group on Fridays and the occasional pediatrician appointment for Clara, my calendar was blushingly bare.

Next, I searched my texts. Had she texted me about plans? My only one-on-one text with her was just after I'd attended my first meeting, after which we'd exchanged numbers. She'd sweetly said, **So nice meeting you and Clara! She's adorable, like her mom. Looking forward to getting to know you both better!** Our only other communication was in group texts with the other moms. I searched my Gmail to be safe. My sole email correspondence with her was when she emailed me the details of the moms' group meeting, following her (delayed) response to my Facebook post.

I couldn't find any trace of communication with Isabel on my phone that I'd forgotten about. No reason why she would think we'd have plans on Thursday the first.

None of this made any sense. Why did Isabel think we had plans? And at 7:00 p.m., meaning it wouldn't have even been a playdate. It would have been just the two of us. Had she planned on asking me to get together, and then never did? Was she interested in one-on-one time with me for a specific reason? And, most importantly, if she had wanted to see me outside of our meetings, why hadn't she asked?

The detectives' visit to my apartment would have felt routine, like I was just a check on a long roster of all the people she knew, if it weren't for this calendar entry. This felt dangerous. Like I was a suspect or something.

I finally put my phone down and went to the bedroom to scoop Clara from her bassinet; her fussing had turned into decisive *Come get me NOW* cries. I returned to the living room with her, flopped onto the couch, and yanked my shirt down, not caring that I was ruining the ancient, pilly Gap V-neck that probably belonged in the trash. I hoped Clara would latch quickly so that I could get back to the business of Isabel, and she did. She began nursing eagerly, and only then did I notice that as she drank, she was scratching my chest gently with her fingernails, which were indeed a bit long. But not hard enough to make cuts—not even close. So the mysterious cuts covering my knuckles that the detectives had inquired about remained unexplained. *What the hell did I do to my hand?*

I decided to open up my *Isabel* search to my entire phone, just to see if anything else at all came up. First, my search history, which yielded only evidence of very recently googling her name after she disappeared, and then, from further back, my Ingrid & Isabel maternity wear purchases. Then I checked my notes. There were notes that made little sense to me and that I barely remembered writing:

9/17 3:23 a.m. Pretty Baby don't look for me a good marriage the Herd

These, I realized after a minute, were four separate titles of books I wanted to read but sadly probably wouldn't anytime soon.

9/21 1:21 a.m. pump tube thingy???

I needed to order new valves for my breast pump but had apparently forgotten what they were called when writing this note.

9/23 2:01 a.m. Mom I miss you so much please come back

Reading this one made my eyes sting and heart hurt.

There was nothing about Isabel in my notes.

I opened up Google Docs. I hadn't been using the app much, since usually I only did so for lesson planning and work-related stuff. So it was surprising that there was a new Doc. Untitled. Friday, September 25. Appeared to be only one line. I opened it.

Isabel doesn't matter.

My heart leaped out of my chest. It was a surprise that Clara didn't propel off me.

What the hell were these words doing in my documents? I hadn't written these. I couldn't have. What did they mean?

My mind jumped to the same explanation I had offered the detectives about myself: Could this be about a different Isabel? But I really didn't know any other Isabels. Certainly none whom I would have written this about. But I couldn't imagine writing this about *her*, either.

Next possibility—could this be someone else's Google Doc that I was invited to view?

I checked the file's ownership settings and saw my own Gmail address there.

And no other people had viewing or editing access to the Doc.

Had I—could I possibly have—written this?

And on Friday, September 25.

The last time I had seen Isabel.

Why would I have written this?

I thought hard. Admittedly, sometimes I left our meetings feeling a little down. The other moms, Isabel included—even Kira, if I was being honest—just had their shit together more than I did. So sometimes our conversations left me feeling more inadequate than uplifted. Sometimes I felt a bit excluded on the basis of wealth, too: the talk of Comotomo bottles, SNOO bassinets, BabyBjörn chairs, private twos programs, and Jacadi clothing made me feel like not only was I failing Clara in emotional ways, I was also coming up short by not being able to give her all this great stuff that the other moms were giving their babies.

But the frustrations I felt during our meetings were mild, for the most part. I liked these women. A lot. I admired them. I enjoyed and felt I was benefiting from seeing how other moms were managing the roller coaster of new motherhood. I valued their insight and advice. And I loved getting wine with them after.

Didn't I?

Isabel doesn't matter. Had she said something that hurt me? What had I meant by this?

I couldn't have written this. And yet, here it was. On my phone. In my Docs. Undeniable.

And, truthfully, there were plenty of other things I couldn't remember these days.

I could never remember how many feeds or soiled diapers Clara had in a day; when they asked me this question at our biweekly pediatrician appointments, I inevitably shrugged helplessly.

I never left the house with everything—whether it was diapers, a sweater, or my keys, I could be sure that I was forgetting something I would invariably need.

I forgot whole conversations with Tim, resulting in him looking at me incredulously, saying, "You really don't remember us talking about this already?" before backtracking after he realized he was hurting my feelings.

I had forgotten Clara's middle name while filling out a form at the doctor's office. I actually had to text Tim so that he could remind me that it was Violet. It simply wasn't in my brain. I knew it was a flower. I could not for the life of me remember which one.

I had neglected to upload Clara's birth certificate to file my maternity leave with the Department of Education, resulting in some nightmarish calls with Human Resources to sort it out.

I watched the same episode of *Sons of Anarchy* three times because I didn't remember having seen it. It was Tim who asked me, half paying attention to the show while he worked beside me on the couch one night, "You really like this episode, huh?"

Most concerningly, it was only about a week ago that Tim had woken me up from a sound sleep—while I was standing over Clara's bassinet. "Babe, what are you doing?" he'd asked softly, putting a hand on my back.

"Checking on the baby. One of us has to," I'd snapped. (Even in a total fog, I was good for some unwarranted passive aggression.) There was only one problem.

"The baby's in the bed," he'd said, pointing to where the baby was indeed fast asleep on her DockATot atop our comforter. I had been sleeping standing up, hovering over an empty bassinet.

Was there any way I could have written this about Isabel and forgotten about it? Or written it in my sleep?

And if so—could the apparent anger I felt toward Isabel have played a role in her disappearance? Could *I* have played a role?

I tried to claw my way out of this thought tunnel. I deleted the file hurriedly and then deleted it from my trash folder. I wouldn't be able to forget it, but I needed to make sure no one else saw it. There had been detectives at my home to ask me about a missing woman, whom, according to my Google documents, I had some kind of issue with, and with whom I'd apparently had plans the night of her disappearance.

Suddenly, the water I was swimming in felt much, much too deep.

I looked at my tiny, perfect daughter, half dozing but still latched to my breast. The one thing I was sure of: I had too much to lose for anyone else to see what was written on that document. But I also needed to figure out why I'd written it, or how it had gotten there. Because if I had written it and had forgotten—and had forgotten what had caused me to write it—what else might I be forgetting?

May 1

Dear Baby,

Very soon now, you'll be in my arms instead of in my belly. You and me against the world. We, us. A team. Will I be enough for you? I'm going to try my hardest, that's for damn sure. And I'm going to make your world as beautiful as I possibly can.

In a way, I wonder if the strange mess that brought you to me will make us closer, right out of the gates. I hope it will.

And I hope you know that, whenever you read this, you can ask me anything you want to.

So here goes—the truth. Our truth: you were conceived during an ill-advised one-night stand.

If you can even call it that.

I stayed behind at a bar after my friends left one night. I wanted one more drink—it had been an exhausting week at work, and I was too wound up to go home yet.

And there was a guy, and he was alone, too, and he was suave and persistent and handsome. There were drinks, too many of them, and there was his hotel room, right upstairs.

I don't remember that much, but what I do remember is not pretty.

I'm sorry I don't have a better story for you. Mom and Dad met, fell in love, got married, baby makes three. This isn't that, or anything close to it.

When I decided I wanted to be your mom—and again, please know that for me, it was a stunningly easy decision—I vowed I'd put him out of my mind. That he wasn't part of this, wasn't relevant, never would be.

But it wasn't that easy. I thought about that night a lot. And I got curious, because I knew you would one day get curious, too. And I wanted to get ahead of that.

One problem—I knew almost nothing about him. Nothing to tell you not if, but *when*, you asked, no way of contacting him in the event that I felt I should, for whatever reason. What if you needed a kidney donor one day, for God's sake? I knew that I should at least know who the hell he was, even if I have no interest in ever seeing or speaking to him again.

Of course I tried googling him—he'd told me that his name was Brendan Wallace, that he was a sports agent from Cincinnati. Google could not find such a person.

Fortunately, your aunt is the kind of woman who can track anyone down on social media or the internet, even if all she had was a cocktail napkin they'd used, or the first name of their second cousin's dog. So I enlisted her help.

The fact was, I hadn't even wanted to tell her I was pregnant, at first. She's sort of been more of a mom than a sister to me; she's eight years older, and our mom died when we were young, so she always helped take care of me (while also being extremely judgmental of what she perceives as my many shortcomings). I knew she'd have some strong opinions about my choice to keep the baby. Sorry, to keep *you*. So I waited until pretty late in my pregnancy to tell her.

I should have given her more credit. She was supportive, or supportive-ish, and promised to love you like mad.

Anyway, when I told her I wanted to find out more about your father, she went back to the bar where we'd met that night. She sweet-talked the bartender into printing out the credit card receipts from the night we were there. The bar wasn't crowded that night. There were forty-one receipts. Twenty-five of them men. She googled and pulled up pictures of every single one of those men until we found him.

I looked him up—the real him. Suffice it to say, none of what he told me about himself that night was true.

For one thing, he's married. Of course he is. When I found that out, I felt a lot of emotions, but surprise wasn't one of them.

Is it too soon for me to give you advice, having not even met you yet? If you find yourself in a situation with a guy, or girl, and things aren't going the way you anticipated—if it isn't what you wanted—*say* so. Scream it! It's hard for me to say that to you, because I don't want you to think that I regret the outcome of that night—you—and yet, I do regret not trying everything I could to stop it while it was happening. Because it wasn't what I wanted. Or what I thought it would be.

I also know better than to blame myself. Officially. But while it was going on, and even now, that's exactly what goes through my head: *You shouldn't have stayed there alone. You shouldn't have drunk so much. You shouldn't have been wearing that top. You shouldn't have kissed him.* It's what women are trained to do—blame themselves. I promise to teach you better.

Only one thing matters to me, now, though: you. Kicking, churning inside me. My sweet love. I will see you soon.

Love you forever,
Mommy

Chapter Ten

Monday, October 5

As much as I didn't want anyone to find out what was on my phone, I was also desperate to talk to someone about the detectives' visit and what they'd asked me about my alleged plans with Isabel the night she disappeared. It made no sense, and the more I thought about it, the more certain I was that this was a simple misunderstanding with an accessible explanation. Maybe one of the other moms would be able to make sense of it. I told Tim that detectives had stopped by to talk to me, but he was surprisingly nonchalant about it and didn't ask me too many questions about their visit. He said it was logical that they'd talk to everyone who had seen her recently. For reasons I couldn't explain myself, I didn't tell him about what they'd said about me having plans with her, though.

And of course, I didn't mention the Google Doc to him. I would never mention it to anyone. I needed to make sure no one ever saw that again. Including myself. As much as I yearned for an explanation—and surely there was one—it was more important that it stayed buried and forgotten. Forever.

Add it to my list of secrets.

Days had passed since Isabel's disappearance, and there were no leads that I was aware of. I kept looking for news items on Isabel, even though her name was already plugged into my Google Alerts. There was a brief item in the local *West Side Rag*: Search Underway for Local Missing Mom: Foul Play Suspected. The comment thread on this article had devolved, just like the one following the Upper West Side Moms Facebook post, into an argument about whether it was safe to house the men at the Two Parks Hotel.

I supposed that if Isabel were found dismembered on the side of the highway, it might be newsworthy. But for whatever reason, as it was, the search for her was still largely not being picked up by the press.

Punctuating the stress I was feeling about Isabel still being missing, and the Google Doc that must never be excavated, was the fact that I was also one week closer to ending my maternity leave—just three weeks to go, in fact. My principal had called me about a week ago to "check in," and the conversation had left me nauseated. She'd brought up various tasks I would need to complete before returning, such as syncing up my syllabus with the substitute's, submitting my first unit plan for my yearly portfolio, and drafting an assessment map for the year. These tasks, which I had once executed with relative ease and enthusiasm—actually enjoying poring over rubrics, geekily thinking about each and every word in every grid box—now sounded completely foreign to me, like I was being given a to-do list in another language. I didn't even know where to begin. *Tying my shoe* tired me. Literally. I was pretty much exclusively wearing slip-ons. Opening up an Excel document and generating grading criteria for a thesis statement would surely kill me.

I had been uneasily dwelling on my conversation with her ever since—a conversation that had, ironically, ended with her asking if I was excited to have a break from the baby. As if work were some kind of a break! As if the thought of being separated from Clara didn't make me salivate with both desire and nausea. My feelings were ineffable, but "excited" wasn't the word. The strangest part was that my principal was in her early forties and had three young kids herself. So I couldn't understand why she seemed to have no idea how I was feeling right now, how impossible my return felt to me. It just served to confirm that I might really be the only person, or at least one of the very few, who found all this so very hard.

On this Monday morning, Tim had stuck around putting final touches on the design he was pitching at a meeting closer to our apartment than his office in Brooklyn. I think he also felt guilty about leaving me alone with the baby all day on Sunday.

I kind of liked watching him work. His brow was furrowed and he was completely focused, sitting tall at his slanted desk by the window, visibly present in both his body and brain, pausing only to push his glasses back up on his nose. He used to work from home frequently, but since Clara was born, he preferred to go to his office, or a shared work space he sometimes used in our neighborhood. Anywhere but here, pretty much. But I was glad he was here this morning because it gave me an opportunity to talk to him about something I'd been thinking about vaguely for a few weeks now.

He saw me looking at him and smiled slightly. "What's up, babe?" His pet name filled me with guilty bile rather than warmth. I didn't deserve his love, though I had no intention of telling him this.

"I don't know." I shrugged. Not a strong opening. "Remember I mentioned I talked to my principal a few days ago? It's got me thinking that I might not be quite ready to go back yet."

He blinked. Which was fair: that was a blink-worthy comment. "Really?" he said. "I thought you were psyched to go back to work? What about Diana?"

We had already found a fantastic nanny through a referral in Upper West Side Moms. (Occasionally, the Facebook group was good for more than helping me pass mindless minutes nosily reading about other people's problems.) She came highly recommended from someone in the group whose children were now both in elementary school and no longer needed full-time care.

"Yeah, I know. I hate to lose her. But maybe we could offer her a few afternoons a week until I go back full time—sort of a peace offering? And it would be amazing for me to get a break."

He'd turned fully toward me now, his eyes slightly obscured behind the windows' glare playing over the lenses of his glasses. "Yeah. I hear you," he said, his voice carefully modulated. "But I don't know. We'd be stretched pretty thin if we were paying for a part-time nanny *and* you aren't working."

He was only being practical. I knew that. But it felt like my options were either round-the-clock childcare with no shower breaks, or to return to a job that I simply wasn't ready to do. "I get that. So maybe we'd lose Diana. It'd be too bad, but . . . it's just weird to go back to school in November, right in the middle of the semester. It makes a lot more sense for me to go back in January. Or even next year. Have a clean start."

"Next year?" He was holding himself very still, but his Adam's apple bobbed as he swallowed dryly. He'd leaned toward me a little, just enough so that I could see the flecks of green in his soft brown eyes. I certainly had his whole attention. "Look, I support whatever you think is best. It's your call." And, to his credit, he sounded sincere. "But . . . I thought you hated being alone with Clara all day? And loafing around with the Lululemon moms? I figured you'd be eager to get back to work and have someone else helping you out with Clara."

Lululemon moms. Okay, I'd originated the phrase, but still. I was one of them, wasn't I? And "hated" was such a strong word, and it stung. Did he think I hated being a mom? Was that how I seemed? I felt damned if I did, damned if I didn't. If I stayed home with Clara, I *would* be kind of miserable—what did that say about me? But if my only reason for going to work was to avoid my baby, that made me even more terrible. And again, his characterization of the moms' group—he was only repeating my own words, but for some reason, hearing it from his lips irritated the hell out of me.

"We don't 'loaf around,' first of all. We're actually pretty busy taking care of children. You know, like yours? And maybe the reason we're all in yoga pants is because we're too tired to put on real clothes—from never sleeping? And our vaginas are still healing. From pushing humans out of them." Man, I was even more fired up about his comment than I'd realized.

"Okay, okay." He put his hands up surrender-style, realizing he'd screwed up. "I'm sorry. Bad choice of words. Before this turns into another fight, is this actually about wanting to continue staying home with Clara? Or something else? You haven't been . . . yourself lately. And now your friend is missing." He'd kept his tone calm, and now it softened even further. "I'm worried about her, too, obviously. But it's you I most care about. And I just want to make sure that more time off is part of a solution, and doesn't end up making you feel even more stressed out, with more time to worry about . . . everything you've got going on."

I made myself take a breath. What he was saying was fair. I honestly wasn't sure if prolonging this stage—my day-to-day grind with Clara, and now obsessing over Isabel, too—would be healthy. All I really knew was that I physically could not put on black pants and a sweater, kiss my baby goodbye, and facilitate discussions about literature all day. Attend staff meetings. Grade papers. Email with parents. I wasn't there yet: I couldn't visualize it, couldn't fathom it, certainly couldn't do it.

"I'll give it some more thought. But I just wanted to put it on your radar that this is something I'm considering."

"Okay. Again, I support whatever you decide to do. Shit, I'm going to be late." He started putting the papers in front of him into a folder.

"Wait, before you go—random question for you?"

"Shoot."

"Did I say anything to you about having plans a while back, the week before last? With Isabel?"

He scrunched his forehead, sending his glasses sliding down his nose again. "No, I don't think so. Why?"

"No reason. It was something the cops mentioned. It was surely a mistake. Just kind of weirded me out, that's all. But I've been home every night, right?"

"Yeah, definitely. I mean, you went out some weeks back with your teacher friends"—I gulped—"and then there was that random night you went walking."

"What?"

"You remember. It was probably a week or two ago. You came home at like, eleven p.m. I didn't even know you'd been gone. I knew you'd gotten up, but I figured it was to help Clara. But when you got back in bed, you said you couldn't sleep and went for a walk."

None of this sounded remotely familiar to me. I had definitely taken a few evening walks following days where I hadn't managed to leave the house, or when my blood was boiling with the stress of the day, but I didn't remember ever taking one so late at night. "What night was it?" My pulse was suddenly racing.

"Oh man. I have no idea. It might have even been a few weeks back. That's probably why you don't remember, because it was a while ago. It wasn't a big deal. It's not like it was the middle of the night. Lots of people take walks to calm down. It's a little strange you don't remember, but you're tired. Don't sweat it."

He put his folder into his shoulder bag and then walked over to the counter and poured his mug of coffee into his ancient yellow Michigan thermos, spilling a few drops without noticing.

"Okay, I really gotta go. Bye, babe. Bye, smaller babe." He kissed us both and was off to a day of being around other adults, using his brain and his degree. I wondered if he even thought of us while he was at work.

And I wondered where the hell I'd gone on this walk that I had no recollection of. And when exactly it had taken place. If there was a chance it was the Thursday that Isabel disappeared at around 10:30 p.m. Because all these questions led to the most important and frightening one, a question I didn't even want to think, let alone utter out loud: *Could I have had something to do with Isabel's disappearance?*

Chapter Eleven

Monday, October 5

I was desperate for some company and someone to talk about Isabel with. I had texted Kira, my usual first line for one-on-one hangouts, a couple of times in the past few days, actually, but she said she'd had some bad nights with Caleb, was super tired, not up for leaving her apartment. I would have offered to go there, but it seemed a little too pushy.

I thought about reaching out to my best friend, Jules. We'd been friends since freshman year of college when I'd had to tell her that I'd accidentally used her toothbrush in our hallway bathroom because our toiletry caddies were identical. "Um, you can keep it, obviously," she'd said to me with a wry grin, and we were inseparable from then on. Jenn and Jules. We'd proudly declared ourselves J-Squared when we were drunk once, and laughed about it for hours, only to wake up the next morning and realize that it was not the least bit funny or clever, which made us laugh even harder.

Now Jules did interior design for stores, so she was frequently out and about rather than stuck in an office, and she'd told me several times that she could stop by whenever I wanted company while I was on maternity leave. But the truth was that we'd been off ever since I'd had Clara. It was hard to explain, but being with her made me feel more tired than I already was. She had so much energy, was so blatantly well rested, had so much *freedom*. She was super interested in Clara, and so sweet with her, but I worried that if I had to kick her out at a moment's notice, like if Clara had a meltdown, or if I simply wanted to take advantage of her nap time to nap myself, she wouldn't understand. Or if Clara was screaming and I couldn't figure out why, she'd talk about me later over wine at 9:00 p.m. at some cute spot in the West Village with one of our other friends: "Oh my God, Jenn is struggling, huh? She looks like hell. Poor thing. When I'm a mom, I'm definitely going to . . ." and proceed to list all the ways they'd do it better, differently, than me, when it was their turn. Our relationship was also complicated by the fact that she was still single and I knew she wanted to be married with a baby, too, so I felt guilty complaining to her, even though my situation felt far from enviable. More often than not, I decided against calling her, after going through all these made-up scenarios of ways in which it could go poorly in my head.

I knew Vanessa was working, which still blew my mind, so I went out on a limb and texted Selena: Hey! Plans today? Any interest in coming over this afternoon? We weren't necessarily super close, but I knew it would make me feel better to socialize.

She texted back right away and said Sounds good! Does around 3:00 work?

I tried to force myself to clean the apartment, though one mess just led to the next, making the task seem more and more insurmountable. If I ran the dishwasher, I'd have to put the dishes away. If I put clothes in the washer, I should really strip the bed and do the sheets, too. And then I'd have to put them in the dryer, and later fold them. If I scrubbed the bathtub, I'd have to clean the toilet and mirror, too. So instead, I did a half-hearted surface-level tidy while Clara took a twenty-minute nap in her bassinet and called it good enough when she woke up wailing, having somehow wrestled her arms out of her swaddle.

Selena knocked on the door right on time at 3:00 p.m., holding Miles. She always appeared to have plenty of energy, too, and today was no different. "Hey! How are you guys doing? Thanks for having us! You look tired. She's still not letting you sleep? Hi, Clara! You look so cute today! I love your outfit! But you have to let your mommy sleep, okay? Leave the stroller in the hall?" she asked, which was the only option because my apartment definitely didn't have room for two strollers in its narrow entryway. *Too early for wine?* I wondered. To be safe, I offered her "something to drink," leaving it vague and putting it on her to interpret the question, in case she judged me for offering wine so early on a weekday. But I hoped she was as ready as I was for a glass or two.

To my disappointment, she responded to my offer with "Water would be great." Ugh. Oh well, she couldn't be here for more than an hour or two, and then I'd be able to pour a nice big glass of ten-dollar chardonnay, which I knew was waiting for me, already opened and chilling in my fridge.

"Crazy about Isabel, right?" I brought her up pretty much immediately, unable to restrain myself. "I really can't stop thinking about it. I can't believe she hasn't turned up. And that we haven't heard anything."

"Ugh. Yeah. It's so awful. I really hope she's okay." Miles lounged on her lap calmly as she sipped her water.

"You know, Vanessa and I went to her house. Her husband was nice enough. But he didn't even know she'd been in a moms' group. Kind of weird, right?"

"Yeah, I mean, to be honest, that sounds like typical dude stuff. Cameron has a pretty vague notion of what Miles and I do all day."

"Yeah. I guess that's fair."

There was a long silence. It was becoming rather obvious that we'd never hung out solo before. We didn't have a great rhythm.

I cleared my throat. "So you're a lawyer, right?"

"I am. I'm a divorce lawyer and handle other 'life changes,' too."

I actually already knew this through Kira. Selena was being modest when she said she was a divorce lawyer—she had started her own boutique firm that specialized in helping people manage the legal logistics of major life events: divorces, deaths, illness, and so forth. She worked with individuals but was also hired by corporations as a benefit for their top-level employees (since people with big jobs got divorced so often, apparently). A legal entrepreneur in her early thirties, she was a total boss.

"When are you going back to work?" I asked.

"I've been doing a bit here and there, but I'll probably go back full time in early December. It will make it easier to settle back in, since things quiet down around the holidays. People tend to save their divorces for January, to give their kids one last Christmas as a family, so I'll need to be ready by then! Luckily I have an amazing team who can handle things while I'm home with him."

"Are you excited to go back? I'm supposed to go back at the end of the month, but I'm pretty nervous." *Understatement.*

"It'll be hard, obviously. I'm definitely not looking forward to pumping milk in my office all day like a cow. But I have to say that I'm excited to wear real clothes and use my brain in that way again. I love being with Miles, but there's this whole other part of my identity that's just kind of dormant right now. And I'm looking forward to waking her up. I grew up with a working mom—my mom worked for a senator, actually. She still works a bit, but she's finally scaled back. Partly because she's a grandma now." I felt the familiar lump of bitterness and anger rise in my throat, thinking of how much my mom would have loved to be a grandma, how amazing she'd have been at it. Selena smiled in Miles's direction. He was on his stomach on our play mat now, gumming a Sophie the Giraffe toy. "She'd kill me if I became a stay-at-home mom. It's a feminist issue, for her. I really don't have a choice. My mom has a lot of opinions, and she isn't afraid to share them." Her eyes flashed ever so slightly, and I realized, for the first time, that as much

Mother of All Secrets

as I wished my mom were still around, the new grandma / new mom relationship was probably not without its own set of complications.

Fearing a reciprocal question about my parents was on its way, I was eager to return to the subject of Isabel. "Isabel didn—*doesn't* work, right?" *Good save on the tenses, Jenn.* Isabel had never explicitly mentioned not working, but she'd certainly never mentioned a job, either.

"I don't think so, no. In fact, I'm not even sure what she did before Naomi. She mentioned something about an off-off-Broadway performance she'd been in once, but it was kind of vague. I have the sense she hasn't worked in a while." I thought perhaps I detected the faintest whiff of disdain in Selena's tone, but I was probably imagining it.

"So, can I ask—maybe you'll have more intel on this as a lawyer— why do you think Isabel's family doesn't want to have a bunch of missing persons alerts on her? Like, no rewards offered, very little press coverage? Don't you think that's kind of surprising? I would think this would be a pretty high-profile disappearance, given their wealth."

Selena sighed slightly. It wasn't clear whether she was just weighing the question or was annoyed by it. "Well, to be honest, I think there are a lot of reasons that families might choose to keep stories like these to themselves. If they're thinking abduction, the press could spook a perpetrator. I've heard it often endangers the victim more than helps, unfortunately. Not to mention, once the press is involved, the detectives will be inundated with false leads, tying up their time and taking them off course. Perhaps, even, they want to avoid traumatizing Naomi years from now when she's old enough to dig into news archives. Though of course if Isabel is found dead, there won't be anything they can do to stop reporters from sharing the story, if they want to."

It sounded like Selena was pretty pessimistic about the possibility of Isabel being alive and okay. I imagined Naomi as a teenager, googling her dead mother, seeing pictures of a dismembered body. It made me shudder.

93

"Anyway," Selena continued, "you'd be surprised how many missing persons cases never make it to press. Especially in New York City. There are tons of runaways, plenty of parents who abandon ship—dads mostly, but some moms, too. And the press only cares about certain missing people. Like if it's a Black adult from Queens? You'll never hear about it. Please." Her eyes narrowed. Clearly this was a loaded topic for her. Of course it would be. I could only nod my understanding. "In that respect," she said, "it *is* a little odd that they haven't been all over Isabel. A white, attractive mom is very appealing to reporters. But it's still really recent, too. She's only been missing a few days, and it's so unclear what they're investigating at this point, it'd be difficult for reporters to report on it, frankly." She took a sip of water and glanced toward the door.

"The detectives came to my apartment," I blurted out. "It kind of freaked me out. Did they come to yours, too?"

She nodded. "They did. Don't worry about it. It's totally standard for them to contact people who see her regularly. See if something seemed off with her. Or if she had said anything that could be a clue."

"There was a little more than that." The words were tumbling out—I hadn't meant to tell her this, hadn't planned to. But I needed to tell someone. To try to make sense of it. "They said I had plans with Isabel the night she disappeared. That in her phone, it said 'drinks with Jenn D.' scheduled for Thursday night. The Thursday she disappeared. But I don't remember ever having plans with her. We had never even hung out outside of our meetings." I stared at her intently, desperate for her to say something that would help all this make sense. I knew I was coming across like a total creep, but it was a relief to unload.

She pursed her lips, processing. "That's weird. But I'm sure there's an explanation. It probably means that she meant to ask you for drinks, and put it in her calendar that day to hold the date, but never actually asked you. Or maybe you forgot? God knows I can barely remember to brush my teeth these days." She was trying to bring lightness back into our conversation, or perhaps get us back to our comfort zone, commiserating about our "mom brains." But I wasn't ready to put it to rest quite yet.

"Yeah. I'm sure you're right. It's really bothering me, though. Also, I have another really strange question."

"Sure," she said, without enthusiasm.

"Did Isabel ever do or say anything in our meetings that was like . . . offensive? Or mean?"

"What do you mean?"

"Like . . . did you like her? Did it seem like I liked her?"

I was aware that my creepiness had crossed over into full-blown lunacy. I was just determined to figure out any reason why I would have written what I wrote about her. And my mind was coming up empty. So maybe something had happened that I had forgotten but others, like Selena, would remember.

Selena spoke slowly, deliberately, looking at me with concern. "Of course I like her." Her return to the present tense made me feel guilty for once again having assumed that Isabel was dead in a ditch somewhere. "I don't know her that well. And she seemed a bit distant in those meetings—just a bit more subdued or measured than the rest of us. Probably because she was facilitator or whatever, she was trying to be somewhat professional or something. Or maybe she just had a hard time being vulnerable. I don't know. I've never exactly felt close to her. But she's always seemed like a perfectly nice, sweet person, yes. Definitely. Why are you asking me this?"

"Didn't you say you'd had a playdate with her once? That's why you knew her address when Kira and I went to scope it out the day we found out she was missing?"

"Yeah, so?" Selena's eyes were locked with mine.

"So you knew her—*know* her—better than I did. I honestly barely remember my interactions with her, which is so frustrating, because—"

"Jenn, slow down," Selena said, putting one hand up. "I had one playdate with her that lasted an hour. It doesn't mean we're best friends, though I'm not sure what my relationship with her has to do with anything." Selena was starting to get fed up and it was obvious.

"I just feel like I'm missing something. I really don't think she would have left, or hurt herself"—I was thinking of that day I'd seen her at the park with Naomi, again—"and we've probably spent more time with her than anyone over these past few weeks, so maybe there were clues we just didn't see. Do you think—would you want to go visit her house with me again? I want to get a better read on Connor. Her mom said come back anytime, and she seemed more than willing to talk to me and Vanessa when we were there, so maybe she'd even know something about why Isabel thought I had plans with her, and—"

Selena was shaking her head as I spoke and this time held both hands up to stop me midsentence once more. "Look, Jenn." Her tone had shifted from patient to exasperated. "I am really not interested in playing detective with you. I thought you wanted to hang out to get to know me. To have the babies play together. Not to talk about a missing woman whom we really do not know all that well and whose case we know nothing about. What do you even mean, *you're* missing something? It's not up to you to solve her case. It has nothing to do with us, okay? It's very sad, but we aren't involved. In any way."

I knew she was right and I also knew that I seemed unhinged. I felt involved, though. My name was in her phone and hers was in mine. A baby whose cheek I had touched and whose paci I had retrieved from the floor was missing her mother. If that were me who was missing, I would want anyone who'd ever met me to feel involved, to try to find me and bring me back to my girl. Selena may disagree with my meddling, but I disagreed with her apathy. Just because we hadn't known Isabel long, that didn't mean that her disappearance shouldn't mean something to me.

"But it just seems like we could help," I protested lamely.

"If we wanted to help, we could have reached out to help her *before* this happened, because anyone could have guessed that she was having a hard time. The fact is that she probably killed herself and tried to cover it up so as not to hurt her family or ruin her reputation." My ears rang at this, but she kept on. "I've seen it happen before—mainly with people whose companies have gone under and who feel they'll never be able to recover financially. That they've failed their families. Maybe even because of some shady business dealings. They kill themselves but try to make it look like an accident—to save face, and sometimes for insurance money. Of course, Isabel didn't need money, but otherwise, this could very well be the same thing. She'd had enough but doesn't want people to know that this is something she chose. Having detectives in the mix may honestly be a polite formality on the part of the police. And the lack of press may be because it's obvious to both police and her family what really happened. Who knows."

So she did have opinions that she had been withholding. Frightening ones, too.

I absorbed her words, slowly, painfully, like a blunt knife. This whole time, I'd been operating on the assumption that Isabel was kidnapped, hurt, maybe murdered, but possibly still alive. In my mind I'd already ruled out suicide, but maybe that's just because I was trying to deny my own culpability—for indeed, I'd been so caught up with my own sleep deprivation and depression and anxiety over Clara and grief over my mom that I hadn't once said to Isabel: *Hey—are you okay? Really okay? I'm here if you need to talk.* Even though I'd noticed her dark undereye circles and wondered about her anxious watch checking, I'd never asked, truly asked, how she was. And maybe if I had—

But no. I clung to the conviction that she wouldn't choose to leave Naomi. I knew that as hard as things were for me, too, the idea of not being with Clara was unfathomable. Impossible. Worse than anything else. "Do you think we could somehow get access to her phone?" I heard myself saying. "Her mom would honestly probably let us look at it, if they have it."

Selena looked at me with disbelief. "And we'd be looking for what, exactly? Jenn, do you understand that for me to meddle in a missing persons case is not, like, some fun distraction? I'm just trying to take care of my baby and enjoy new motherhood, just like you. Look, I'm deeply disturbed that Isabel is missing, too, but honestly, would you really even consider her a friend?"

"What do you mean? We're all friends—"

"If you think we're all friends, then you must not have any real friends. This is mommy networking bullshit. Not friendship."

I felt like I'd been slapped. "If that's how you feel, why do you even do the group?"

"For my son, Jenn. I hang out with a bunch of whiny white women because, for better or worse, I live in this neighborhood and your kids are Miles's peers. Good parents learn from other good parents. So I'm in this group, and then I'll be in the PTA when he's older, and whatever other freaking committees I need to participate in to make sure that I don't slack on one single thing when it comes to raising my son. Because as a Black woman, I *can't* mess up. You get that, right? Your biggest problem may be that your husband doesn't help with laundry or what-ever, but mine is that my son will be looked at as less than because of the color of his skin. Or that he'll be arrested for something he didn't do. Or worse. I have to be very, very careful as his mom, until the day I die, and God willing that'll be long before he does. So yes. My due diligence as his mom entails spending a few hours a week drinking chardonnay with the sisterhood of the traveling BabyBjörn. I have no choice but to make nice with the 'nice white parents,' and I'll do it for him, gladly." Her eyes stayed on mine the whole time she spoke. "But my *real* friends and I talk about things other than bottles and swaddles. They're the ones I talk to about the fact that, you know, when people see me pushing a stroller in this neighborhood, they assume I'm the nanny. Stuff like that." She shook her head with tightly controlled, mirthless frustration.

She continued before I could begin to recover or formulate a response. "But, Jenn, the main thing is—and please, hear me when I say this"—she slowed down, speaking to me as if I were a wayward child she was scolding—"the main thing is that I'm not interested in being involved in your little game of Nancy Drew. I have no idea what happened to Isabel. But it's outside my lane. And whatever you've got going will not end well. So my advice for you is to drop it and find another way to occupy your time and mind. And if you aren't going to do that, then at least leave me the hell out of it."

I was speechless, and I'd never felt so stupid. I knew that she was right about every single thing she'd said. Why had it never occurred to me to think how she might feel being the only Black mother in our group? And that, because of pervasive and harmful stereotypes, she didn't have the *luxury* of being a "hot mess mom" like me or Kira? She *had* to have her shit together. I felt embarrassed for my trivial problems and my utter selfishness.

"I'm sorry" was all I could say. Lamely. Miles and Clara lay on the floor looking at the mobile and reaching for toys, unaware that their mothers were having it out.

Selena shook her head sadly, like I was a lost cause. "I know. Thanks. We should go." She reached down and started to gather Miles's toys and paci.

"No, wait—I totally get it—I shouldn't have asked you to do that. I know I'm obsessing, I just—"

"It's okay, Jenn. I don't think you do get it. But it's not your fault." She shrugged in a casual, unsurprised way that made me feel even worse. "I'll see you soon, okay?"

And with that, she scooped up Miles, who kicked excitedly, and her diaper bag and let herself out, leaving me with more questions than I'd had before and a rising, hot sense of shame in my chest.

June 15

Dear Baby,

This is going to be brief because I'm effing exhausted, but YOU'RE HERE, MY GIRL! And I thought I knew what love was but I didn't. Because it's this. It's you. Ten fingers, ten toes, twenty-one inches of perfect.

Delivering you into this world is and will always be my proudest accomplishment. Holy Mother! I knew it would hurt, but man . . . those contractions take hold of your body and let go only when you're writhing in pain, sure you can't take any more . . . and then, just as you've tasted a sweet second of relief, they're back with a vengeance. Then, my God, there's the rectal pressure, the pushing and straining to get you out, the tearing, the blood. The postbirth shakes, the aftershock contractions. The sharp, raw first latches, made more painful by the fact that there's no milk to drain yet, only gummy colostrum. The frightening showerhead spritz of bloody pee. And of course the diaper. Mine, not yours. Why aren't more people talking about this stuff? I honestly had no idea.

But I did it, and I did it alone. And if I can do that, then I can do this, too. I can be your mom. I know it. Whatever I had to go through to get you here—labor, and what happened with him, your father—it was worth it.

I have to confide something—in the midst of all of this, I can't stop thinking about his wife. Your father's. Here you are, in the world—proof of what he did—and she probably has no idea who he really is. I feel terrible for her. But I know the best thing is to just try to put them both out of my head, forever.

We're home now, and it hasn't been an easy week. Little sleep, lots of crying. From both of us. I've never been this tired. Everything hurts. But then you stir and reach for me, make some unknowable expression in your sleep, and I know it's all worth it. I can't stop kissing your fingers and your lips. You are so, so amazing. And, happily, you're all me— your eyes, your cheeks, your chin—you're my girl. No doubt about that.

Right now you're sleeping, and I know I should be, too, but I just can't stop looking at you. My little girl. I'll always be your mom, and you'll always be my daughter. You're the best part of my life. For the rest of it, that will remain true.

You and me against the world, girl.

Love you forever,

Mommy

Chapter Twelve

Monday, October 5

By the time Selena stormed out, it was already getting dark; my dressing-down had apparently gone on for quite a while. As soon as she left, I helped myself to the chardonnay in the fridge like I'd planned to, though I hadn't anticipated how badly I'd need it. I was mortified about everything I'd said. And about everything she'd said. All I could do was look at Clara and say, "You still like me, though, right?" But I also knew that me wallowing in embarrassment did nothing: I vowed to apologize to Selena for real and to be more mindful of and curious about her experiences as a Black mother going forward. To try to earn my place as a real friend. And certainly, to stop trying to get her to join me in attempting to snoop around Isabel's house. *Seriously, what is wrong with me?*

Tim got home shortly after Selena left, but had to duck right into our bedroom for a Zoom call. I remembered he'd mentioned that he had an afternoon meeting in the neighborhood, so he had probably decided not to return to his office afterward.

After an hour of trying to play with Clara but actually just mentally replaying everything both Selena and I had said and cringing, I poked my head in to say hi to Tim and see how much longer his call would be, Clara on my hip. He smiled at us, laptop open in front of him, but held up his finger to indicate he wasn't off the call yet. I bounced Clara to the kitchen and poured myself another glass of wine.

I grabbed my phone and prepared to commence my new search routine—instead of browsing Instagram, I scanned Google hits on Isabel for news items, my Google Docs to make sure the note I'd written was still deleted, and my calendar app to see if our alleged plans had somehow reappeared. Although what I'd apparently written remained safely deleted, I couldn't stop thinking about it. I was terrified it would resurface somehow. I checked my Google Alerts next. Nothing new; still the same half-hearted single-paragraph coverage on *West Side Rag*. Search Continues for Missing Mom, it offered, though the article contained no new or meaningful information. Clara started wailing from the play mat. Six thirty p.m.: time to eat. I decided to give her a bottle; I was nearly done with my second glass of wine, after all. Besides, maybe a bottle would fill her up more, resulting in a longer stretch of sleep.

I put the refrigerated bag of milk in warm water and cleaned an already-clean Comotomo bottle, which I'd felt shamed into ordering after our most recent moms' group meeting—the meeting that Isabel hadn't shown up to—despite the absurd price tag. So far, it seemed like any other bottle.

Clara nosed around my chest while I tried to give her the bottle. She made several scrunched, dissatisfied expressions as I put the bottle near her mouth but started drinking reluctantly nonetheless. Once she had some momentum and seemed settled, I again reached for my phone to continue my Isabel searching, finding it nearly impossible to maneuver my phone, the bottle, and Clara's head all at once; maybe breastfeeding was easier in some ways, after all.

I entered her name into my text messages, ready to reanalyze our group messages, looking for clues that I'd missed. Instead, my search came back completely blank. Where was our group text? Had I deleted that, too, somehow?

I went to my call log instead and entered her name once more, distracted by Clara's fidgeting. I tried burping her while holding and squinting at my phone, confused. There was one outgoing call to and one incoming call from Isabel Harris; both were from a few weeks ago. I didn't explicitly remember ever talking to her on the phone, but these calls were placed in early September, shortly after I'd joined the moms' group. So perhaps we'd communicated about logistics of a meeting. How many conversations and interactions could I be forgetting, though?

More perplexing, I'd just conducted this same search yesterday and hadn't seen any calls from Isabel Harris.

Isabel Harris.

Something wasn't right. Whenever I met another mom, I always put the baby's name in my phone along with the mother. So that I could be polite and remember the names of their kids. And keep straight all the mom friends I planned to make, at some point in the future when I was feeling more social. More myself. *Selena, Miles's mom. Vanessa, Phoebe's mom.* And so forth.

She had been in my phone as *Isabel, Naomi's Mom.* Not *Isabel Harris.*

And that's when I realized that this wasn't my phone.

It was Tim's.

He had recently changed his wallpaper to the same picture of Clara that I had on my phone ("Copycat," I had teased him half-heartedly). It was an adorable picture of her in her stroller, smiling broadly, on the verge of a laugh, even. The afternoon sun was reflecting on her head, making it look like she had a halo. Now that we had the same wallpaper, our phones were completely identical except that his case was dark gray and my case was light gray. It was the most subtle difference.

We even had the same passcode; I'd forgotten mine a couple of months ago in a delirious, exhausted haze and was incredibly frustrated to be locked out of my phone all day, unable to pull the four-digit code from the depths of my withered brain. When muscle memory finally kicked in and brought it back to me, he changed my passcode to match his own—Clara's birthday—so that he could easily remind me if I forgot it again.

We had unsurprisingly mixed up each other's phones a few times now, him grabbing my phone first and then putting it down to cross the room and retrieve his own; me about to pick up an incoming call on what I thought was my phone before realizing it was his boss. A couple of weeks ago, he'd even taken mine when he left for work, before returning ten minutes later to swap them with a sheepish grin. "I think we need a new system," he'd said, blowing me a quick kiss before leaving again.

So this was Tim's phone. With "Isabel Harris" in his contacts. Not only in his contacts, but in his outgoing and incoming call logs.

What kind of couple shares a phone password? The kind with nothing to conceal from each other, I'd once thought. But that was before I'd proved my own theory wrong, with the secrets I was keeping. So now, I feared that it was the kind who had become so distant that each assumed the other wouldn't even be interested in snooping. The kind of disjointed couple for whom it was perfectly easy to hide things in plain sight.

Why was my husband calling Isabel? Why was she calling him?

Surely there was a reasonable explanation. Perhaps I had used his phone to call her—but no. I knew that I had never called Isabel. As confusing as these past few months had been, I wasn't going to convince myself of things that weren't true, just for a false peace of mind.

He was just in the next room, working. Nothing was stopping me from going in and asking him right now. Except for the fact that I was shaking. I wasn't sure I could take any surprises. My life felt like it was hanging by a thread as it was.

I pushed past it. I had to confront him. This was my husband. He was safe. I *knew* him. And I trusted him in my bones. It was just a couple of phone calls. He'd have an explanation, I was sure.

Clara was nearly done with the bottle and had slowed down, playing with it more than drinking. I shifted her to an upright position and rubbed her back for a few minutes, waiting for her belch. I murmured over and over again, "You're such a great girl. You're such a sweet, smart girl." She burped loudly in reply.

Then I walked toward our bedroom holding her and entered without knocking. Tim was finally off his Zoom call and just about to close his laptop.

"Hey. Sorry about that. Just wrapping up. What do you want to do for dinner? I'm starving." He took his glasses off and cleaned them with his shirt. He looked tired.

"This is your phone," I replied bluntly, awkwardly. I sounded angrier than I'd meant to.

"Oh. Okay, thanks." He reached for it, giving me a funny look. "Would you want to try to take C to the diner so we can get a quick drink before we put her to bed? Think she'll allow it?" This was one of our favorite things to do together—a very quick happy hour with Clara at the diner around the corner. I needed to get to the bottom of this, though, before I could imagine enjoying a beer and some mozzarella sticks with Tim.

"I think it's a little too late. Maybe tomorrow. Can I ask you a question? Why is Isabel's number in your phone? And why are there calls?"

He paused. Sighed. Rubbed his head. Was he buying time? Deciding which version of the truth to tell me?

"Have a seat. I should have told you about this before. It's nothing bad."

"So tell me." I reluctantly sat on the bed, scared of what I was about to hear.

Tim took another deep breath. "I was worried about you, Jenn. I *am* worried about you. You've barely smiled since Clara was born. You're a shadow of who you were. You just seem so . . . worn out."

106

A *shadow* of who I'd been? "I *am* worn out, Tim. I sleep for like, two and a half hours a night. It's pretty tiring, caring for a newborn with almost no help."

"I know, I know." Tim kept touching his glasses. *Was he nervous? Was my husband afraid of me?* "And I know I haven't been as hands-on as I could have been, or in the ways that you've really needed. But I also have no idea what I'm doing. I am trying. I love you both so much. I just feel like nothing that I do is right."

"Okay, but that doesn't answer my question. Why were you calling Isabel?"

Tim looked down with dread, or shame, before answering. "I called her to ask if she thought you were okay." A ringing sensation started in my ears. "You'd been doing the moms' group thing for a couple of weeks and you'd mentioned that she was the moderator. To be honest, I had no idea what a moms' group was. I thought it was like therapy, so I thought she was, like, the counselor or something. That's why I was so enthusiastic about you joining a moms' group to begin with. I thought she was a professional who helped moms and families. I didn't realize it was just like a friendly, social thing. I mean, what do guys know about moms' groups?"

I was suddenly and eerily reminded of Isabel's husband. He certainly didn't know anything about our moms' group, either. Maybe Connor's apparent disinterest wasn't so incriminating after all.

"Anyway," he continued when I said nothing, "I just wanted to talk to someone about . . . whether what you're going through is normal. If you'd come back to yourself soon. And what I could do to support you. Most of my friends don't have kids yet, plus it's weird for me to talk to other guys about this kind of stuff anyway—and I so wish your mom was here, so that I could talk to her, and so that *you* could talk to her, but—"

"Yeah, me too."

"I know—I know. I'm so sorry. I know you're hurting so badly, and without her here, I'm the one that's responsible for you. Not in a bad way—I'm your family and that's my job. It's a job I want to do. But I feel a bit in over my head right now, because I'm worried about you, and I don't know how to help."

His frantic backpedaling only made me feel even more like a burdensome child. My cheeks burned with angry humiliation. I already knew I was a failure as a wife and a mother, but I hadn't realized how obvious it was to Tim and probably everyone else who saw me that I was unraveling. I knew I seemed tired, but I thought that only *I* knew the depths of my mental and physical exhaustion, the dark thoughts that sometimes laid claim to my brain and being. Not to mention—the other thing. God, I really was awful. Awful, awful.

When I said nothing, he continued, hesitantly. "So I got Isabel's number from your phone and called her to get her two cents, or just to check in, or whatever. Again, Jenn, I thought she was some kind of a therapist. She didn't answer, but she called me back the next day. It was a super awkward conversation, because obviously, I'd misunderstood her role; she's just a mom in the neighborhood who had been trying to make friends, like you. She thought it was very strange that I was calling her and had no idea what to say. I mean, you guys had only met a couple of times when I called. She barely knew you. And it wasn't her place to, like, assess you. I'm an idiot. I know that."

I was silent. Clara was still in my arms, her body digesting her milk as I took in not only what Tim thought of me but that he had shared that information with Isabel. I wondered why she hadn't said anything to me; she probably didn't want to embarrass me. So she knew for weeks that my own husband thought I was crazy, but concealed it from me. Or perhaps, protected me from it.

"Anyway, I should have told you, but honestly, I was mortified for being so incorrect about what the moms' group entailed and for meddling in a way that was totally disrespectful of your privacy, not to mention unproductive. I asked her not to say anything to you, and I guess she didn't."

"But how could you not say anything to me even after she went missing? You acted like you'd never heard of her when I told you, but you'd talked to her yourself."

Tim nodded, looking at me intently through his glasses. "I mean, of course I am completely weirded out by her disappearance, as I know you are. But she's still a stranger to me, despite having had one very ill-advised conversation with her. I never even met her."

"What did she say when you talked? What did she say about me?" Now I was curious to see if even Tim could perhaps shed some light on my relationship with Isabel, offer a reason I might have written what was said in that Google Doc.

"It was a brief conversation. Super brief. However, she did tell me before we hung up that she thought you were a lot stronger than I was giving you credit for."

My chest warmed for a moment. I closed my eyes. *Thank you, Isabel. Thank you.*

"Did the police talk to you?" I demanded. "About your little phone call?"

He paused yet again for what felt like a full minute but was probably only a couple of seconds, choosing his words carefully.

"They did. I'm sure they were just, like, going through her call log and stuff, following up with anyone who was a question mark, which I totally get why I would be."

My heart started pounding, activated by disbelief and betrayal. "And you didn't tell me that, either?" Clara had started squirming, so I put her on the bed on her stomach; she stared back and forth between us, captive audience to our fight. I wondered if we were traumatizing her by arguing right in front of her.

"It was just yesterday. After they came here to talk to you. They called me at work. I told them exactly what I'm explaining to you, about why I called her, and I haven't heard from them again." He put his hand on Clara's back and stroked her with his thumb.

"Talking to detectives is a huge deal, Tim, no matter the reason or the outcome. I told you about the detectives coming here. I was so shaken. Don't you think it would have made me feel better to know that they'd followed up with you, too? That they were talking to literally everyone who'd been in contact with her?" It wouldn't have made me feel any better about her calendar entry or my damning Google Doc, but I wasn't going to mention that. Now I was being choosy with my truth, too. As I'd been for weeks now. As I would have to be for the rest of our marriage.

"I would have told you, but I actually thought it would make you more anxious about the whole thing, not less. Because then I would have had to tell you all of what I'm telling you now, and I'd already resolved to just keep it to myself. I didn't want to risk hurting your feelings and making you feel even lower than—"

"—than I already am. Got it. Well, I'm glad to know what you think of me, at least." I was willing myself not to cry. To focus on the anger, not the hurt. I didn't want to cry in front of him and confirm how weak he thought I was. He'd robbed me of the freedom to be vulnerable in front of him without feeling judged.

"Babe, I am sorry. But you have to understand that what I did was out of love and concern for you. It was misguided and stupid, but it wasn't malicious. I would never intentionally hurt or embarrass you." He reached for my hand but I pulled away.

I was humiliated and hurt at what Tim had done but also fully aware that it was my own fault for being so unhinged to begin with. If I were just a regular mom, in love with my new baby, suffused with my new-mother glow, happily folding freshly laundered pink blankets while my baby slept in her bassinet, doing postnatal yoga videos in our living room, he never would have contacted Isabel to begin with. He wouldn't have been worried and confused about where to turn. He would have had nothing to hide from me.

I couldn't help but wonder, though—was there a chance he was lying? Was he really *this* clueless about moms' groups? Or had he concocted an excuse that I couldn't fault him for as a cover for an even more untellable reason for his contacting Isabel? A small part of me didn't trust his explanation. Though I knew that the reason I wasn't able to trust him was because I was burying a secret of my own, even deeper than I'd buried the Google Doc. Something I would do everything in my power to never, ever tell him. I knew that my anger toward him was unfair, since I had betrayed him, too—he simply didn't know it. And I hoped he never would. But I couldn't help but wonder if he was as undeserving of my trust as I was of his.

Suddenly I felt like I was stuck on a stalled elevator. I needed to get out of the apartment immediately. It was almost Clara's bedtime, but I hoped she would tolerate a quick walk. And if she fell asleep in the stroller and it resulted in a more challenging night for both of us, then so be it. It's not like my sleep could get much worse. I gathered Clara's blanket, paci, burp rag, and Sophie the Giraffe, trying hard not to forget anything, not to further prove my incompetence to my husband. I also poured the rest of the bottle of chardonnay into a coffee thermos and put it in the stroller's cup holder. Tim didn't attempt to come out of the room and continue our conversation. Fuming, I buckled Clara into the stroller and stalked out of our apartment.

Chapter Thirteen

Tuesday, October 6

The next morning I was still reeling from my conversations with both Selena and Tim. Whenever someone was mad at me, or I was convinced that someone didn't like me, it was practically the only thing I could think about, casting a shadow over me for days. This time was ironically a little bit easier, because my exhaustion made it impossible to care about anything as deeply as I probably would have if I had been rested. The two confrontations were also canceling each other out in my mind. I couldn't worry too much about either one before I switched to worrying about the other.

Basically, I was doing great.

When I'd gotten home from my walk with Clara the night before, Tim had still been in our room, working. He cleared out so that I could put Clara down, and when I came back into the living room after getting her settled, he simply said, "I know you need a little distance right now, so I'm just going to put my headphones in and you can pretend I'm not here."

I wanted to respond, "How do you know what I need? Why not let me tell you, instead of vice versa?" But I said nothing, and went on to ignore his presence for the rest of the night, as instructed. When he left in the morning, I pretended I was still asleep, though I wasn't sure I'd actually slept a wink all night.

By midmorning, I was tired of stewing and was hoping some fresh air and a walk would clear my head. Clara fell asleep in her stroller pretty much as soon as we left, which was a bit unusual for her but a welcome surprise. She'd woken up a lot during the night, so it made sense that she was tired. I grabbed a latte and a cheddar scone at PlantShed, a hybrid coffee and flower shop on Eighty-Seventh Street (right around the corner from Isabel's), to treat myself and combat my fatigue. It was sunny and cool, a perfect October day. A woman in line behind me peeked at Clara, whispering, "She's so cute! Congratulations!" I thanked her and smiled graciously, for the moment enjoying playing the part of a mom who actually had it together. For a few minutes, as I sipped my coffee and walked along, I felt almost normal. Like myself, but a mom, the two blending together naturally in the way that I had wrongly assumed they would. This was what I had imagined maternity leave would look like: walks in the park, fancy coffee in the cup holder, peaceful sleeping baby in the stroller. Maybe if it had been more like this, I wouldn't be such a basket case.

I saw other moms on the street, some solo but many in pairs, walking along, chatting in sweaters. Some had older children that they were taking to school, two seats in their strollers. They all smiled at me knowingly as we passed each other, like they understood just where I was in life, but I couldn't help but think that there was no way they'd been like me when they were new moms, with these messy parts I was trying and failing to hide. Messy parts like the fact that every time Clara and I managed to leave the apartment, I immediately collected a list of terrifying and morbid worst-case scenarios in my mind: Clara's stroller rolling into oncoming traffic and being instantly flattened by a FreshDirect truck while I obliviously fiddled with my diaper bag. Holding her near the ledge at Riverside Park to show her the view of the water and accidentally dropping her fifteen feet into the woods.

Fumbling with a faulty lid and dumping hot coffee all over her face, giving her third-degree burns. One tiny mistake on my part could be disastrous, devastating. These suffocating fears made it difficult to function. My sense was that, despite the knowing, chummy looks they gave me, these moms I passed were not like me.

Maybe Isabel was, though, unbeknownst to me. And maybe Selena was right. Maybe it was all too much for her.

I took a left on Eighty-Eighth, resisting the urge to turn right and walk past Isabel's, and instead headed down the hill toward Riverside Park. The leaves on the ground crunched under the stroller wheels: fall was here. Walking past Hippo Playground, I watched the toddlers running around, shrieking and laughing. I felt a rush of excitement for when Clara was old enough to go to the playground—I envisioned her climbing the ladder and going down the slide, or laughing as she swung on a swing while I made goofy faces at her. I could see it all, and despite how low I felt much of the time, I also felt grateful and fortunate that I'd be the one holding her hand, making her laugh, dusting her off if she fell. I'd be better, by then.

I grabbed a seat on a bench overlooking the Hudson, trying to relax and enjoy my coffee, despite—well, everything. Clara had already been sleeping for about forty minutes. I actually wished I had a book with me. I hadn't been able to focus on a book since she was born, but I needed something else to occupy me besides obsessing about Isabel—*what the hell had happened to her, seriously?*—and my inexplicable Google Doc, my mom, Tim, Selena, all of it. I knew that Selena was right—I had no right to go nosing around in Isabel's business by visiting her home again, and I especially shouldn't have been trying to recruit Selena, or anyone else, to join me.

Two women pushing strollers were walking toward the bench I was sitting on; they were older, in their fifties maybe, so I assumed they were nannies. Both of their babies were sleeping in their strollers, with muslin blankets shading them from the sun. I should have thought to do so. Nannies always made it look so easy. Even the ones caring for multiple kids just seemed to intrinsically know how to make the kids do exactly what they were supposed to: nap in the stroller, take a bottle, play safely, wait quietly. I almost never saw babies screaming with their nannies, and if they did, it seemed they were calmed within seconds. I, on the other hand, took all Clara's meltdowns personally, like criticisms. I felt her wails in my own chest, my own head. My obstetrician, a mom of three, had jokingly told me that kids are like dogs: they can smell fear. I'd thought she was kidding, but it made sense to me now, and I wondered if my stress and anxiety were contributing factors to Clara's fussiness.

As the nannies got closer, I realized that one of them was pushing Vanessa's daughter, Phoebe. I couldn't actually see Phoebe, as she was ensconced in her bassinet, but I recognized Vanessa's chic beige stroller, as it stood out from the huge, clunky black ones that most other moms, myself included, had.

The nannies were talking in hushed voices, so as not to wake the babies, but I heard Vanessa's nanny—I thought her name was Cynthia—say "Naomi."

They were talking about Isabel.

Though I'd half-heartedly resolved to take Selena's advice and butt out, I was overwhelmingly curious. They might know something, have seen something, maybe.

I decided to follow them. It was innocent enough—I was going for a walk in the park with my baby, just like they were, like so many other mothers and caregivers were. I just happened to be walking at the same pace as them, and at a relatively close distance that allowed me to hear their conversation.

Completely innocent. Casual.

"She was at their apartment a few days before she went missing," Vanessa's nanny was saying, gesturing to Phoebe in the stroller. "So sad. Poor woman. I remember she was crying when she was over. The baby was napping, so I mostly stayed in the kitchen, to give them their space. But she was very upset."

Everyone touts their proximity to tragedy. It's human nature. She could have been exaggerating the degree to which she'd borne witness to Isabel's troubles. But this was interesting, to say the least. I hadn't realized that Vanessa and Isabel hung out on their own. And it sounded like they were close, that Isabel had confided in Vanessa.

"It's so terrible," the other nanny said. "What do you think happened?"

"Who knows," Cynthia said, shaking her head. "Nothing good, though. Poor woman. She was over all the time, you know."

Vanessa certainly hadn't made it seem like their relationship was that extensive when we brought food over to Isabel's. She hadn't said anything about Isabel being over "all the time."

"What was she like?" the other nanny asked.

"Very considerate. Spoke to me by name. Usually the boss's friends don't even acknowledge us, right?" The other nanny rolled her eyes and nodded knowingly. "But she always went out of her way to ask me how I was doing, where I grew up, that kind of thing. She did seem overwhelmed by the baby, though. Not sure why—Naomi seems easy enough. But she seemed intent on being the perfect mother. If Naomi spit up even a drop on herself, Isabel would change her entire outfit immediately. And I heard her tell Vanessa all about how she wasn't sure if she could do it, it was too much, something like that. I remember feeling that way when all three of my kids were born—a lot of it is the hormones, of course. And you just do what you think you can't do, and as time goes on you realize that you're doing it—then, lo and behold, you're a mom. Fake it until you make it, right? None of us know what we're doing in those early days." She paused, and I could tell she was about to say something else. I picked up my pace to inch a little closer. "Honestly, I'm a little surprised that she was looking to *Vanessa* for help."

"Why is that?"

"She's a great boss. Don't get me wrong. I'm very lucky. But she's not exactly the warm and fuzzy type. Nor was she in a position to empathize with Isabel having a tough time."

"What do you mean?" Nanny #2 asked, patting the blanket down over her baby's legs.

Cynthia paused; I couldn't tell if it was for dramatic effect, or genuine hesitation. She seemed to be enjoying sharing both her gossip and her wisdom. "It's just . . . easier for some women than others. I've been with them since Phoebe was six weeks. Vanessa had her on a schedule, was already back in the gym. No squeeze bottle or witch hazel pads still lying around. No pumping bras and nursing pads to wash, since she formula feeds." This was news to me. Vanessa had implied many times in our meetings that she was nursing. I thought so, anyway. Maybe I was wrong. But hadn't she said something about stopping by her place to feed Phoebe during the day? I supposed that could have meant bottles, though. "Hell, if you'd asked me," Cynthia continued, "I would say there was no way she could have just given birth! Some women are blessed like that, though. Just snap back into their bodies like they were never pregnant at all. Point is—Isabel was going through something that Vanessa wasn't. Assuming that Naomi was what had her so upset, of course."

I hoped the other nanny would press her further, and thankfully, she did. "What did she say to Isabel when she was upset?"

"From what I heard, she just kept telling her to press on, that it would be fine, which actually isn't terrible advice, when you think about it. Look, she's a lovely woman and a great mother. I'm grateful to be with them. She's just not the person I'd choose as a shoulder to cry on, that's all. She also doesn't seem . . . as worried as you might expect, about Isabel. She's going about her business like her friend isn't missing. But of course, people hide their fears and sadness all the time. Especially people like Vanessa. Miss Perfect." She clicked her tongue with overwrought sadness. "Poor Isabel. Pray they find her safe and sound."

"I hope so, too. For that little baby's sake. Poor thing. Probably missing her mother. Babies know when their mother is near." I'd heard that before, but in the context of my presence somehow being hindersome to my baby's feeding and sleeping schedule. Hearing it in this new context put things in perspective once more: how lucky I was to have my baby close to me, both of us safe and sound.

"Do you mind if we sit for a second? I have to make a bottle." They sat down and Cynthia took out a Comotomo bottle filled with water and dumped powder from a plastic baggie into it. She shook it vigorously, carefully lifted Phoebe out of her stroller, and started feeding her. "There's a girl. There's a sweet girl. Drink your milk, baby. By the way, how is your son doing at college?" And with that, they moved on from Vanessa and Isabel.

I turned left out of the park, exiting onto Eighty-Third Street and Riverside Drive. I was winded, either from the short hill or the adrenaline rush from overhearing what I had.

Clara woke up with a scrunchy face and a wail. I knew she would be hungry, and I didn't want her to cry all the way home. I felt like whenever she started crying in the stroller, people glared at me—as if I didn't *know* I was inadequate and they needed to confirm it with their concerned looks. Even the most well-meaning interventions, like a woman who'd recently asked if I needed help as Clara shrieked through the last few minutes of a walk in Central Park, left me shaken. "I promise it gets better!" she'd said with a sympathetic smile. I knew she was being kind, but I was still embarrassed.

I sat on another bench on Eighty-Fourth and Riverside, shaded by trees and overlooking the section of park where we'd just been walking, and fumbled with my nursing bra, nursing cover, and Clara's head, until at last she was latched, tangled in my layers.

I allowed my mind to race, replaying their conversation. Lots of women bounce back quickly from delivery. (Not me, obviously, but I'd seen pictures on Instagram of Kristin Cavallari in a bikini, like, nine days after giving birth, and Hilaria Baldwin on a run the day after coming home from the hospital. So I knew it could happen.) The fact that Vanessa looked trim and was already exercising when Cynthia met her didn't mean anything. It didn't mean that she was incapable of understanding the plight of other postpartum women who were perhaps struggling more than she was. Nor did it mean that she wasn't also fighting her own private battles. *Especially* since she was doing it all on her own.

That she had lied about formula feeding, or at least perhaps implied that she didn't, only made me feel sorry for her, that she'd been embarrassed enough about her choice that she'd tried to hide it. Because there was nothing wrong with formula feeding at all—I knew that, absolutely—and yet I wondered if I, too, would deny it, or just not mention it, when I made the switch. There was so much judgment around the whole issue, and most mothers I met were *so* quick to mention that they were nursing. That dreaded "Breast is Best!" chirp—who came up with that? I'd like to smack whoever did.

But her apparent close friendship with Isabel felt like a big omission. That day when we visited Isabel's house, it seemed to me like we were each somewhere between acquaintances and friends with Isabel, that we both weren't totally sure if we really belonged there. And Vanessa had only lived in New York City for a few months—how could they be close enough for Isabel to be crying in her arms? And days before disappearing, no less. Isabel had obviously confided in her about something—what could it have been? Was she simply feeling overwhelmed by new motherhood, as Vanessa's nanny had assumed? Or could it have been something else, and if so, could whatever it was be related to her disappearance?

I couldn't answer any of these questions without logging some more time with Vanessa. I resolved to do that, as soon as possible.

I quickly switched Clara from right boob to left and, with my free hand, rattled off a quick text to Vanessa. Hey! How are you? I know you're working, but let me know if you have any time this week. Would be great to get a drink or have the babies play (or both).

I saw three dots appear right away and then disappear just as quickly. I imagined her at work: crisp, fitted black dress under her white coat, hair in a low bun, red lipstick, smiling and laughing with patients, putting them at ease as she scraped moles, injected cysts, and prescribed creams, making even these routine, unappealing tasks seem somehow glamorous.

Her response came through after Clara and I had finished her feed and were walking up Eighty-Sixth Street toward home. Yes! Let's do it. I actually finish at 1 today. Would you and Clara want to come over this afternoon, maybe around 3? I know it's super last minute so if today doesn't work we can definitely find another time!

Tim and I had dinner plans that night: of all things, it was our anniversary. I had a babysitter coming over for the first time. But I'd made a late reservation, to allow for me to put Clara down to sleep myself, so I figured I could still easily squeeze in this afternoon playdate. I didn't even know if we were still on for dinner, anyway, considering where we stood right now. Regardless, I was invested in learning more about Vanessa and trying to gain some understanding of what I'd overheard. I responded that Clara and I would be there, and could we bring anything? (A question women are legally obliged to ask, though the answer is always "Not a thing!")

Clara beamed at me from her stroller, and despite everything going on, I instantly felt warmer. Whenever she smiled at me, I felt (albeit briefly) like maybe I wasn't doing such a terrible job, after all. "Are you my assistant detective?" I asked her in a voice I'd once told myself I would never use. "Yes you are!"

June 27

Dear Baby,

I'm not sure if I can form sentences here, because I am so freaking fried, but I'll try.

Let me start by saying that you are perfect. You really are. So if it seems like I'm complaining about you, I really don't mean to. Am I having a hard time right now? Yes. But the easiest part of all of it, the only easy part, actually, is loving you. That part is no problem.

But wow. I thought I was prepared. I had the diapers, the bassinet, the onesies. I'd read a few books. But I had no idea how much babies needed. You're out of my body, technically, yes; but you still need some part of me all the time, at all moments of the day.

When I look in the mirror, I wonder what the hell happened to Allison. I see a different person now. A very tired one.

And I think the sleep deprivation is doing something to my judgment, because I did something that I really shouldn't have done.

I called his wife.

Ugh. I know. Crazy, right?

But you know what? I think your birth sort of reignited my anger at your father, at what he did, and at the utter lack of consequences he faced and will ever face.

And I just felt like I wouldn't be doing my duty as a woman if I let her continue to go on in her life, oblivious to what her husband was out there doing with and to other women. Because I highly doubt what happened to me was an isolated incident.

I didn't tell her about you, because I figured that she would confront him, of course, and I don't want him to know that you exist. God forbid he wanted to be involved in some way—unlikely, given the kind of person he is, but it's not a risk I want to take. I didn't even tell her my name. I didn't get into any specifics. I simply told her I'd met her husband and if I were her, I'd want to know that he was not a good husband. Or human.

And you know what she said? "I'm so sorry." I thought she'd be furious with me, but it was the opposite. *She* felt sorry for *me*. She asked for no details. And she hung up quickly.

She already knew about him. And I knew then that your father was even worse than I realized.

There's one other thing—she hung up quickly, but not before I heard something: a baby's cry in the background. A cry that sounded just like yours—the cry of a newborn.

They have a baby, too. You have a half sibling out there in the world.

I know—it's a lot to process.

Or maybe it was a friend's baby, or a niece or nephew. No way to know for sure.

If it's hers, theirs, though, a part of me is relieved for her. She isn't alone. Just like me, she has someone who's making her life worth living, even if her husband is a piece of crap.

I have to let it go. I need to focus on what matters, and that's you. I just need to buck up and get him out of my head, forever. As far as we're concerned, he doesn't exist. From here on out. Okay?

I can't help but worry about his wife, though. She sounded so . . . small. I wish there was something I could do for her.

Whew. What a mess, right? At least we're in it together. Let's try to get some sleep tonight, okay? I could really use it. My head is all fogged up right now.

Love you forever,

Mommy

Chapter Fourteen

Tuesday, October 6

The day crawled to 3:00 p.m. Clara had some major projectile spit-up when we got home from the park that concerned me a bit, so I was worried I'd have to call off our plans with Vanessa and Phoebe, but she seemed totally fine after that and didn't have a fever or anything. We dozed together on the couch for a while, and when we woke up, she was hungry and smiley. I really didn't want to cancel. I was desperate to spend time with Vanessa and try to figure out if she knew more about what had been going on with Isabel than she'd been letting on.

Vanessa's apartment building on Seventy-Ninth Street and West End Ave.—right next to her dermatology practice—was magnificent. The doormen of her building looked more like the queen's guard or *squires* or something. There was a massive courtyard with lush flowering hydrangeas shading deep iron benches. The doorman kept calling me "miss" and insisted on helping me manage the cobblestones with my stroller. I suddenly felt underdressed for this playdate, even though I was wearing my "fancy leggings" (SPANX brand, so not actually fancy) and a sweater and ankle boots, a slight step up from my dirty "casual leggings" from Old Navy and ancient crewneck Colgate sweatshirt.

Vanessa opened the door to her apartment and greeted me with a big smile, then grabbed my shoulder to pull me in for a cheek kiss.

"Perfect timing! Come on in! Phoebe just woke up, so the girls can play." The notion of three-month-olds playing was amusing to me; they would lie on the blanket together, putting toys in their mouths, staring up at the ceiling—whether they were even aware of the other one was questionable. But maybe on some level the socialization was beneficial, even important. Every other mom seemed to think so, judging from the plethora of pricey classes available in this neighborhood for infants, as I'd learned from all the recommendations on the Upper West Side Moms Facebook page.

The light in her apartment wafted over me and instantly made me feel calmer, as if I'd just taken a deep breath. I didn't even have to leave my stroller in the hallway; there was plenty of room in her massive foyer, which opened into a spacious living room. Everything was bright and clean. While she did have baby gear in various places—a play mat on the floor, a Boppy cushion on the couch—her apartment was incredibly uncluttered for having a newborn. Vanessa was predictably put together in her own fancy leggings, which really did look fancy, and a camel-colored duster over a white turtleneck. She was barefoot, with perfectly pedicured smoke-colored toes. I was surprised, and relieved, when she offered wine—3:00 p.m. on a Tuesday could totally go either way, especially with someone as seemingly straight edge as Vanessa, but I was certainly ready for a glass.

She poured us each a generous serving of an expensive-looking California cabernet sauvignon in glasses with bowls as big as the babies' heads. We sat down on the floor next to Phoebe's elephant play mat, on a white rug as thick as a mattress. Red wine, a white rug, and two squirming babies seemed like a recipe for disaster to me, but Vanessa looked unconcerned.

I had so many questions I wanted to ask her—if she'd heard anything about Isabel, first of all, and if they'd really been as close as her nanny had implied—but I knew I needed to ease in. I couldn't come in as hot as I had with Selena and risk angering Vanessa, turning her off from opening up to me.

I figured I'd start with something unrelated to Isabel: Phoebe's birth story. Every mom I'd met loved talking about this, probably because giving birth feels like a superhuman feat; women understandably enjoy bragging about it, and have earned the right to. Forever. It was actually weird I hadn't already heard it at one of our meetings; I knew all the gory details of Kira's second-degree tearing and Selena's arduous C-section recovery.

"So, remind me"—playing it safe in case she *had* told me before— "was Phoebe born in DC or New York?" I took a sip of my wine. It was velvety perfection.

"DC. We moved up here not long after she was born."

"Was she born on time?"

"She was about a week late. I was so ready for her to be born. I was just so excited to meet her, to confirm that she was actually real, you know? It was a smooth labor. I mean, you know . . . as smooth as it can be," she said laughingly, as we both knew that "smooth" entailed contractions that made you wish you were dead, the feeling that a broom was stuck in your butt when it was time to push, the moment of tearing, and the blood, oh, the blood. Smooth, indeed. "What about Clara?" she asked, sipping her wine demurely.

"She was born here in the city, at Mount Sinai West. She was also a little late. I was induced, which was not so pleasant," I said, the biggest understatement I'd ever made. I'd endured thirty-six hours of contractions with an epidural that only worked on one side, vomiting throughout most of it. "That must have been such a crazy time to move! I can't imagine moving with an infant. I could barely move from my bedroom to my bathroom for a while there."

"Yeah, it was a little nuts," she said, laughing lightly. "But I had a great opportunity to join this amazing practice that I'd admired from afar forever, and plus the whole situation with Phoebe's dad, which I mentioned to you the other day. So it felt like the right time to have a fresh start elsewhere. It's so much better for me to be in a dermatology practice with a predictable schedule—my schedule at the hospital in DC was crazy. I was always working. And obviously, that's a lot tougher with a kid! Especially since I'm on my own. And we're loving being in New York, so far."

"And you're already back at work. Is it hard to be away from Phoebe? I can't even imagine being at work right now. My brain still feels totally like mush. I'd probably, like, forget to wear a shirt or something." I wanted someone to tell me how great it was being back at work. How everything clicked back into place upon returning. Maybe if I heard more of that, I could actually start to gear up to do it myself.

"Well, I kind of *have* to work, but it hasn't been bad so far." My cheeks flamed. Of course she had to work. She didn't have a spouse with an income taking some of the pressure off her. What was wrong with me? She softened and retreated quickly, looking embarrassed, too. "But I'm lucky to have a lot of help. I had a night nurse, and now my amazing nanny. So it's manageable. I miss Phoebe when I'm at work, though. But we're right next door, so I can pop over and see her sometimes between patients and feed her." Perhaps this wasn't an implication of breastfeeding at all, as I'd once thought. She was talking about togetherness, not logistics. She cleared her throat. "To be honest with you, I wasn't sure I would have kids—Phoebe was a surprise. The best kind of surprise. So now, when things are hard, or I'm exhausted, I just remember how grateful I am for Phoebe, and everything else seems suddenly trivial."

Her attitude toward being a mom was something I could probably stand to emulate. Sometimes I felt like all I did was feel sorry for myself, when I knew deep down how lucky I was.

"Well, Phoebe is lucky to have you as her mom, too. Do you have any family close by to help?"

"Unfortunately, no. My parents—well actually, my dad and step-mom, my mom died when I was young—they live in California, but they're not in the best shape. They're on the older side, and my dad isn't well. I guess that's also why what's happening with Isabel is even more upsetting for me. I don't have a lot of people up here, and I know none of us have known each other all that long, but Isabel and I were just starting to get close. And then out of nowhere, she's just—gone. I wonder if there was something I could have done. But it's hard to even think about that when it's so unclear what's happened to her." She sipped her wine again and looked down.

So she wasn't trying to hide her close relationship with Isabel. On the contrary, she was the one to bring it up.

"For sure. It's been upsetting for me, too," I assured her. "I didn't necessarily know her super well, but I just feel so awful that wherever she is, she isn't with Naomi. I keep thinking about if that were Clara. I know that's a little selfish, to automatically go to 'What if it were me,' but it just makes me want to do anything I can to help. And, um, also, my mom got cancer and died when I was pregnant," I blurted out. "So I can kind of relate to feeling like—well, you know, just not having family around and—" I was rambling and had no idea why I'd felt the need to tell her I was also a member of the dead mom club, as if it were some coveted, exclusive group. Usually I avoided bringing it up at all costs. It had come flying out of me, unexpectedly.

"Jenn, that's terrible. I had no idea." Vanessa's face was warm and open, eyes filled with genuine sympathy.

"Yeah. Thanks. This isn't how I imagined new motherhood, you know? I always pictured her being around, helping me with the baby, showing me what to do. I miss her so much." I was opening up to Vanessa more than I'd confided in anyone since Clara was born. I wasn't sure why.

"I'm so sorry. This isn't how I had always imagined it, either, for what it's worth."

I felt like this was my opportunity to ask. She had shared, I had shared. She had again alluded to her split. We were bonding. I pushed it a bit further.

I took a breath and a swallow of wine. Liquid courage. "Can I ask? What happened with Phoebe's dad?"

She nodded. "Well. It's a long story, but let's just say he wasn't who I thought he was, and I'm not who he thought I was, either. That's for sure." Her tone changed a bit; she sounded strangely proud. "He wasn't interested in being Phoebe's dad, and she's better off without him, in my opinion." For once, I mustered restraint and refrained from asking her to be more specific, though I was disappointed in how vague her answer had been.

She reached over and tickled Phoebe's belly, immediately eliciting a big smile and squeaky, gurgly laugh from her. She bent all the way down and nuzzled her cheek. "It's his loss, obviously. Who couldn't love this girl? But we're okay. I will be all the parent she needs." As she and Phoebe smiled at each other, I noticed how they both had brow lines that sloped upward, giving an earnest, inquisitive quality to their faces. They both had a dimple that only appeared when they smiled really deeply. They had the same warm green eyes.

"What about you?" she asked. "How are things with your husband?"

"A little bumpy, to be honest with you," I said, way too quickly. "He tries to be helpful, but he hasn't had that much time to bond with her yet, because he's always at work. We've been . . . a bit off, since Clara was born." I felt guilty whining about him after what Selena had said to me yesterday, and knew that my problems with Tim *were* trivial, especially when Vanessa was doing this all on her own. After all, a well-meaning, albeit slightly clueless, partner was still more beneficial than no partner at all. But I also didn't want to be disingenuous with her. Maybe it was the wine, but I felt like we were truly connecting. And opening up felt good. Though I certainly wasn't going to mention the piece about Tim contacting Isabel. It was far too mortifying.

"Just curious," I continued, "since we're on the subject of husbands"—*smooth, Jenn*—"did Isabel ever complain to you about Connor? He didn't seem very involved, when we were over there the other day. I'm not saying he has anything to do with her disappearance, but—I don't know. I got a bad vibe, to be honest. Right?"

She looked at me intently. "She did allude to feeling a bit trapped in her role within their marriage, between you and me. He didn't want her to work—of course, she didn't need to—but she . . . expressed some regret about not having more autonomy in their partnership." She was choosing her words carefully and still studying my face as she spoke. "Did you know him at all, before the other day? Not like *know him, know him*, but just—know *of* him, or anything?"

"No, not at all. I mean—I googled him," I admitted. "After she disappeared. Otherwise, no."

"Didn't he say you looked familiar when we were over there?"

He had—I'd almost forgotten about that strange moment. "Yeah. Not sure what that was about. Probably just passed him on the street or something."

She nodded slowly. "Well. At least he's got tons of money, so I'm sure he's doing everything he can to find Isabel and bring her back." *Is he, though? Why are there no news alerts?*

Out of nowhere, Clara started wailing. It was already 4:00 p.m.; she would soon be ready for her final short nap of the day. And I needed to get ready for a dinner with my husband that I couldn't really imagine sitting through right now. I thanked Vanessa for having us and promised to be in touch during the week. I was no closer to figuring out what might have happened to Isabel, but still, it was nice to be leaving feeling closer to Vanessa. Apparently, Isabel had felt the same way about her.

Chapter Fifteen

Tuesday, October 6

Even notwithstanding our fight, going out for a fancy dinner was pretty much the last thing I felt like doing. All I really wanted, all I ever craved these days, was to log some time on the couch after the baby was sleeping. To be by myself without anyone touching or talking to me for an hour while I numbed out to some trashy TV show. But October 6 was our wedding anniversary—three years—so we were obliged to go out and celebrate.

Tim and I had gotten married at a bed-and-breakfast in Vermont. It was unseasonably freezing that day, but I didn't care. In all our pictures, we're laughing about how cold we are, my goose bumps visible, since the photographer basically insisted that we take our coats off for the photos. Our wedding was casual. We had lots of good food and local craft beers, only eighty guests, a Ben & Jerry's truck at the end of the night (which, obviously, we'd booked before we knew it would only be forty degrees). I danced with both my mom and my dad, eschewing tradition. I loved everything about that day. I didn't feel the stress that so many brides describe. And I assumed that our marriage, like our wedding, would be smooth sailing.

But adding a third person to our relationship had presented challenges neither of us had anticipated. It was embarrassing to recall how nonchalant we'd been about having a baby. "We can just bring the baby with us on trips and hikes and stuff; it's not like she'll take up much room!" we'd declared, laughing. We'd taken a two-hour childbirth class a few weeks before Clara's expected arrival. The midwife leading the class had declared, "Partners, the mother-to-be *will* poop during labor. She will. You need to prepare yourself for that."

I'd looked at Tim and shaken my head, whispering, "I totally won't." Spoiler alert: yes, I did. Suffice it to say, things were not shaking out the way we'd arrogantly assumed they would.

And now, I was rocked by the realization that Tim thought I was a basket case, and that's *if* he was even telling the truth about his communication with Isabel. There was still a small part of me that wondered if that's all it had been. But if not that, then what? I had assumed that I was the only one in our relationship harboring a dirty, unutterable secret. More than one, now, with my deleted note about Isabel. But maybe it was both of us. More likely, though, I was projecting: I knew that I didn't deserve *his* trust, and I was unfairly taking that out on him.

Despite where we were, how tired, frustrated, and mixed up I felt, part of me knew we needed this dinner. Even if it wasn't the romantic night we'd hoped for when we made the plans, we needed more time to talk things through. Plus, I had a ridiculously expensive babysitter lined up: Selena's former night nurse, in fact. She happened to have a gap in her schedule this week before she started with another family, so she was very happy to help us for a few hours—especially, I imagined, given that she'd likely just be watching TV and eating takeout that I'd ordered for her, since Clara would theoretically be sleeping the whole time we were away, by my own design. As much as I was struggling to meet Clara's daily needs by myself, the thought of handing over the reins to someone else made me even more anxious. How would they know the angle she liked to be fed at, or that I counted her fingers and toes for her every night before putting her in her bassinet, or the specific way I rocked her upright after a feeding, the rhythm and inflection of my "shh shh

shh"? It was times like these I so wished my mom were around so she could babysit, so that I could actually feel comfortable leaving Clara.

Clara's bedtime went down without a hitch; I pumped and fed her a bottle so that I could leave for dinner completely drained, as comfortable as possible, and so that I could make sure she had a good feed so she'd be more liable to have a long stretch of sleep. Tim let Jackie, the babysitter, in while I was putting Clara down. I changed as quietly as possible in our room after placing Clara in her bassinet. I realized that it was only my second or third time putting on a regular bra since I'd given birth, and I could barely squeeze my floppy, freshly drained breasts into it.

I put on a flowy, long-sleeved, short black floral dress—my legs still looked okay, I thought, and the dress pretty much hid all the parts of me that I was self-conscious about. I hurriedly put on a little bit of makeup in the bathroom, but even holding an eyeliner pencil felt awkward. It was like writing your name and the date on a piece of paper on the first day of school after the summer. It just felt wrong. I barely ever made myself up anymore. Gone were the days of taking thirty minutes to get ready for a night out; with Clara already asleep, I was officially on the clock, as we'd have likely no more than three hours until we'd have to be home for her first waking of the night.

"You look great, Mama," Tim said sweetly as I walked into the kitchen. Jackie and I talked shop for a few minutes—*text me if she wakes up; if she cries, let her cry for a minute to see if she'll fall back asleep on her own before going in and picking her up*—and then we were off.

Tim and I were going to the Milling Room, a beautiful restaurant just a few blocks away with a huge skylight and tons of tall plants, so it felt like you were eating outside. I loved their blue cheese olive martinis, and their chicken put every other chicken to shame. Tim held my hand as we walked down Columbus Avenue, but it felt forced. We'd never really been a hand-holding couple, even at our best. Plus, I finally had a minute without another human on my body, out in the fresh October air, walking along unencumbered by a stroller or baby carrier—the last thing I wanted to do was hold hands. But I didn't want to hurt his feelings or start our night off on a salty note. I didn't want him to think I was still mad about his call to Isabel, even though I definitely hadn't let it go. But I needed our night together to be fun, despite everything going on with us.

We were escorted by the hostess to a quiet corner table. Once we were seated, we looked at each other and smiled.

Awkwardly.

No choice but to try to get the elephant out of the room as soon as possible. He began. "Look, again, I am so sorry for calling Isabel. If anything, that should show you the degree to which I have no idea what I'm doing. I may seem uninvolved, but I do care—about you, about Clara, about our family. So much. I know that you've been bearing the brunt of caring for her, and it has to be so tough. I can't imagine. Not to mention, you're missing your mom. But you are doing an amazing job. Clara's the luckiest, most well-loved baby ever. And it isn't fair to you that it's been so uneven. I want to have a bigger role. And I promise that whatever concerns I have, about *anything*, I'll bring them to you first. I'll never go behind your back again." He reached across the table for my hand.

It was all I needed to hear. Knowing that he trusted and valued me. That he didn't think I was doing a crappy job being a mom. If I heard this more, maybe I'd actually start to believe it.

Then again, his kind words also reminded me of what a terrible wife I was. That I didn't deserve him.

"I am having a hard time, it's true," I conceded. "Who knows what's happening with my hormones. And the lack of sleep makes me feel insane. But it's only been a few months—you and I are both still learning. We'll get better. And we both love her, which has to be the most important thing. And I'm sorry that we haven't had time to talk, and connect . . . I miss you." Everything I was saying was true, and yet, I felt like such a fraud.

"You already are a good mom, babe. A great one. And you and I are gonna be fine. Please. We've got this." He smiled the crooked smile that made my heart leap.

My eyes welled up. I knew this guy. I loved this guy. We would be okay.

It was then that I saw a familiar face in profile. Connor, Isabel's husband, was sitting at the bar by himself, drinking an old-fashioned.

I put my hand on Tim's arm. "See that guy? The one in the white collared shirt at the end of the bar? That's Isabel's husband, Connor."

"Oh wow." Tim's face wrinkled, suddenly, as if he'd eaten a bite of lemon. "Kind of weird he's having dinner out, right? His wife is missing, and he has a newborn at home. What is he doing at a restaurant by himself?"

"Yeah, I guess. Isabel's mom has been helping them. Maybe he just needed to get out. He still has to eat." I had no idea why I was defending him. Tim was right. It *was* a little strange that he was here, alone.

"At the Milling Room? If he wants to get out and grab a slice of pizza, fine. He doesn't need to be treating himself to a five-star dinner when his wife is probably in a ditch somewhere." Tim had taken off his glasses and begun cleaning them aggressively with a napkin.

The sharpness in his tone surprised me, as did the violence of what he had said. "Hey. We have no idea if Isabel is dead. And we shouldn't judge how people deal with their stress. I know that better than anyone." I immediately regretted saying this, though there was no way Tim could have known what I was truly referring to. I cleared my throat, trying to shake it off and reclose that door. "He probably doesn't even eat pizza, anyway. He's probably, like, a paleo person. Plus, they have tons of money. To him this probably *is* the equivalent of grabbing a slice of pizza."

I was trying to be funny, but Tim took in that comment with a grimace. He always took conversations about money personally. If I remarked that private school likely wasn't in the cards for us, for example, or noted that we weren't financially ready to move to a bigger place, he got very defensive, which was all ridiculous—he had a great career as an architect and loved what he did. And he made a good living. Plus, I thought the notion that the man should be the "provider" was a horrifically antiquated expectation, and Tim knew that. Still, I tried to tread lightly when the subject of money came up, so as not to hurt his feelings.

As our food arrived, I could see that Connor was talking to the bartender loudly, practically shouting at him from across the bar. I couldn't make out what he was saying, because the buzz of conversation around the restaurant muffled his words, but the fact that I could hear his voice at all from our table meant that he was at top volume. The restaurant was bustling.

I tried to ignore Connor and focus on Tim and our meal, but he was in my direct line of sight, and I couldn't stop glancing over at him. He ordered two more drinks in about twenty minutes. He wasn't talking to the bartender anymore, just staring at his phone, holding it about four inches from his face. Squinting slightly with one eye. I knew this expression too well. He was drunk.

We got a **she's stirring** text from Jackie at around ten as we were sharing a piece of cheesecake, so we signed our check and made our way to the restaurant's front door. Connor was still at the bar. Tim had his hand on the small of my back, and unlike earlier when he'd held my hand, it felt natural, and right. It made me feel like he was proud to be my husband. It made me feel like our relationship could be simple again.

"I think I should say hi to Isabel's husband," I said to Tim as we were about to pass the bar. I hadn't been planning to, but I couldn't resist. I was dying to know if there had been any leads in the case. It was frustrating having so few ways of learning anything. I wasn't a close friend. I didn't know her family. All I could hope for was random leaks of information here and there, on the internet, or secondhand from one of the other moms in our group. And the information I was hoping for was as much about myself as it was about Isabel: an explanation of what I had written and deleted. What I would never speak a word of. Maybe at some point, I would learn something that could help me resolve it. But only if I was somewhat proactive about searching for answers.

"Really?" Tim looked skeptical. "I figured you'd be eager to get home to Clara."

"Yeah, I am, but it'll just take a sec. Just want to see how he's doing. It seems rude not to, right?"

We walked up to Connor's stool, Tim reluctantly trailing behind me. "Hi, Connor," I said timidly. He didn't even turn around. "Hi, Connor?" I tried again a bit louder. He craned his neck to face me without moving his body. His face was flushed with alcohol and showed no sign of recognizing me. "I'm Jenn. From Isabel's moms' group. We met the other day, at your house? This is my husband, Tim. We saw you at the bar and just wanted to come over and ask how you are." Tim stuck out his hand but Connor didn't register it, so Tim quickly returned it to his pocket, reddening slightly.

"Well, not great, Jenn." He whirled around in his chair to face me completely, leaning forward so his face was only about a foot from mine, so close that I could feel his hot breath on my face. It was a strange mix of whiskey and menthol, and as it washed over me, a jolt of electricity went through my body, like a dizzying hot flash. It passed quickly, fortunately.

"I know. I'm so sorry. It must be so hard. Have they made any progress on finding her?" I shifted my weight uncomfortably. I'd just felt my breasts fill up and knew I had only a few minutes before I would need to pump in order to avoid leaking into my dress.

"Well, indeed they did," he said sarcastically, bitingly. He seemed like a completely different person from the polished, self-possessed man I'd met at their home. "They found her rings. Covered in blood, I should add. So that's 'progress,' I guess." He threw my choice of word back at me cruelly, gripping his glass and flashing me a bitter, mirthless smile.

"What? No, that's—that's awful. Where did they find them?" I felt sick.

"Some mom found them down by the river, on the rocks right by the water. Her kid was exploring, I guess. She noticed the blood and called it in. They're Isabel's. So there's that." He started to turn away as if the conversation were over. But I couldn't end it there, obviously.

"Well, that doesn't necessarily mean—I mean, at least it wasn't, like, a limb," I said. I was awkward even in pretty standard social situations, let alone conversations about bloody rings and dead wives, but this was a horrifying new low. *At least it wasn't a limb.* God.

It didn't seem to faze Connor. "Yeah, I guess," he said. "But *something* bad happened. I know Isabel, and she's just not—" He paused and laughed, rolling his eyes slightly. "She wouldn't leave. That's for sure. She's not the type." He seemed not to mean this as a compliment, and I felt offended for her. "So now I get to live with my mother-in-law while the search continues." He rolled his eyes again. "Kill me now." He slammed the rest of his old-fashioned—probably half the drink—in one long open-mouthed swig, basically pouring it down his throat. In the same motion, he flagged the bartender and signaled for another. The bartender looked at us accusingly, like our association with Connor made us to blame for his behavior.

Tim spoke up. "I'm so sorry about your wife, man. That's such a bad hand. Really, really sorry."

He again didn't even acknowledge Tim, keeping his gaze on me instead. "Don't I know you from somewhere?" He really was wasted. It was our second time meeting, and I'd just explained that I was in the moms' group. Again. Tim's grip on my lower back tightened.

"Um, well, yeah. I'm in Isabel's moms' group? I came by the other day with Vanessa to drop off some food?" I hoped these clues as to who I was were specific enough for him.

"Hmm. Yeah, I guess that was it." A fresh drink was placed in front of him begrudgingly by the bartender, who gave us another wary look. Connor took a small sip and glanced around. Maybe he was finally pacing himself.

"Can I ask? Why haven't there been any . . . missing persons alerts or anything? Maybe someone saw something that could help but they just don't realize that she's even missing." I knew I was overstepping as usual but was emboldened by the cocktails I'd had, and it was clear Connor was drunk, too. Maybe I didn't have to follow the rules.

"Well, Jenn," he began condescendingly. "Imagine you're an investor and you're thinking of giving me millions of dollars of your money to invest. Would it make you inclined to do so if you knew that I had a missing wife? I'm guessing not. It's not a great look for me, or my business. Because people always think it's the goddamn husband. No one would care that I'm a hundred percent cleared. All they'd hear is 'missing wife,' and then they'd look at me as at worst a killer, at best, can't keep my own family safe and in check. Luckily, I'm well enough connected in the media world to keep it quiet. I've gotten a lot of calls, but so far, everyone's been smart enough to give me the privacy I've requested. At least for a few days, or until there's more of a story." He shook his head in disgust. "Last thing I need." I was amazed at his ability to make all this about him.

"But . . . what if it could help her be found?" I pressed.

"Guess we'll never know. Not a risk I can take." He slammed his drink. Again. Tim gave me a slight but meaningful nudge that said, *It's time to go.*

"Okay, well, we have to get home, but . . . I'm so sorry about the ring thing"—*Ring thing? What is wrong with me?*—"and please let me know if there's anything I can do to help. Anything at all."

"See you." He gave us a quick salute and me a wink, which struck me as a very strange way to end such a heavy conversation, and pivoted to face the bar once more. It was then that I noticed the twentysome-thing girl a few seats away from Connor at the bar, alone and swaying slightly, eyes blank and drowsy with alcohol. I felt a powerful urge to ask her if she needed help getting home, but I resisted, of course; we had to get home ourselves, and it would be completely overstepping in any event. She wasn't a child; she was just living her young life. Maybe my brief flash of concern for her was just a sign that I was becoming a mother, after all.

We walked out of the restaurant into the night. I spoke first. "Wow."

"Yeah," Tim said. "What is wrong with that guy?"

"Well, I guess he's worried about his wife and dealing with it in all the wrong ways," I said generously. "I meant about the bloody rings. That's really scary. What do you think it means?" Surely, this latest news did not bode well for Isabel. Puddles of blood down Eighty-Eighth Street and now bloody rings by the river. This was turning into a grisly scene from which I could not imagine her emerging.

"No idea," he said. "But like you said, she could still be alive." He paused. "I did not like that guy, Jenn." He looked truly angry. I wasn't sure if I had ever heard Tim say that about anyone—he was so reasonable, so mild, the type to get along with everyone and always extend the benefit of the doubt—especially to someone who was going through a tragedy. "Let me know if you see him again, okay?" he added. I promised that I would, without being exactly sure why he was so fervent about it.

When we entered our apartment, Jackie was rocking Clara on the glider. "She woke up so I just settled her back down," she said, smiling, as if settling Clara down were the easiest thing in the world. "How was dinner?" She wasn't even trying to keep her voice down, but Clara was sleeping as soundly as she ever had, swaddled flawlessly and resting comfortably in Jackie's strong, confident arms, having been coaxed back to sleep without any milk at all. Her face was perfectly serene. So was Jackie's.

Before Jackie left, she put Clara back in her bassinet, transferring her in with apparent ease, a feat I'd managed only a handful of times. After we paid her (an exorbitant sum, though no more than she deserved, for keeping our daughter safe), she said, "She's a dream! So glad I got to spend a little time with her. Let me know if you ever need help again. I'd love to work with you guys." Was Clara a dream? Was she just an easy baby who everyone else was better at handling than I was? Why was I so bad at this?

Predictably, Tim initiated sex that night. It was our anniversary, after all; if ever there was a night to be romantic, this was it. I was nervous; it had been over three months since we'd done it, and I felt like a different person. What if he could tell that I was no longer the woman he'd fallen in love with? But I was surprised at how good it was to be close to him again, to feel his familiar warmth. When it was over, we held each other for a few minutes before letting go.

After that, Tim was snoring within seconds, but I couldn't fall asleep for at least an hour, thinking about Isabel's body lying somewhere, yet to be discovered on the bank of the Hudson, and her husband angrily complaining about the inconvenience of her disappearance over drinks at the Milling Room. I thought ever so briefly, too, of the drunk girl at the bar.

But I also knew deep down that the reason I was lying awake thinking of Isabel and Connor was so that I could avoid thinking about the shameful fact that, while I was certain this had been Tim's first time having sex since we'd had Clara, it hadn't been mine.

Chapter Sixteen

That night, in between feeds, I dreamed of severed arms and legs. That I was tripping over feet and wrists and fingers and elbows while running through the woods. There were rings and bracelets and anklets attached to them.

I wondered if any of the other moms knew about the rings. Maybe Vanessa, who was perhaps checking in more regularly with Isabel's family. I considered texting them to tell them but decided it would be much easier to talk about it in person; it was too unseemly, too grim to write in a text. I was so relieved that we were meeting today—Vanessa had texted us all late yesterday afternoon, shortly after I'd left her apartment, to arrange an unscheduled meeting. *It would be good to see each other, talk about everything,* she'd said. It was the first time we'd all be together in person since learning of Isabel's disappearance last week. Had that been only five days ago? It felt like a year had passed between then and now.

My buzzy anticipation of our meeting, of being able to talk about Isabel, gave me a little more energy than I usually had—I was actually able to do some cleaning and some laundry, and once again put on my fancy leggings and a sweater instead of staying in my sweats all morning.

Clara seemed to respond to my energy positively, too, giving me lots of smiles during the day and taking one decent nap in her bassinet.

I walked into the WSWC ten minutes early, the sight of strong working women as always giving me a jolt, a harsh reminder of how foreign their world was to me right now. Productive women getting dressed up, pitching marketing decks, closing deals, probably after eight hours of sleep and a five-mile morning run or a Peloton ride. They might as well have been aliens.

Despite being early, I wasn't the first to arrive: Selena and Miles were already there. I hadn't spoken to Selena since our heated conversation a couple of days ago. I was all ready to apologize, but she broke the ice first with a cautious smile.

"Hey, I'm sorry about all that," she said effusively, not needing to clarify what "that" she was referring to.

"No, no, *I'm* sorry. You were totally right. I shouldn't have asked you to . . . I don't even know what, like, conduct some kind of amateur deep dive into Isabel's disappearance? I think I'm just looking for an outlet that takes me away from obsessing about Clara a little bit. But that is obviously not the right one. I certainly have no right to be nosing around in her family's business—and I definitely shouldn't be, like, recruiting friends to join me! I don't know what's wrong with me, to be honest." Hearing how true my words were made me feel even worse and refreshed my embarrassment.

"I totally get it," she said. "Look, it's really upsetting. And I don't want to seem callous. I've been thinking a lot about her, too, obviously. But it has nothing to do with us."

Why did she keep saying that, though? While I could certainly recognize that the way I was dealing with the Isabel situation—trying to involve myself, uncover clues—was weird, and possibly dangerous, Selena's reaction and insistence on distancing herself from all of it seemed just as off to me.

She continued, squeezing Clara's toe affectionately as I placed her on the mat next to Miles. "Anyway, I hope we're okay. And I didn't mean to imply that I don't like you guys, because I do. That was too much, and I didn't mean it. I do value your friendship, and I hope you'll keep what I said between us. That was the stress talking. But my situation is different from yours—it just is. Sometimes my stakes feel so high. Like I'm not allowed to make a mistake. And getting involved in all of *this*, for me, would be a mistake." There was a note of finality in her tone that told me it was time for me to let it drop, and I wouldn't ignore her cues, like I had the other day.

"Of course. I completely respect that. And again, I'm sorry for not being more considerate, and for making you uncomfortable." Kira and Caleb walked in at that point, bringing a natural end to our conversation.

Kira looked like hell. And coming from me, that was saying a lot. Her face was shadowy, her sweatshirt was stained, her hair looked like it hadn't been washed in several days. When I pulled her in for a hug, I even noticed a bit of a scent to her.

"Hey!" I said, too enthusiastically, as if I could magically transfer her some energy. "You doing okay?"

"Yeah. Sleep's been a little tough lately, I guess. We're trucking along, though," she said, barely returning my hug, smiling slightly but not meeting my eyes.

Vanessa and Phoebe walked into the room then, Phoebe content-edly tied to Vanessa's chest in her stylish Boba wrap, Vanessa wearing her like a gorgeous, prized accessory. Vanessa looked serious as she greeted all of us, lightly kissing everyone in her classy way.

No one had brought snacks that day. We hadn't discussed it explic-itly, but perhaps it felt too casual, too normal, suddenly inappropriate for our new circumstances. Besides, Isabel was the one who normally designated snack duties.

Once we were all seated, Kira nursing Caleb (who was predictably and adorably dressed in a purple-and-pink striped onesie), the rest of the babies on the play mat, Vanessa spoke solemnly. "Ladies, I hate to start off with bad news, but I think it's best I tell you right away. I got a call from Louise, Isabel's mom, yesterday evening. Apparently, the police found her rings on the Hudson riverbank." She glanced at each one of us, gauging how we were processing the news.

Selena and Kira gasped, putting their hands to their mouths almost in unison.

"So what does this mean?" Kira asked, rubbing her eyes with confusion as she tried to register it. I looked at her coffee cup on the floor beside her: *3x*. Three extra shots of espresso. Sleep really had been bleak for her, apparently. "Couldn't that be a good sign? Like maybe she threw the rings in the water and peaced? I mean, not that that's *good*, per se, but better than . . ."

"The rings were covered in her blood," Vanessa added flatly. "Sorry. Should have said that first."

"But we knew there was blood from the stains," Selena said. "This isn't necessarily bad news. Or at least, not worse than what we already knew." She was trying to rationalize, but the fear and concern in her eyes betrayed her words.

"I mean, it's better than finding a body, but it's very concerning, to say the least," Vanessa said. "And if someone killed her, they may not have wanted to keep or sell her rings for fear of being caught, so . . ." She trailed off, not needing to finish her thought.

I cleared my throat awkwardly. "I saw Connor last night, actually, and he mentioned it."

Kira whirled on me. "What do you mean, you saw Connor last night?" She finger quoted my words with so much force that Caleb became unlatched. Selena was looking at me agape, too.

"Tim and I were having dinner at the Milling Room, for our anniversary, and Connor was there, at the bar. He was kind of drunk, actually. He told us about the rings."

"Why didn't you tell us right away?" Vanessa asked.

I was surprised by the vehemence of their reaction. "I knew we'd be seeing each other today, and I felt weird sending it over text."

"So he's just like, what—out at bars, telling everyone all about his dead wife?" Kira said indignantly and still a bit too sharply.

We all winced. Vanessa, with infinite grace, said gently, "She might not be dead."

"Who confirmed that it was her rings?" Selena said. "Was it only her blood on them, or anyone else's? Were the stones still in the rings, or was it just the settings?" She'd assumed her lawyer role, asking logistical questions, trying to get more information to have a complete picture of the situation.

Vanessa took a breath. "Louise ID'd the rings. They are hers."

Another collective silence. We were all thinking the same thing: it felt intentional, meaningful, *personal*, that her rings had been removed and left there. It would have made it seem like a suicide, except that the blood dripping down Eighty-Eighth Street didn't. And it just begged more questions, like where were the rest of her belongings? Clothing, a wallet?

I broke the silence, finally. "Again, why did they clear Connor so quickly? I know he didn't do it himself, but he could have easily hired someone, right? I have to say: I don't like him."

Selena nodded fervently but then shrugged. "There would have been paper trails—you know, a large bank withdrawal, emails—some kind of red flag. It's not the kind of thing that's easy to get away with. So I guess they don't have any of that. I'm sure they looked. They're probably still looking. This newest evidence will make them look harder."

I was intrigued by what Selena said, but I knew that part of my desperation for Connor to be guilty stemmed from the fact that I still hadn't resolved my terrifying suspicion of myself: what our plans that were never plans meant, why my unspeakable Google Doc had been written, my forgotten walk, the cuts on my hand, which had now mostly healed. If Connor was guilty, it meant I definitely wasn't and that any clues implying otherwise were irrelevant, coincidental.

"Jenn, to your point, Connor may be an asshole," Selena continued, "but if the police are sure he didn't kill her, that's that. A lot of guys are jerks—it doesn't mean he murdered his wife. Vanessa, how's her mom doing?" She'd changed the subject quickly. Too quickly; I hadn't been ready to move on from discussing Connor.

"As well as can be, I guess," Vanessa said. "I was kind of surprised that she thought to keep me in the loop. I guess Isabel didn't have that many other friends, at least locally—we're kind of it, is what her mom made it seem." This surprised me. Isabel had lived in the city for a while, I'd thought. I had assumed we were fringe friends, not primary. It also made me question Selena's stance on the whole situation; if we were her only friends, we needed to be more involved, not less. Isabel needed us right now, and instead, we were bailing on her, just complacently waiting for her to reappear dead or alive, instead of actively searching, asking questions.

Kira had been silent for the past several minutes. She took her phone out and checked the time. "Guys, I'm sorry but I need to go. I have so much to do at home, and I have to feed Caleb soon." Caleb was dozing soundly in his stroller, now cocooned in a fleece blanket, having literally just been removed moments ago, unconscious, from Kira's boob. God knows I was no expert, but it seemed his next feed should be at least a couple of hours from now.

"Wait—before you go." Vanessa cleared her throat. "I know this is super weird timing, with everything going on, and crazy last minute, too, but a partner in my dermatology practice offered to let me use his Montauk house this week. His son made soccer playoffs here in the city so they can't go, but the house is apparently all stocked and clean and ready to be enjoyed. It's a really big house. He told me to invite anyone I wanted. I have the rest of the week off—part of my efforts to 'ease back in'—which is why he offered it to me. Anyway, I was wondering if you guys would want to go tomorrow, just for the night, no babies? I think we could all really use a night away. It could be super relaxing—just us, the ocean, plenty of wine. It might help us take our minds off things. What do you think?" She glanced around at each of us, again trying to assess our reaction, the same way she'd done when she told us about Isabel's rings minutes before.

The idea of being at someone's beach mansion was, on the one hand, extremely appealing, but it did feel odd to be treating ourselves to a girls' getaway when someone in our group was probably at the bottom of the Hudson. Then again, Vanessa had been closest with her, so if she felt it was okay, I should probably defer to her judgment. The even bigger issue for me, though, was whether I could really leave Clara for the night. I wasn't sure if I was ready. And I wasn't sure if Tim was ready—if he was even available. Asking him to take a day off from work at the last minute was a big request.

"That sounds amazing," Selena said. "I'll see how Cameron feels about it. He actually just started his paternity leave; we wanted to overlap for a bit. So this could be good timing." I was a bit surprised by her positive response, given what she'd said about all of us when she'd been at my apartment. But she had said she hadn't meant it—maybe she really hadn't and this was her way of showing me.

"That would be incredible," I found myself saying. "I'm not sure if I can swing it, but I'll definitely discuss it with Tim. Thanks for the invite." I was surprised that a big part of me actually did want to go. And was it such a huge thing? We'd successfully left Clara with a babysitter last night; this could be just like that, but for a little longer. Besides, being away from Clara might be less daunting if I were in the company of women who knew exactly how it felt to be separated from their babies for the first time. We could talk each other off our respective ledges. Still, I knew better than to get my hopes up. I kept coming back to how unlikely it would be that Tim would be available, especially on such short notice.

"I won't be able to go," Kira said glumly. "Jack's just getting back from a work trip tomorrow morning, so it'd be a bit too chaotic. Besides, he's changed, like, four diapers. I can't even imagine how many questions he'd be texting me if I left him with the baby for a whole night." She'd begun hurriedly packing up Caleb's things. "If you do go, though, please drink seven bottles of wine for me," she added. "My FOMO will be raging."

"What about your mom?" Vanessa suggested suddenly. "Didn't your parents move to the city to be closer to you and the baby?" Though she was only being helpful, it seemed a significant breach of her usual perfect etiquette.

Kira looked at her, surprised, too. "I'll think about it and check. Thank you for inviting us. It does sound great," she said, softening slightly.

"Okay, well, keep me posted. And I hope everyone gets some sleep tonight. Text the group later." Vanessa started tying her Boba wrap back on, apparently adjourning the meeting. We hadn't even discussed anything baby related that day. Perhaps this was another sign that we really were ready for some moms-only time at the beach. It sounded too good to be true.

July 9

Dear Baby,

Well, we've survived our first few weeks together! (Barely, it sometimes feels like. But here we are.)

I have to be honest with you (as always)—I fear I'm not too good at this. This whole mom thing. Maybe I'll be better when you're older—I think I'll be a great toddler mom, or teenager mom. I'll be fun and energetic and creative and real with you. I'll always treat you like the full human that you are. But right now—well, I'm failing and flailing all over the place, it seems.

Sometimes I have no idea when your last feed was. I try to remember to time them, space them out, but the numbers on the clock look like hieroglyphics to me. And it takes me about twelve minutes to change a diaper, and you're crying the whole time. I just want to make sure all the poop is out of your vagina. I read that that was really important. But I can tell I'm hurting you. Your poop is green when it's supposed to be orange, and it seems like you're uncomfortable when I feed you. I have no idea what to do about that. I try to burp you in every position, but rarely do I hear the release of air come from your little body. I google everything I can, and I've got tons of books. I really am trying. I just . . . sort of suck at this.

I can't get you to take a pacifier to save my life. I know it would help, but you just don't seem to want it. We went for a walk yesterday—a short one—and you started screaming. Some old woman on the street said to me, "Can't you give her a pacifier? She'd be much happier." I nodded and told her I would try. Then I sobbed when we turned the corner. You and I were both crying. I know she was just trying to help. But she might as well have been saying, "Why can't you take care of your own child?" Which is exactly what scares me. That I don't really know how to take care of you. That I'm in over my head. That I'll never be the mother you deserve.

I used to be someone I think you'd be proud of. Not too long ago. A cheerful, confident person. I liked myself. That's so weird to say, but I did. I liked spending time with myself. I liked being me. It was so easy to smile. I hope that person comes back soon so that you can meet her.

It might seem like I'm being too open with you, too unfiltered. I have a feeling that all this, what I'm telling you, was NOT what the Pinterest board that recommended writing letters to baby was suggesting! Ha. But the thing is that I don't really have anyone to talk to about this stuff. I can't tell your aunt, because she'd just give me some judgmental old "I told you so" lecture. Talking about baby stuff with her is sensitive, anyway. She has a rough past when it comes to babies. My coworker suggested, right before I gave birth, that I join a new moms' group, but how do I even find one? None of my friends have babies or are anywhere close to having them. I've had a couple of visitors, but no one who I can really open up to about how much I'm struggling.

You know what's kind of funny? There is one person out there in the world who knows just what I'm going through: your father's wife. Assuming, of course, that it was her baby I heard on the phone. Maybe I should call her again. Ask her if she wants to swap notes on sleep sacks and wake windows.

Ha. That's the sleep deprivation talking.

I wish I could talk to my mom. I told you she died when I was young—well, I was only a year old, and she died by suicide. Maybe if she'd known she wasn't the only one having a hard time, it would have somehow been easier for her. So my hope is that, if one day you have a new baby and you're struggling, you'll reread this and remember that you aren't alone, that I went through it, too. And that you can always talk to me.

There you go, waking up from a nap. You're stirring right beside me, making your "hangry" face, contorting with a cry that's still brewing but hasn't yet been released. Gosh, you're cute, even when you're about to wail.

And that's the funny thing—no matter how exhausted I am, I'm always happy when you wake up. Excited to see you, even though you've been beside me the whole time. Relieved you're alive. Relieved you're *real*. It's such a strange but lovely feeling.

I love you, and I'm sorry I'm a mess. And thank you for being patient with me while I figure all of this out. Because even though you're just a baby, I can tell you love me, too. Even though I probably don't deserve it.

Love you forever,
Mommy

Chapter Seventeen

Wednesday, October 7

Usually we all walked out of our meetings together, even if our pace was ridiculously slow because someone had to keep stopping to wipe drool from a mouth or pick up a dropped sock. Our politeness was even stronger than the rush to get home or to happy hour. But this time, Kira just bolted. I decided to try to catch up with her. I hadn't talked to her all week, and she seemed off. Plus I wanted to get her take on the Montauk invite; in the unlikely event that I'd be able to go, I'd much rather she be there, too. The idea of it being just me, Vanessa, and Selena was a little intense.

I placed Clara in the stroller and buckled her in quickly, then practically had to run through the WSWC lobby to catch Kira, leaving Selena and Vanessa behind, just outside our meeting room, still chatting and easing Miles and Phoebe into their respective stroller and wrap.

"Kira! Wait up!" I called, nearly crashing into a statuesque brunette woman in a herringbone blazer as I speed walked toward the exit.

Kira halted her headlong rush for the door and turned. "Oh, hi, sorry. Didn't mean to run out, but I feel like Caleb's about two minutes away from losing it." Caleb was in his stroller happily sucking on his shoulder strap, staring at the ceiling. "Anyway, what's up? How are you?" Her eyes flashed between Caleb and the door, never quite settling on me.

"Yeah, fine. Weird week. Long week. Already. How are you doing?"

"I'm all right. Haven't been getting much sleep, that's all, because of a certain someone in purple." She gestured toward Caleb, as if worried she'd offend him by calling him out directly. "And I'm also very worried for Isabel, too. Goes without saying."

I nodded in agreement as we exited the WSWC and started walking south on Central Park West. The bright sunlight and crispness of the day were in stark contrast to Kira's dark undereye circles and mood and the distressing news about Isabel's rings that we'd discussed inside. "I was curious," I began. "What do you think of Vanessa's Montauk invite? Do you think you're going to be able to go?"

"I don't know. It sounds great, but I mean, realistically, there's no freaking way. Plus it's weird she asked us to go so last minute. If I *was* going to do a girls' trip, I would need to prep Jack for, like, weeks ahead of time. I can't just pitch it to him the day before."

I knew it wasn't fair to spring it on Tim, either. And yet, God, I wanted to go. I *needed* a change of scenery, a palate cleanser, some salty air. Maybe if I went, I would return from Montauk a new woman. That'd be a win for all concerned, wouldn't it?

"Do you think your mom would help, like Vanessa said?" I pressed, cautiously.

"I'm sure she would be happy to help, and then when I get home, I'll be subjected to a tirade of criticism masked as 'helpful advice.' When she babysits him for an hour, she suggests about fifteen things I should be doing differently with his schedule, his room, his clothes. Can't imagine the kind of feedback I'd get if she stayed with him for a whole night. So I'm not really jumping at the chance to invite even more of that than usual; I can only take small doses at a time." I tried not to show any reaction on my face, but what I would have done for any-size dose of my mom—with or without criticism. "And anyway, I'm really not sure how relaxing this night away would be for me. I'd just be worrying the whole time. It's probably not worth it. It's easier if I just stay and take care of him myself." She sounded like me; as hard as it was to do things without help, it was easier, too, in a damning sort of way. She started walking faster, as if she were getting heated as she spoke.

"Are you okay?" I asked her, struggling to catch up again. "You seem . . . stressed. I mean, obviously, all of this"—I gestured vaguely at the babies, back toward the WSWC, the world in general—"is stressful, but you don't seem like yourself, and we've barely talked since Isabel disappeared. I'm—" I stopped myself at telling her I was worried about her; the last thing I wanted to seem was condescending, as if I had my shit together and she didn't, which couldn't have been further from the truth. "I just want you to know you can talk to me, if you need to."

Kira gave me a long look, eyeing me, as if determining how much she could open up to me. Apparently she decided to go for it, because she said, hesitantly, "Do you want to get a drink after all? I could definitely use one."

Chapter Eighteen

Wednesday, October 7

We walked a few more blocks south to Vin Sur Vingt, a cute French wine bar that was usually fairly quiet in the afternoons and surprisingly welcoming of strollers and babies given that it was a French wine bar (though restaurants that weren't kid friendly around here tended to be quickly and viciously skewered on Upper West Side Moms, a fate I imagined they all wanted to avoid).

We sat down outside to make stroller parking easier, and since we were both in sweaters and it wasn't too cold out. We each ordered a Chablis, which appeared moments later in large, cold glasses. Kira took a long sip of her wine—half the glass, practically. Caleb and Clara were both happily sitting in their respective strollers, kicking their legs from under their blankets, seeming to enjoy being outside looking around. Caleb didn't seem on the verge of a meltdown at all, as Kira had implied while we were leaving the WSWC.

Kira took a deep breath. "Okay, so, this is crazy, but I've been a little freaked out because"—another deep breath—"I sort of know Isabel's husband. That's why I wanted to leave her house so quickly the other day, when we found out about her disappearing. I recognized him. And I didn't want him to recognize me." She finally looked up and met my eyes.

"What? Are you serious? How do you know him?" I leaned closer to her, practically salivating at this revelation.

"We went to high school together. On Cape Cod." She blinked hard. "I had no idea that he was Isabel's husband until we saw him that day at their house, after she disappeared. I mean, she'd only ever mentioned him by his first name, which I thought nothing of. But of course when I got home that day after we found out she was missing, I googled them, to check if it was really him, and sure enough, it was. I felt so weird bringing it up to you guys. Like it wouldn't seem believable that I hadn't realized she was married to someone I knew. And then when I didn't mention it immediately, I felt like I shouldn't mention it at all. It's not like I'm *friends* with him. We hadn't seen each other in a long time."

"That's definitely a weird coincidence," I said carefully, processing, "but . . . you didn't do anything wrong by knowing him. I'm sure Isabel didn't make the connection, either. And you hadn't seen him since high school—that's like forever." I wasn't sure why having gone to high school with him was something she felt like she had to hide.

"Well, *knowing* him isn't the whole problem." She took another deep breath and another long sip of wine. Her glass was already almost empty. "I *hadn't* seen him since high school . . . until about four years ago. It was when I still lived in Boston. I ran into him at a bar. I saw him but didn't even plan on saying hi—I didn't think he'd remember me. But eventually he came up and said I looked familiar, which surprised me, because I was sure he'd never noticed me in high school. He was a total hotshot jock, and I, on the other hand, was very obsessed with my school's literary magazine—literally worked on that thing every night and weekend like I was the editor of the *Times* or something—and even though we were in the same year, I don't think we had a conversation the entire four years of high school.

"Anyway, I was out with some work friends when I saw him. I had just accepted a new job in New York, so this was kind of a send-off for me. Eventually, it got really late and my friends left, but Connor and

I were kind of making eyes at each other, or I thought so, anyway, so I stayed. As soon as they left, he was all over me—buying me drinks, flirting. We were drinking whiskey, which he kept ordering. I should never, ever drink whiskey. Seriously. If you ever see me holding a whiskey, send me home immediately." She laughed a little, but sadly. "The thing is that in high school, I was always kind of that funny, quirky girl that guys were friends with but never dated. I read, like, five books a week instead of going to parties. Hence why I got into publishing, I guess. And Connor was—well, everyone knew Connor. He was six foot three with a five-o'clock shadow when we were, like, thirteen. He was *that guy*. The guy that never got turned down, that could be with anyone he wanted to be with. Even the senior girls liked him when we were freshmen. He never would have looked at me twice in high school. But I guess, maybe I looked good on this night that I ran into him—my braces were finally off, at least—and we were buzzed. I was way more than buzzed, actually. And I was enjoying the way he was looking at me. At first. You know how it is, when you see someone from high school and it kind of transports you back. Suddenly, I was seventeen-year-old Kira, relishing the attention from the hottest guy in school. I guess I was having a *She's All That* moment or something. So pathetic. Anyway, one thing led to another, and . . ."

"And what?"

"You need me to say it, Jenn? I feel so weird even telling you this. We're close, sure, but the fact is that we really haven't known each other that long. And I'm telling you that I had sex with the husband of our missing friend. While they were married." She looked at me wide eyed, waiting for me to say something.

Now I was the one guzzling my wine, trying to modulate the shocked expression on my face. "Did you know he was married, when you—"

"Of course not." She looked hurt, and I immediately regretted my question. "I didn't ask, though. I wish I had. But who gets married that young? I just assumed he was single. He *seemed* very single."

I tried to think of something reassuring to say but came up empty, so she continued, nervously. "Obviously, no one can find out. And, to be completely real with you, our hookup was awful. I thought it would be hot, because he's hot, but . . . it was really bad. *Really* bad. I was actually messed up for a while afterward. It just—it wasn't what I had in mind. Do you know what I mean?" *Do I ever,* I thought. All this was hitting way too close to home for me. "I met Jack pretty soon after, and I wouldn't sleep with him for the first few months that we were dating because of it. I've tried to just forget the whole thing." Her eyes darkened briefly. I waited for her to elaborate, but she shifted instead. "If it got out, it just wouldn't look good for me, given the circumstances, what with Isabel now missing and me knowing her *and* having slept with her husband . . . God, it's just such a mess. So you cannot say anything to the other girls. Or anyone else. Please." She locked eyes with me, waiting for me to promise.

I looked at my empty wineglass. Clara was starting to fuss in her stroller, so I picked her up and put her on my lap, holding her close and kissing her fuzzy head. "I won't. I promise. And I'm sorry you went through that, and that you've had to relive it because of all of this. But do you think what happened between you and Connor years ago could possibly have any implications on Isabel disappearing? Like, with him maybe having something to do with it? If he was cheating on her, and you had a bad experience with him . . . well, he obviously wasn't a good husband. Maybe this is kind of like . . . a lead, in a way. Who knows what else he would do?"

Kira sighed. "Of course I've thought about that, too. But if he's involved, the police would figure that out on their own. Her disappearance has nothing to do with me." I was brought back immediately to my conversation with Selena, when she insisted the same.

Against my better judgment, I pressed. "But don't you think maybe you should tell them, just in case? I just feel like an unfaithful, creepy husband is pertinent information in a case like this one." I *knew* there was a reason I didn't like or trust Connor. And I wanted the police to know, too.

"He's already cleared, though, so what would be the point? It's better if I just let the police do their job. Besides, if what happened with me was a habitual thing for him, there would be others that they would probably find . . . though I'm sure he covered his tracks. But regardless, my . . . *encounter* with him, let's call it, surely has nothing to do with what's happening with Isabel, and I don't want to wreck my own life offering up irrelevant information." She put her hand on Caleb's leg protectively. "It was so long ago, anyway. Maybe he's cleaned up his act."

I doubt it. But I nodded, considering. "Do you think Isabel knew he had cheated?"

"I have no idea. Hell, for all I know, they could have an open marriage, right? They're Manhattan millionaires—these people have all kinds of crazy situations behind closed doors. But as far as me and Connor, there's no way she knew. It was *such* a onetime thing—we literally didn't even exchange numbers or spend the night together. I didn't tell anyone about me and him, either. I don't really keep in touch with that many people from the Cape, and it wasn't exactly something I wanted to brag about. There's just no way she knows. No way at all."

Caleb started fussing in his stroller. Kira grabbed him swiftly, lifted her shirt, and put him to her breast with ease, without using a cover. I loved how confident she was about breastfeeding at a restaurant. I so wanted to be someone who did my part to "normalize breastfeeding," but I could barely bring myself to breastfeed in a secluded area of the park, let alone at a wine bar on a crowded street.

She shook her head, as if trying to shake the memory of her night with Connor out of it. She'd gone as far as she was willing to go, it seemed. "Anyway," she said, "it's all an unfortunate coincidence. A *very* unfortunate one. But I wanted to tell you because I want you to know why I've been so weird since she disappeared. Because I like you and I know this is a hard enough time, for all of us, and I didn't want you to think my being distant was about anything else, other than this." She reached over and squeezed my hand.

That meant a lot to me. It was as if she were saying, in the nicest way possible, "I know you have the tendency to agonize, so I'll try to save you the trouble."

"Thank you. I won't say anything," I repeated, for good measure. "You can trust me." And I meant it. I would keep her secret. But I couldn't help but think, regretfully, of Selena's stance that none of us even knew Isabel that well, that her disappearance wasn't really ours to fixate on or explore, that it wasn't our business, despite sharing time with her in our moms' group. And now here was Kira, declaring that her encounter with Connor was moot, meaningless, not worth revealing to anyone. What if Kira had just handed me a key but then made me promise not to use it? Connor had cheated on Isabel and traumatized Kira. This went beyond his not knowing she was in a moms' group. Surely, all of it *meant* something. He must have been involved in Isabel's disappearance, in one way or another. What if we were capable of helping Isabel but instead we were all just standing aside?

Maybe Selena was right—maybe we weren't really friends at all.

Chapter Nineteen

Wednesday, October 7

As I walked home from the bar pushing Clara, brooding over what Kira had disclosed, I couldn't deny that there was something else upsetting me, too: a part of Kira's story that stirred something in me I never wanted to confront again. I had worked so hard over the last month to shove that "something else" far beneath the surface of my being, to suffocate it, but Kira's admission about her night with Connor brought it back to life: a bubbling, festering, infected wound.

When Clara was six weeks old—right before I joined the moms' group—I went out with a couple of my teacher friends whom I hadn't seen since having Clara. It was my first night out. Two hours tops, is what I had told Tim. I had almost canceled about ten times, especially while attempting to get dressed and finding nothing that fit. I was nervous about leaving Clara and was so tired, as usual, that I would have preferred to just watch TV for an hour and go to bed. But I forced myself to keep the plans. I didn't want to be the person who was always canceling on everyone now that I had a child. Tim was all for me going, telling me it would be good for me, would make me feel like my old self again.

And it did, for a little while. I finally found an outfit that made me feel kind of sexy. A tight black dress that, with the help of SPANX, sucked my pooch in and accentuated my firm new milk boobs. I was happy to see my friends and catch up on school gossip, like how Mr. Getelman, a history teacher known for throwing kids' phones out his third-floor window, had finally retired over the summer, and Mr. Fernandez, the assistant principal, had gotten engaged to Ms. Zanko, the speech therapist, even though they'd only been dating for four months. It was a little hard to hear about how normal my coworkers' summers had been—lazy mornings, lots of reading, some travel— whereas mine had consisted of scrolling, strolling, getting pooped on, and being milked like a cow. But overall, it felt good to be out with them.

After two margaritas, I was feeling almost like a real human being again, not just Clara's grouchy, slovenly mom. It was ten o'clock before I knew it, and my friends were ready to call it a night; they were planning to go into school to set up their classrooms the next morning. Originally, I had doubted that I'd even last this long. But I had just gotten an unexpected All good! Clara took a bottle and is sleeping next to me in the DockATot. Hope you're having fun. Take your time! text from Tim. A few drinks in, and so relieved to be separated from the baby for a few hours, I found that I really did not want to go home yet.

My friends felt bad leaving me there by myself, but I shooed them out and told them I'd be right behind them, that I was going to use the bathroom and maybe try to get some fries to bring home. But instead, after they left, I sat down at the bar and got a tequila shot, which I hadn't done in practically a decade. It burned my throat in the best possible way, a punishment and a reward all in one, and made me feel twenty-two. I ordered another margarita, too. I was sort of pretending I was in a movie. I didn't even feel drunk; all I felt was relieved. Like I could breathe for the first time in months. It felt so good to be alone. And a frumpy, exhausted, frustrated, still-grieving new mom would never have a tequila shot, so as long as I was here doing exactly that, I was Old Jenn. Or, Young Jenn, more accurately.

And knowing that Clara was fine, safe at home with Tim, made my little taste of freedom all the sweeter. We could be apart and she would be okay. It was like a revelation. And it just made me love her even more.

I'd had enough, though; all I needed was a taste of freedom. Just a taste. I was ready to go home. I was going to ask for the check when another shot appeared in front of me. The bartender gestured vaguely—warily, in retrospect, perhaps—and there down at the end of the bar was a tall, brown-haired guy with an expensive-looking haircut and a narrow gray suit, raising his own shot toward me with a slight smile. I was surprised. Flattered. I felt rude not taking it. Or uncool, or both. *Why the hell not,* I thought to myself.

I smiled back and downed it.

It's blurry after that. We moved toward each other at the bar and talked a little. About what, I couldn't say. I remember at least two more shots and a beer, drunk in rapid succession. I can't recall laughing. Or his name, if I ever learned it.

I remember it all in scenic flashes only. Leaving the barstools. Entering the bathroom, him ushering me along like I was a child. I don't think I quite knew where we were going until I saw the toilet and heard the door lock. Him kissing me, hard and brief, in the bathroom. His rough stubble, which had looked sexy from afar, hurting my cheeks. That was the first time I said no. He responded by turning me around and shoving my head into the wall. I remember staring at my wedding ring as he entered me from behind and feeling momentarily nauseated. I was sure I'd throw up during sex. *At least that will put an end to it,* I thought. *Who would want to have sex with someone who was puking?* I felt myself floating outside of my body, looking down at myself, thinking, *What is happening, Jenn? What the hell is this?* But this was what I had wanted, wasn't it? To be someone else for a little while. I'd accepted a drink from him, and another, hadn't I? Pretending I was a character in a movie, right?

None of this felt like what I had wanted, though. I so badly wanted to scream for him to stop, but instead I only whispered it—once, maybe twice—my efforts feeble and futile. In truth, I felt like I had already let it go too far to shut it down. It was happening. The only thing left to do was see it through until the end.

It hurt. He wasn't gentle. I was irrationally terrified that all my organs would fall out of my still-healing vagina. But he kept saying "You're so tight," which had to have been a lie. He also kept saying "You slut," which, though I knew I deserved, still made tears fall from my eyes.

The encounter felt like it lasted hours, but in reality, it was probably a matter of a couple of minutes. He came quickly, pulling out and finishing himself off with a grunt. He said we probably shouldn't leave the bathroom together and that he would leave first. When I followed a minute later, dazed and in shock at what had just happened, he wasn't in the bar anymore. I already knew he wouldn't be.

One minute I was in the bathroom with him breathing heavily behind me, my eyes shut tight, praying for it to be over. The next I was in a cab, heading home to my husband and baby, not sure of who the hell I was, in disbelief at what had just transpired. My underwear was in my pocket because it was ripped and I couldn't wear it anymore. I called my mom's voice mail from the back of the cab, to hear her voice, something I did more often than I should have. I closed my eyes and imagined myself curled up in her hug, on her bed, eating pizza. Pizza in bed had always been her solution to everything—a bad day at school, a fight with a friend, a broken heart. But no amount of pizza in bed could make me feel better about what had just happened. And then, for the briefest moment, I was relieved she was dead, because what would she think if she could see me now?

When I got home it wasn't even that late, barely midnight, but so much had changed between when my friends left the bar and when I got home. I peeled off all my clothes and got into the shower, turning up the heat to an almost unbearable temperature. I deserved for it to hurt. My skin started to turn red. *Good,* I thought. I scrubbed my face, watching black mascara peel off in bits and fall into the drain. I knew tears were running down my face, too, but I was too disconnected from my body to really register that I was crying.

I could hear Clara whimpering when I got out of the shower. I pulled my robe on and walked into our room. Tim shifted in bed. "Hey, how was your night? You gonna feed her, or do you want me to?"

"It's okay, I got her. Go back to sleep," I told him, grateful that it was so dark that I couldn't see his face and that he couldn't see mine, either: the face of a lying, dirty, betraying wife.

While Clara's cries usually made me feel a bit panicky, tonight, they offered me surprising relief. It was as if she were pulling me back to safety, back to my real life, where I had the crucial job of keeping this precious baby alive, and away from the deed I'd just committed, of screwing some random jerk in a filthy bar bathroom. The two people could not possibly be the same. And I was this one. Not the one in the bar. I chose this one. A million times over.

I was disgusted with myself. Yes, my husband was rather useless when it came to night feedings, and his sneezes were loud enough to wake a corpse, let alone a dozing baby. But he was a great guy who loved me and who'd done nothing but try his best to support me through both my mom's death and new motherhood, and he deserved so much better than this. Better than me. He should have been with someone who could handle one baby without epically melting down every day and then acting out in this horrifically self-destructive way.

I fed Clara a bottle from the breast milk stash in the fridge—obviously, I couldn't nurse her, after all I'd drunk, though I felt stone-cold sober by that point. My breasts were painful, rigid torpedoes, especially after the hot shower, but I didn't pump after putting her back in her bassinet—I didn't deserve the relief it would bring, and I didn't deserve to sleep well. I never deserved to sleep well again.

July 14

Dear Baby,

My thoughts don't feel like my own.

My crazy, sleep-deprived brain is taking me to places I don't want to go.

I think of him all the time—I can't help it.

Even when you're sleeping, I can't. Despite that being the golden rule. Sleep when the baby sleeps! As if it's that simple. What a bunch of BS.

And when I do sleep, my dreams terrify me. I dream all my teeth have fallen out. Or that my breast milk is poison and it makes you sick. Or that you're crying but I don't have arms so I can't pick you up. Or that you fall down a well like in that movie *The Ring*. I've never even seen a well. But that's what I dream about.

And sometimes it's even worse than that.

Sometimes I dream of killing him.

I know how that sounds. But I just wish he weren't in the world anymore. He could be preying on other women as we speak. And who knows what he's doing to his wife.

I think of his hand on the back of my head, pushing me. The things he was whispering in my ear, his hot breath against my cheeks. How he walked out and slammed the door afterward, never even acknowledging me.

And when I'm not thinking about that, about him, I'm just thinking about what a crappy mom

I am. How I'll never be good at this. How I don't deserve you.

How I'll never sleep again. Unless I die. Then I could get a good long sleep.

I'm trying hard to shake thoughts like that out of my head and remind myself of the one thing that really matters: I love you. I love you. I love you.

Love you forever,

Mommy

Chapter Twenty

That night, as Tim and I were eating pizza from Arte Café and watching our recorded episode of *The Bachelorette* after Clara had gone to bed, Vanessa sent around a text with a link to the Montauk house. It was extravagant: six bedrooms, five bathrooms, a pool and jacuzzi, a home theater room, ocean views. Let me know who's in, she wrote. I really hope we can make this happen. It would be great for all of us. We deserve this! She included some wine emojis for good measure, as if the house itself weren't tantalizing enough.

I had gotten so caught up with what Kira had told me about Connor that I hadn't even had a chance to press her on the Montauk trip. But given what she'd told me, I assumed that she wasn't even considering it. In addition to her very understandable stress about leaving Caleb, it seemed like her inclination might be to distance herself from her association with Isabel, and that meant the moms' group. I wondered if she might even stop attending our meetings. I hoped not, but I could certainly empathize with doing everything possible to just forget that something like that had ever happened.

So I was shocked when she was the first to respond to Vanessa's text about Montauk with an enthusiastic I'M IN! Jack was on board, after all.

Looks amazing, this will be so much fun. And much needed. Thanks so much, Vanessa!

Against all odds, my conversation with Tim had been just as easy. "I think it's a great idea, babe! You definitely deserve it. It will force me and the C-monster to become best friends," he'd said, giving me a big hug. "It's good timing for me, too, since we wrapped up this presentation today and now we're just kind of waiting on feedback. I can finish up early tomorrow and take Friday off. Shouldn't be a problem."

I was rendered momentarily speechless. My guilt about what I had done at the bar was and would probably always be a lingering weight for me to carry on my shoulders, but never was it heavier than when Tim was so helpful, so sweet, so eager to do anything to make me happy. Maybe that's why I'd been so short with him these last few weeks, over such small things: it was easier to be mad at him about stupid stuff than angry at myself about something monumental. Of course I had thought about telling him—so many times—but I wasn't sure which was worse, telling him or not telling him. I already knew that I was a terrible person—making sure he knew it, too, felt more cruel than altruistic. If I'd only be doing it to seek forgiveness, to relieve myself of the guilt, then I shouldn't do it. I didn't deserve to feel better about it. And I certainly didn't deserve to be absolved.

I shook away my thoughts about that night, as I'd done so many times before by now. "Really? You're sure? You think you can handle all of it? Feeding her, dressing her, her naps, everything?" I was skeptical, knowing firsthand the tedious intricacies of each day spent with a newborn. But after all, he was her father, not some teenage babysitter—he was more than capable.

"I mean, will it go perfectly? Probably not. Will she be alive when you get back? Almost definitely!" He smiled at his own joke and turned back to his phone, seeming to signal that we were all good here, that this was settled, as if me leaving the baby for a night really were that simple.

Maybe it was.

"Okay, well, it's not definite or anything," I said. "I haven't really decided myself. And I don't know if the others can make it, either. I just wanted to check your temperature on it." But shortly after Kira responded, Selena also sent a simple IN and several thumbs-up emojis. So maybe this really was happening.

His joke about keeping Clara alive only made me anxious, though. What if something did happen? What if he was looking at his phone while crossing the street and they got run over, or what if they were walking in the park and a dog came up and bit her leg, or what if she spiked a fever and he dismissed it as nothing and it turned out to be something serious, or what if she wouldn't take a bottle and she practically starved all day? What if she simply stopped breathing in her crib? What if something happened to *me*? My train could go off the rails and blow up. And then I'd never see my baby girl again. All because of my selfish, frivolous Montauk getaway.

I told my churning brain to *stop it*. I did this all the time, even when I was home, even when Clara and I were simply sitting on the couch. Dreamed up a thousand worst-case scenarios, all of which resulted in death. I knew that these weren't rational thoughts and that they were the product of anxiety and hormones. Yes, I'd always worry about Clara, for the rest of my life. But I so badly wanted her to grow up with a happy mom, like I did. Maybe doing things for myself—things other than drinking too much wine and spending too much time scrolling Facebook—was an important first step toward that.

I took a deep breath and responded to the chain: I'm in too. Can't wait! Let us know what we can bring. Suddenly, I was excited. Fresh ocean air, a solid night of sleep, and good conversations with women whom I was really starting to think of as friends might be just what I needed to push me over the hump that I'd been trying unsuccessfully to clear for months now. I was determined to come back from Montauk recharged.

Chapter Twenty-One

Thursday, October 8

The next afternoon, we were on the Long Island Rail Road en route to Montauk. The evening commuters spilled out after we switched trains in Jamaica, and there isn't really much of a Hamptons rush during the fall, especially on a weekday, so we had the train largely to ourselves. I left when Clara was sleeping, telling Tim it would be easier for her not to see me leave, but really it was more for me; I would have cried saying goodbye to her. Tim was reassuring and positive and promised to FaceTime me with her that night, to prove that he was in fact keeping her alive.

I couldn't remember the last time I'd had so little stuff to keep track of: no diapers, no wipes, no bottles, no Ergobaby carrier, no burp rags, no Sophie the Giraffe. Just my own small bag with toiletries, pajamas, and a change of clothes. That's it. I felt lighter than air.

Kira had brought cans of sparkling wine for us to drink on the train, which helped quell my lingering anxiety about leaving Clara. It was just Kira, Selena, and me on the train, because Vanessa was already in Montauk, having driven up that morning to prep the house, leaving Phoebe with her nanny. For the first time ever, all three of us were in jeans rather than yoga pants, a sure indication of how excited we were about this trip.

As the train made its way through the Hamptons, I felt my shoulders relax and my breath slow down. From the train, we could see fields of corn flanked by huge clumps of swaying seagrass, open gray skies, marshy lakes, horse farms, and enormous houses set atop vineyards. It was all so beautiful, and such a necessary reminder that a big world was still turning outside my one-bedroom apartment. It had been doing so the whole time; I just hadn't looked up much in the last three months.

At Montauk Station, we got into a pink taxi and gave the driver the address that Vanessa had texted to us. "First time in Montauk?" she asked with a voice that indicated her last cigarette couldn't have been more than five minutes ago. It was the first time for all three of us. I'd been to the Hamptons in my twenties but had never made it as far as Montauk. "It'll heal you," the driver promised. "Remind you what really matters. Give it a chance. Great chowder, too—try Gosman's."

She drove along the rolling hills of Old Montauk Highway, where we could see flashes of pristine beach past the dunes, and eventually made a right, slowing the car in front of a looming dark-wood, modern haven with huge full-length glass windows. "Very nice, ladies!" she said, shaking her shoulders a bit in an "ooh la la" fashion. "Looks like you'll have a great time." We thanked her and paid her, and the pink van lumbered off.

Suddenly I felt a bit embarrassed by this lavish night off we were having when someone who should have been here with us was still missing, maybe hurt, maybe dead. It felt a bit wrong, despite Vanessa's reassurance that we needed and deserved the getaway.

Before I succumbed to my guilt spiral, Vanessa came out to the front steps as we ascended them. "Yes! You're here! Welcome! Come on in!" She pressed her cheek quickly to each of ours after we'd climbed to her, and led us into the house. It was sparkling clean, with massively high ceilings and a huge chandelier hanging over the entryway.

"What a shithole, Vanessa!" Kira cracked. "You really expect me to sleep here?" We all laughed.

"I'll show you the bedrooms," Vanessa said, walking a step ahead of us. "You can choose your own, of course! My stuff is already in one, but other than that, you can divide and conquer as you see fit." She showed us down the wide hallway, motioning to bedrooms on either side of her. "This is an upside-down house, with the bedrooms on the ground floor," she explained. "It's so you get the view of the ocean from the kitchen and living room upstairs." One of the bedroom doors was shut. "Not that one," she said lightly, so I assumed that one was hers.

"Whose house is this, again?" Selena asked incredulously. "It's unreal."

"Just someone I work with," Vanessa said vaguely. "Okay, so come on upstairs once you're settled! I'll have a spread ready for us."

We each politely chose a room without scoping them all out first, not wanting to appear like we were grubbing for the best one. Mine ended up being the smallest, but I didn't care—it was a night alone in a queen-size bed with no crying baby or snoring husband. I'd have been thrilled with a Motel 6, so long as those terms remained.

There was an ornate mirror above the dresser in my room. I paused to look at my reflection for a second, applying ChapStick and trying to fix my hair a bit. The Montauk humidity had already taken its toll. But other than my frizz, I was pleased with my reflection. I looked different in this mirror. Less tired. A little brighter. Maybe it was just different lighting, or even my imagination. But I thought that the Jenn who looked back at me looked more like *me* than the reflection I'd seen these last few months.

Selena, Kira, and I all exited our rooms at the same time, laughing as Kira exclaimed, "Oh, heyyy!" as if she were surprised to see us. We walked upstairs together. Vanessa had laid out an array of gooey soft cheeses, sliced sourdough bread, olives, salt and vinegar chips, shishito peppers, hummus, and tzatziki. There were empty wineglasses on the counter, waiting to be filled with the white wine that was chilling in an ice canister beside them.

"It's still pretty nice out, so I figured we'd snack on the deck," Vanessa suggested. It was just starting to get dusky outside, but the air was thick with humidity, softening the chill. "Why doesn't everyone plate up and we'll head out?"

I put myself in charge of filling the wineglasses, pouring generously in each, sending albariño tumbling out of the bottle. Kira and Selena took their glasses gratefully. I was feeling slightly nervous, and I wondered if they were, as well; as ideal as this situation was, in many ways, it was all a little overwhelming, too. We really *hadn't* known each other that long. Going from hour-long meetings and short wine dates to a sleepover at the beach was an abrupt leap in our friendship.

We all filled our plates modestly. If I'd been alone with this spread, I would have gone to town on it. But I tried to exercise self-control for decorum's sake.

When I walked out onto the deck, Selena and Kira behind me, I saw that there was someone else already sitting at the table. Her back was to us. *Weird that Vanessa invited someone else without telling us,* I thought. It seemed worth a heads-up at least, though of course, it was her invitation to give, and she was free to extend it to anyone she wanted.

The woman turned around, smiling shyly. "Hi!"

It took me more than a full second to realize that the woman sitting at the table was Isabel.

Chapter Twenty-Two

Thursday, October 8

Isabel looked markedly different from the timid, tired woman who'd engaged with us in conversations about nap schedules and nighttime pumping. She'd always been undeniably lovely, but there had been too many distractions from it: her obvious exhaustion, the shadows on her face, her jumpiness. Now, her face practically glowed, and she looked relaxed in loose jeans and a hooded sweatshirt, a far cry from her usual tailored jumpsuits and cashmere cardigans.

"Surprised?" she asked, sounding almost sheepish.

Kira was stark white and looked like she was going to be sick. Selena's expression was entirely unreadable, perhaps employing her courtroom-practiced poker face. But I could see that her hands were shaking. My whole body felt numb.

Vanessa walked out balancing a plate of food and two glasses of wine, clutching the tops of the glasses in her fingertips. "Oh great! You guys found each other. So we can get started." She placed the plate and one of the glasses in front of Isabel, who patted her hand gratefully. *Get started?*

"Thanks," Isabel murmured, taking a graceful sip of wine.

I couldn't have formed words if my life had depended on it, so I was relieved when Selena was the one to speak up and said exactly what I was thinking, which was simply, "What is going on here?"

To her credit, Isabel held Selena's gaze unflinchingly. "It's a long story. I'll get to it all. But let me first say that I am *so* happy to see you guys. I really am. I feel so connected to you. I know we haven't known each other for that long, but you were my support system during one of the most challenging times of my life, and I honestly have missed you over this past week. I know this is weird—okay, more than weird—and I'm going to explain everything. But I'm just . . . glad to see you. Truly." None of us said anything. "And I hope you're relieved to see me, too. I mean, I'm not dead, so that's good news, right?" She laughed hopefully.

"So you're really okay?" Kira's color had not returned.

"Well, I think I will be. But that all depends on you," she said, seriousness returning to her tone.

"What do you mean?" I managed to choke out.

"And what are we doing here?" Having shed her poker face, Selena was looking at Vanessa angrily. Vanessa knew something that we all didn't, after all; she was the one who had brought us here.

"Well, it depends what you mean by 'here,'" Isabel said quietly, thoughtfully. "Here in Montauk? Or here in this moms' group? Though I suppose the answers overlap."

Selena looked at her icily, not appreciating having her question answered with a question.

Registering her annoyance, Isabel quickly began again. "I'll start from the beginning: the fact is that we all have so much in common, don't we? We're all new moms to precious babies. We're all Upper West Siders. We're all smart, kind women, too, I'd say. But there's one more thing that we each share that never came up in any of our meetings." She paused. "You all know my husband. In the same way."

She took a beat again, slowly turning her gaze to each and every one of us. "And now that we're gathered together, I'd love if we could talk about why you didn't *tell* anyone about Connor's misdeeds after I went missing, *because that was the whole point.*" She took a deep, frustrated breath. "And more importantly—let's discuss how we can make it right."

Chapter Twenty-Three

Thursday, October 8

For a moment, I was genuinely baffled. Indignant. I'd met Isabel's husband only twice, and both times had been in the past week since she'd gone missing.

Then the light bulb went off. The guy in the bar bathroom. Slim suit, perfect build, haircut out of a J.Crew catalog. *Connor. That was Connor.* Of course it was. How hard my brain must have been working to conceal that fact from me when I'd seen him again. Flashes of him came back to me now. His cocky half smile as he slid another shot over to me. His stubble against my cheek as he stood behind me. This explained why I hadn't liked him from the moment I'd laid eyes on him, or laid eyes on him *again*, at their house.

Not only had I had an awful experience just like the one Kira had disclosed to me—I'd had it with the same man.

And apparently, Selena and Vanessa had, too.

My instincts about Connor were right; I only wished the same instincts had kicked in sooner, on the night that I'd met him, before I'd let him walk me into that bathroom.

I was silent, as were the others. Slowly, we raised our eyes one by one, looking around at each other.

And suddenly I was terrified, because it dawned on me that, as Selena had been insisting since Isabel disappeared, we didn't know her that well. I had no idea what she was capable of, or what she planned to do to us, these women who'd played a crucial role in her husband's betrayal of her and of their marriage.

"I'm sure you all have a lot of questions," Isabel said. "We'll get to all of them. But let's have a toast first. This is still a moms' night, after all." We all stood silently, unsure of whether she was serious, but she waited for us to congregate around her to raise our glasses. "Cheers to new friends and new beginnings," she declared pensively. "And of course, to our precious babies, for whom we would do anything. *Anything.*" We all clinked, but as our glasses touched, a sense of dread built within me as I wondered what "new beginnings" would entail, on Isabel's terms, as well as what exactly was contained within that second "anything."

Chapter Twenty-Four

Thursday, October 8

Kira broke the silence. "So, have you been here the whole week?" I almost laughed. The question sounded way too casual, given the severity of the situation. But I supposed it was as good a place as any to start.

Isabel nodded. "Vanessa rented this place for me, and I haven't seen a soul all week. My great-aunt had a cottage in Montauk when I was growing up, and I used to come out during the summers. Montauk is so quiet, especially in the fall; it's the kind of place where if you want to be left alone, you can be. People here tend not to ask a lot of questions. I knew I could disappear here. Of course, I've been worried sick about Naomi and missing her like crazy. It's not like it's been a vacation. But this is all for her, in the long run, after all."

I felt more confused than ever. "What about all the blood?" I ventured. "You're not hurt? We thought you were dead."

"Yes, well, that's how it needed to look. Like something really, really bad had happened to me. Vanessa helped me with the blood; we drew and saved it in her office every few days for the past few weeks so that we'd have a lot. I couldn't have it look like I just left on my own terms; I needed it to be a bloody scene because I hoped that, once my disappearance and likely murder was made public, there would be a parade of women coming forward, yourselves included, revealing that you had been with Connor and knew just what kind of man he was. After all, the honorable thing for any of *you* to do, after learning that this terrible man now had a missing wife, would be to offer up your piece of the puzzle." Isabel slowly looked at each of us, gauging whether we understood.

"See, it couldn't come from me," she continued, eyes wide and earnest. "If I were to tell the world, 'My husband is awful! He's abusive and misogynistic and sociopathic,' Connor would somehow turn it around and make it look like I was crazy, unwell. He'd find a way to come off looking like the good guy. He always does. And I'd be back in my prison of a marriage, where I've been for the past ten years, punishment awaiting me. But if *other* women, one after the other, were the ones to say, no, this is a bad man—and say so publicly, urgently, in the context of my being missing—then he'd never be able to hurt me or trap me again. I needed the spotlight on him, and I needed others to be the ones to shine that spotlight. My vision was a public takedown on a grand scale, woman after woman coming forward and sharing their story about what a predator he was, so that Connor could never recover from the shame and scandal—and, more importantly than revenge, I could finally be free of him."

Kira spoke up. "I'm still not sure I understand. Were you trying to frame him for your murder?"

Isabel shook her head. "I knew he wouldn't actually go down for a crime, since there was no crime, and no real evidence linking him to my disappearance. Besides, I always planned to return, and soon, too, for Naomi. But if his reputation were destroyed in the process of my disappearance, then he'd be knocked off his pedestal for good: he'd be fired from his job, and he'd always be googleable, so any woman he might meet in the future could quickly learn who he really is and save herself. I could finally divorce him easily without him threatening me. The eyes on him would be my protection." She paused for a second, looking halfway hopeful as she described the plan as she'd imagined it. Then her face fell slightly, as if remembering that it hadn't gone that way.

"But of course, that's not quite what happened, is it? I guess I underestimated Connor's power and his utter egocentricity. I didn't know he'd be able to keep my disappearance out of the media more or less completely. I tried to make it a great story, too—the pools of blood, the bloody rings that Vanessa called into the police station—but news coverage was practically nonexistent, as you all know. So most of the women he was with never even learned that I was missing. There were no pictures of me, of us, in the news."

She stopped talking and shook her head slowly, making eye contact with each of us in turn before saying, "Except for you, of course. You guys knew, and you didn't come forward, either. You were supposed to be my friends, so I was sure you'd reveal the truth, in the interest of potentially saving me. But even *you* didn't step up and say anything to the police, to the media. If you had, surely the story would have gained traction and Connor would have been taken down in its wake. And while I get that you have your own lives and families to think about, I'm not going to lie—it's still pretty disheartening that you couldn't step up for me. Even a few women would have been enough to expose him and cast a safety net around me and my daughter. But not a single person said a word." She shook her head with disappointment and disbelief.

I desperately wanted to ask how she'd found out about us, but it didn't feel like the right time. Bottom line, she knew. Right now, that was the detail that mattered more. Still, I felt compelled to defend myself. Slightly. "Isabel, I'm so sorry, but I truly didn't know that the man I was with was Connor. I was so drunk, and that combined with the shame—I blocked him out completely. You have to believe me—I swear, until just now, I had no recollection that it was *him* that night that I—"

She held up her hand and sighed, but then softened and looked at me with genuine sympathy. "I know, Jenn. I know. That became obvious after I showed you a family picture on my phone in our very first meeting and you had absolutely no reaction. I couldn't believe it.

It complicated things. That's why I put our plans for a night out in my calendar and had Vanessa write that note about me in your phone the day of my last meeting with you guys. To get you to really dig deep into my disappearance, for your own personal reasons—I was hoping to jog your memory, that if you saw enough pictures of Connor in your Google searches, or met him at my house when you went with Vanessa, you'd remember. But even then you didn't, apparently."

"Your password is Clara's birthday. Pretty obvious, you know," Vanessa said placidly, looking at me with a shrug.

As terrified as I was right now, a strange part of me was relieved to have an explanation for the calendar plans and the note—to know for sure that I'd had nothing to do with it, that I wasn't quite as crazy as I'd thought. Still, one big question lingered—*how did she know about me and Connor? About the others and Connor?*

Isabel continued. "But what Vanessa wrote in your phone—*Isabel doesn't matter*—it's the way that I felt. That everyone had forgotten about me, that no one remembered I was even a real person anymore. It's the way Connor made me feel almost every day of our marriage—I was always just a prop in his carefully curated life. When I met him in college, I thought he really loved me. It turned out that he just needed a woman like me to create the image of himself that he was determined to embody. I was completely irrelevant. So I'm used to feeling like I don't matter. But, to be honest, I felt it again when none of you stepped forward to share the truth about Connor, even though it might have been pertinent, potentially lifesaving information. Instead, you just retreated. Acted like you knew nothing. Acted like I was no one to you." Isabel looked genuinely hurt, and I felt terrible.

Kira cleared her throat. "I'm sorry." Her voice was still a rasp. "I really am. For all of it. You're right; I didn't come forward because I thought it would look bad for *me*, knowing you, and knowing him, in that way. I've also just tried really hard to leave it in the past. But you're right. I should have said something. Of course I should have."

Selena nodded. "I'm sorry, too. I was scared. I was dating Cameron when I met Connor, and—well, I guess I was also just desperate to avoid reliving that night. I just—it was easier, cleaner, to squash it. Felt so, at least. But I regret it. *All* of it." She looked down, and I could tell she was remembering her encounter with Connor; I looked at her intently, wondering how similar it had been to mine and Kira's and when it had happened. She glanced back at me briefly, nodded slightly, and gave me a look that said *Later*. I looked at Vanessa, too, and silently questioned where she fit into all this—she'd rented this house for Isabel, had lured us all here. Her role was obviously much different, bigger, than ours.

As if she were reading my mind, Kira looked at Vanessa and said, "And Vanessa—you too? Connor?"

Vanessa shook her head emphatically. "Not quite. The most important part: Connor is Phoebe's father." *Holy shit. So Vanessa actually had his baby.* "But it's not what you think," she continued. "I'm actually the only one here who *didn't* have the misfortune of meeting Connor while alone at a bar." *So he had an MO.* "A fact I'm grateful for," she added.

Now I was more confused than ever. Thankfully, she continued.

"My sister, Allison, did, though. And she got pregnant and decided, of all things, to keep the baby. She didn't know anything about him—I was actually the one who dug up the truth about who he was: that he was a New York millionaire, married to Isabel. Obviously, it's not what he'd told her about himself."

She looked momentarily exasperated but then coughed, seemingly an attempt to stifle tears that were brewing in her chest. I could see that she wasn't the type who was comfortable crying in front of other people. Once she'd mastered herself, she went on.

"Allison and I were so close. Our mom died when we were young, so I helped take care of her. Allison was always fun loving, spontaneous, silly . . . until Connor came along. She became a shell of herself. She was traumatized after their night together. Depressed. Being lied to, taken advantage of like that—it takes its toll. Not to mention, all of a sudden, she's a single mom. Granted, she chose that path. But still—it was a lot. More than she'd realized it would be."

I could certainly relate to that. "So, where is Allison?" I ventured to ask.

"She killed herself," Vanessa choked out. Kira, Selena, and I produced nearly identical gasps, our hands flying to our mouths. "Overdosed on pills. It was all too much for her to handle. On top of being so low after what had happened with Connor, she was completely overwhelmed by new motherhood. So she took her own life and left Phoebe with me." Tears were rolling down Vanessa's face finally, and she wiped them away with a manicured hand.

"Connor was the catalyst for all of it," she went on. "So I vowed to myself that I would never let Connor do to another woman what he'd done to Allison. And that needed to start with Isabel." Isabel looked at Vanessa gratefully as she spoke. "Allison had already called Isabel once to tell her about what had happened with Connor, but Isabel was like a hostage. I knew she needed more help than Allison had been able to offer. So I offered more." She shrugged modestly and took a long sip of wine.

Isabel put her hand on Vanessa's shoulder and squeezed it, then took over, giving Vanessa a minute to regroup.

"Allison reached out to me, yes," she said. "And frankly, I loved her for that. For trying. And I wish I had let her say her piece, because while I knew about Connor's infidelity, I didn't know . . . what it was really like. What he was really doing to women. I figured he was just finding other consenting women to have sex with. But it wasn't that, was it?" *No. It wasn't.* "I didn't learn that until Vanessa came to me and told me about her sister. Though I still don't know what I could have done to stop him."

I remembered Isabel's dark undereye circles, the ones I'd once briefly thought were bruises, and a fresh flush of shame rose in my face. Shame that I had done nothing, had dismissed any concern I'd felt for her so that I could go back to worrying about myself and my own problems.

"It's been going on for years," she continued quietly, "the obsessive control, the abuse, the other women. All he cared about was that we had this picture-perfect life. He made every decision for me: clothes, food, our house." I thought of Naomi's little dresses and of how Isabel would rush out of our meetings. I also remembered how Connor hadn't even known she'd been in a moms' group; he probably wouldn't have approved. "Not that it's any kind of excuse, but he had a rough childhood; his dad hit both him and his mom. A lot. The psychology could hardly have been any clearer: Connor had to control everything about our life, since he didn't have any control of his childhood. In his effort to create what he thought was the perfect life, he didn't even realize he was doing the exact same thing his father did.

"For a while, when it first started, I did sort of use his past as an excuse for him. I was quick to forgive and rationalize. But that only took me so far. Soon, I just sort of shut down.

"Eventually, I actually grew to view his infidelity as sort of a blessing. Because I hated him so much, and if he was out having sex with some random person, at least he wasn't in the house with me. I know how selfish that sounds, because I really did feel sorry for every woman who crossed paths with him. And that was even before I learned from Vanessa how bad it had been for Allison. And for each of you, I assume." She paused for a moment, and I could tell she felt the weight of responsibility, even though it wasn't her burden to carry.

"He did everything he could to make me feel worthless, like I wouldn't be able to survive if I left him. I did try, or at least, I started to try, a few times. At first, he said he'd make sure I was financially destitute. When that didn't deter me, he leveled up, saying he'd prove that I was unhinged; he even got all these prescriptions for me that I didn't really use and said he'd claim that I was abusing them and have me institutionalized. And finally, his favorite threat—that he'd kill me and get away with it because he'd make it look like a suicide." Isabel pursed her lips sadly. "Maybe I should have tried harder, or just left in the middle of the night or something. But his threats didn't just *feel* real. I knew him well enough to know they absolutely *were* real."

She looked down as if she were embarrassed. "I know what you're thinking," she said, though really, even *I* didn't know what I was thinking—not if I'd had to name just one thing. I could tell the others were as dumbfounded as I was. "You're wondering why the hell I didn't run screaming from him right at the start."

All right. Yes. That was certainly one of the things I was thinking.

"For one thing, he somehow kept the genie in the bottle for the first few years that we were together. The devil in the bottle. Whatever. And we got married so young. I had such high hopes for us. In retrospect, I see that I married him because everyone *else* thought he was amazing. Everyone always told me how *lucky* I was. But I knew it wasn't right between us. Even before he started hitting me, I knew that there was something essential missing in him—an empathy chip. I came to realize he genuinely doesn't see other people as people.

"I fought it, that realization. And continued to make excuses for him. To tell myself I was lucky to have this lavish life. It's scary what you can convince yourself of when you're trying to avoid reality." She shuddered. "But when I met him, he was everything I'd thought I wanted in my husband since I was a child. He was tall and handsome and smart and driven, and I knew he'd be successful." She shook her head again. "I know how pathetic that sounds. I just . . . I guess I didn't grow up in time to make the choice I should have made.

"Within less than a year after we were married, I'd completely lost myself. He didn't want me to work or have friends. He just wanted me to stay home and look pretty and keep our apartment in perfect order. The first time he hit me, we'd been married about six months, and it was because I was in a hurry to get somewhere so I put his dry cleaning back in his closet with the plastic still on."

We all looked at Isabel. My arms were covered in goose bumps, and my fingers were white knuckling the stem of my empty wineglass.

"That time was just a slap. It got worse, quickly. And that stuff came before I even found out about the cheating, so when I did, it almost seemed like the lesser of my problems. There was a ripped thong in his jacket pocket one day . . . I confronted him about it and he didn't even bother denying it. He basically just told me not to worry about it, that what he did outside our marriage didn't concern me." She shook her head in disbelief at her own reality. "I felt like I couldn't tell anyone. For a long time, I even pretended to my mom that everything was fine, because she so badly wanted me to be happy, and I wanted to give that to her. But she didn't believe me, and so for several years, I had to distance myself from even her. To protect her from the awful truth. He preferred not having her around, anyway. But finally, I couldn't do that anymore, and I let her in."

I interrupted her, accidentally, when she brought up her mom. "What *about* your mom?" I blurted. "I mean, right now. She's probably worried sick. Is there a way of telling her you're okay without—"

"My mom is in on all of this, obviously!" Isabel seemed appalled that I would think her capable of distressing her mother. "I would never do that to her."

"She's *in* on it?" Selena exclaimed.

"She thought all of this sounded a bit extreme at first, but when she learned the extent of what Connor had been putting me through over the years, she quickly got on board. She'd do anything for me." Her face relaxed a bit. "And I gave her explicit instructions to mess with Connor as much as possible while I was missing. Vanessa told me about the back rubs; I think there also may have been some incidents related to Nair in his hair products and soap in his green juices over the past week?" She laughed, a true belly laugh. "My mom is epic. I mean, come on. It's a small but important part of Connor's punishment: he has to live with his mother-in-law, indefinitely, for all he knows!"

And here I'd thought that Louise had seemed a bit off, hadn't seemed grief stricken enough. But the opposite was true: she loved her daughter so much that she would do anything that was asked of her— even if it seemed crazy. She'd even been reveling in punishing Connor on Isabel's behalf. She wasn't necessarily the best actress, but she was sure as hell a wonderful mom.

"Anyway, where was I?" Isabel asked dryly. "Ah, right. My living hell of a marriage. But then I got pregnant. I'd always vowed to myself I would never get pregnant with his child. I wouldn't have wanted to subject a child to having him as a father. We rarely slept together, but on the occasion we did, I was so careful. So Naomi was a shock, but when I found out I was carrying her, I couldn't let her go. I couldn't even think about it. I didn't even tell him that I was pregnant until I was about five months along. I just didn't want him to be part of it. And I still don't. And then, right after Naomi was born, Vanessa reached out and told me all about what had happened with poor Allison. She told me about Phoebe. I had no idea he'd fathered another child. Vanessa wanted to help, and had ideas, and I had some ideas, too, and finally, most importantly, I had the strength I'd been missing all along, to do something, something big, to finally get revenge on him and shake him out of my life, our lives, forever. Vanessa gave that to me, but so did Naomi. Becoming a mom has made me aware of my own power, my priorities, in a way that I never was before." I nodded my genuine understanding.

"And so I recruited you, so to speak. Not only did we share the terrible bond of our acquaintance with my awful husband, but we were also new moms. So I knew you were as strong as I was—that you would understand why I needed to finally get out. For my daughter. I knew you were the right people to help me."

"How did you find us?" Kira asked, finally. "How did you know?"

"Well, that was easier than you'd think." Isabel shook her head with loathing. "There's a list."

"A list?" Selena asked, her voice trembling with fear and revulsion.

Isabel nodded gravely. "Yes. Connor keeps a list of names on his computer. The first time I saw it, years ago, it was by accident—I opened his computer to check my email, because my phone was dead, and it was just there, open on his desktop. I didn't know what it meant, at first. But I was curious—and once I started googling names, matching locations to his work travel, finding pictures of the women online . . . I put it together. And the crazy thing is that I had *asked* him if I could use his computer before I did—of course—and he said, 'Sure.' He *wanted* me to see it. To taunt me. Because it was yet another piece of proof I had that he was a monster, but one that I could do nothing about. A list of names isn't evidence. It's not like it's videos and pictures. It wouldn't mean anything to a lawyer, for instance." Isabel was right. A random list of names would never be enough to incriminate Connor. "His whole life is about power, control—the list is no doubt meant as a reminder to me that he can get away with whatever he wants to. And a leg up on all of you, too, because I'm assuming most of you didn't know his name, but he made sure to find out exactly who you were."

My stomach flopped; I felt like I was going to be sick. I did not want to be a name on Connor's disgusting list.

"But the list ended up being handy, because I used it in a way he didn't anticipate," she continued. "When I realized that the four of us all had new babies and lived in the same neighborhood, I knew there was a way to get us together. To let you get to know me without immediately running for the hills when you realized how we were connected. To make us a team, so to speak. Jenn, you were a late add, of course." Of course. I hadn't met Connor until Clara was six weeks old. Isabel hadn't responded to my post until a few weeks after I'd written it, and the group had already met once or twice when I joined. "Anyway. You guys were plan A. That you'd know me and care about me enough to reveal the truth, publicly, about Connor after I went missing. Then I'd come back, he'd be ruined, and I'd be free forever. That didn't happen, unfortunately. But like I said. That was plan A."

"What's plan B?" I asked, my voice trembling.

"Plan B is that you help me kill my husband," Isabel said evenly.

Chapter Twenty-Five

Selena didn't skip a beat. "Absolutely not. I'm sorry, but no. No, no, no. I'm sorry your husband is a sociopathic monster, and I'm even sorrier I *ever* crossed paths with him—believe me—but I am absolutely not killing anyone. Surely you can figure out how to divorce him or leave the country and never see him again without doing all of . . . this." She gestured with her hand wildly. "Divorce is literally what I do for a living. I can help you with *that*, and will do so gladly. But I'm not going to help you kill the guy."

"This is too much, Isabel," Kira agreed. "I know I made a huge mistake, and I want to help you get away from him, but you can't honestly expect us to help you kill him. We're not killers."

I chimed in. "What if we just all come forward now? Tell the police everything that he's been doing?"

Isabel shook her head. "It's too late. The moment is over. It's time for me to come back. I can't risk getting in trouble for staging all of this. Besides, I see now that he's capable of squashing the story, changing the narrative. I can't risk that we try that and then it doesn't work. You'd be in danger then, too."

I knew she was right. If we tried to take down Connor with the truth and it didn't go our way, he could easily come after us. He *would* come after us.

"Look," Isabel said, "I know that the thing I'm asking you to help me with is big. But what it comes down to is this: he doesn't deserve to be alive. He's abusing the *privilege* of living by being so cavalier with the lives of others. I mean, look at what happened to Allison!

"If I could go back to when I was twenty-one and undo my choice of being with him, of course I would. But I can't. And"—she cleared her throat and slowed her words—"as long as he is alive, he will be Naomi's father. Even if we somehow managed to largely cut him out of our lives . . . she'll be damaged by him. I know she will. And I can't accept that. I simply need him out of the world. And I think together we can do it and do it right."

Here she paused, looked around at all of us to see if she was making headway. It was scary for me to admit it to myself, but where I was concerned, she sort of was.

"Listen," she said. "Think of your daughters growing up and meeting someone like Connor in a dark bar. Think of your sons growing up and being friends with him. Idolizing him. Trying to be like him. See, the moms' group gave me the perfect way to get us together, but the truth is, I wanted you guys on my team not only because I had a way to get to you but also because, as moms, you have the best reason in the world to take down people like this man. You are all *so* strong—you might not even realize it, but you are." I thought, with gratitude, of what she'd said to Tim on their phone call. And I knew she had meant it. "And I'm asking all of us to pool our collective strength. We can't rid the world of all the Connors. But we can rid the world of this one. And we should." She nodded emphatically.

There ensued a long pause in which, to the soundtrack of the surf washing the shore, everyone just sat around the table with all she'd said. I could've used a week, but it was clear we wouldn't be afforded anything like that long to wrap our minds around it.

It was Kira who spoke first. "And if we say no? What then?" she asked, discernible fear in her voice.

This time, it was Vanessa who answered. "Please don't make us stoop to threatening you," she said flatly.

Isabel winced slightly at her words, making me wonder which one of them had really been leading this whole thing.

"It feels like you are, though," Selena said, eyes narrowing. "Threatening us."

"Look, I don't like where this conversation is heading," Isabel said. "I honestly have no intention of threatening you. That would make me no better than Connor. I just want you to say yes. So why don't we fill you in on the plan? That might help. It's foolproof, truly. I think you'll feel comfortable with it. Vanessa, do you want to run them through it?"

"Happy to. As you all know, I'm a doctor." She flipped her hair, and I wondered how many times she had mentioned that she was a doctor in the six weeks that I'd known her. A hundred, perhaps? At least. "I can access a drug that will freeze Connor's muscles and stop the flow of blood to his heart. It's used in surgery sometimes to help doctors work on specific organs. The dose we'll give Connor will be much larger and will essentially simulate a massive heart attack. Then we'll maybe push him down the stairs, for good measure, making it seem like the heart attack also caused a fall." She shrugged, far too casually. "You really won't need to do anything. We just want you there for the confrontation so he understands the magnitude of his misdeeds before he passes—we'd like this to be something of a catharsis for all of us, after all—and then maybe to help with a little staging and cleaning, after the fact. And of course, strength in numbers—it takes a village, right?" Vanessa smirked slightly and for a split second looked like an entirely different person. "We need to make sure he can't overpower us. I have another drug to help us with that, too." *Jesus.* "Having this be a group effort is more of a cautionary measure than anything; trust me, I'll be doing the heavy lifting. And since it won't even look like a murder, there's nothing to get caught for, but even if there were, you'd never be the ones implicated." She looked at each one of us, trying to gauge how we were digesting the plan.

The three of us were silent. Isabel smiled at us earnestly. "I really hope you'll get on board. And look, you don't have to decide right this second. I know it's a lot to take in. Take some time to talk it over among yourselves. In fact, you can go down to the hot tub right now if you want to relax a bit while you discuss it."

Relax. Yeah, right.

"And if we decide not to?" Kira pressed.

Isabel's eyes clouded over. "Then I'll need a new plan to get out of my marriage. But I just can't promise the new plan will protect you as well as this one does." There it was. And I knew that, with the information she had on us, she had the power to forever fracture our lives as we knew them.

Chapter Twenty-Six

A few minutes later, Selena, Kira, and I were walking across the dark lawn in our bathing suits toward a steamy, bubbling jacuzzi that was big enough for twelve people. It was painfully hot, simultaneously punishing and cleansing, like the shower I'd taken after my encounter with Connor. We turned the jets all the way up and climbed in, hoping that the noise would steal our words from ears that might be prying. Of course, we brought our glasses of wine, which we carefully placed on the hot tub's edge.

A lot of air needed to be cleared before we could even discuss Isabel's proposition for us. Or demand. I still couldn't determine which it was. "Jenn, I confided in you," Kira whispered. "Why didn't you tell me that you had been with him, too? What the hell? You honestly didn't remember?"

"I truly didn't. I was so drunk when it happened. And I've been so sleep deprived. My brain hasn't been working since Clara was born, and this happened not even a couple of months ago. I honestly didn't remember his face when I met him. I didn't know it was Connor that night. I would have told you." *I think.* "I'm so sorry."

"It happened with him that soon after having Clara?" Kira added. "My God. I barely wanted to *poop* after having Caleb, let alone—sorry, it's just—wow. How did—how did that happen?" Selena, too, was looking at me wide eyed.

My eyes welled with tears, and I was almost unable to respond. "You know what it was like with Connor—it was just as you described, Kira. Not what I had in mind. It wasn't like I made the choice to *sleep* with him. God no. I was drunk, and it all happened so quickly—it's so hard to explain. And once it got past a certain point, it was too late to undo it. Or at least, it felt too late." I took a deep breath. "Also—I didn't tell you this, but my mom died a few months before Clara was born. I'd been—I still *am* in a bad place. And things with the baby have been so hard . . . I wanted some kind of an escape that night, which is why I was out drinking alone, but I certainly didn't want . . . that."

"I'm so sorry about your mom," Selena said. "I wish we'd known."

"Dude, why didn't you tell us? That's terrible," Kira said, squeezing my hand under the water.

"Just not ready, I guess," I said. "I wish I had." I really did. I already felt so much better, more supported, now that they knew. I was hoping the moisture on my face from the jacuzzi was hiding my tears.

Kira spoke again. "And Selena—you too? When did it happen? And when did you find out that he was married to Isabel?"

"Isabel had me over back when the group first started meeting, and I saw his picture in her house." She drew up short, brought the fingertips of one hand to her lips.

"What?" I asked.

She slowly shook her head. "It's just now, it occurs to me that she probably wanted me to see the picture, to see what I would do—she was probably studying my reaction to make sure I remembered him." She closed her eyes, then opened them and looked back and forth between us. "God, I wish I'd just come clean then. Maybe none of this would have happened if she'd had more people willing to be honest with her and stick up for her earlier on.

"I was sick to my stomach when I recognized him." She shuddered, remembering, and then downed a gulp of her wine. "But I didn't say anything to her, when I realized. I didn't want the situation to explode. I was scared that she'd be furious with me, or not believe me, and retaliate by telling Cameron. Or that she'd confront Connor and he'd find me—and of course, the last thing I wanted was any further interaction with him, ever. I didn't want to jeopardize my marriage, my reputation by opening this can of worms. So instead I just kept it cordial but distant with her. And then when she disappeared"—she paused and looked at me—"I wanted nothing to do with any of it. As you know, Jenn. That's why I got so . . . heated when you asked me to nose around with you. When you were so insistent that we should be doing something. Because I really didn't want to do the one thing that I knew I probably should."

"When did it happen?" I repeated Kira's question. "With you and Connor?"

She heaved a sigh and looked off at the ocean. "It happened about a couple of years ago. Cameron and I were dating, but we were in a bad spot. I had found some texts on his phone from an old girlfriend. He insisted that texts were all they were, but I was pissed. I went out that night with a friend, to a hotel bar downtown. To be honest, I wanted to be hit on. I wanted to be reminded that I was hot. That other people would want me, too. That I had *options*. I was in a total *screw Cameron* kind of mentality. But I never actually wanted anything to happen."

She inhaled deeply. "My friend went home. I stayed. I drank too much. But you know what?" She looked at us intently. "I didn't drink *that* much."

We paused for a moment, taking in the weight of her comment.

"I know myself," she said, "and my limits. I'm well practiced at being careful. And I only had three or four drinks that night, over the course of several hours. And yet, I remember what happened with Connor only in flashes . . . I know I was upstairs in his hotel room, but I can't ever remember agreeing to go up with him. I know we had sex, but I just can't believe I'd . . ." She trailed off for a moment, face furrowed with hurt and confusion. "Drunk or not, it doesn't seem like me. Like something I would ever, ever do. And the next morning, I was incapacitated. I felt like I had a concussion. I was bedridden for the next two days. And I always thought . . . I thought maybe he gave me something. But I convinced myself that I was wrong, that I was just looking for a way not to blame myself.

"I never said anything to anyone—I mean, for one thing, I didn't want to have to tell Cameron what had happened—but I've always wondered. And now—knowing more about him, the kind of guy he is—I think my hunch might have been right."

"I'm so sorry, Selena," I whispered, my anger for what had happened to her making my blood bubble like the jacuzzi jets.

Selena nodded at me. "Me too," she said.

"What an absolute prick," Kira said, squeezing Selena's shoulder. We were all silent for a moment.

"As horrible as he is . . . ," Kira continued, bringing us back to the topic at hand, "and don't get me wrong, he's obviously beyond horrible—I mean, like a sociopath, right?—I'm still not sure I can agree to *murdering* him." Panic returned to her face. "Again, I still don't really get why she can't just divorce him and move across the country or overseas or something, like a normal person?"

"It would never be that simple now that there's a child involved," Selena admitted, though she'd advocated for the same solution earlier.

I nodded. "I really felt what she was saying about how she couldn't allow him to be Naomi's father. I would do anything I could to protect Clara from someone who would be that kind of toxic presence in her life. We know how he is with women. Who *knows* what kind of damage he might do to a child."

The hot tub's heat couldn't fully account for the flush surging into my face, the spots that floated in my vision. I took a gulp of wine and went on.

"If Isabel says that divorce won't cut it, even if she were able to get one, I want to believe her. I *do* believe her." I heard myself say these words but was shocked at how much I sounded like I was arguing in favor of killing him. Could that actually be what I wanted?

"Still," Selena said, shifting her position in the jacuzzi, "does that give us the right to just remove him from the world? Play God? I don't know that it does. Besides, how do Isabel and Vanessa know for sure that we won't get caught? They don't. Anything could go wrong. And I don't want to spend the rest of my life in jail."

"But if we do decide not to—if we say no," Kira said, "do you guys think that Isabel and Vanessa will just let it go? Or are we in some kind of danger here? I'm not sure that we're really in a position to just walk away." She rubbed her head with both hands and then stretched her arm out to grab her glass of wine, taking a long sip.

I had been wondering the same thing. "I guess we're taking a risk no matter what we decide. But—and I almost can't believe I'm saying this—the only way to make sure he never does this to another woman is to do what they're asking. And I want that. I don't want any more of us out there." It felt like an out-of-body experience, listening to myself tout the pros of killing someone. And yet, I was pretty sure that's what I was doing.

"Let's try this," Selena said. "I think the question we all have to answer is, Will we be able to live with ourselves if we do it? And will we be able to live with ourselves if we don't? What feels better? What feels safer? What feels more right?"

Kira and I nodded carefully, thinking. Selena, ever the lawyer, was the voice of reason. I was glad she was here. I was glad both of them were.

Kira spoke up, finally. "I want to say yes to Isabel," she said, but her voice was unconvincing. "I really do. He's a terrible, destructive person, and Isabel wouldn't ask this of us if she wasn't sure that this was her only way out. We should have said something when she went missing, and we owe it to her to be here for her now, after we didn't step up when

we had the chance before. But—but it's murder, you guys. *Murder.*"
She looked at us each for a long moment, making sure we understood.

"I'm scared, too," I said. "Terrified. But the thing is that I really do want him gone." Yet again, my own words surprised me. But they felt right leaving my lips. As much as I'd assured myself several times over the past week that I didn't know Isabel all that well, that her disappearance couldn't have had anything to do with me, the truth was that I'd learned everything I needed to know about her that day that I'd seen her on a park bench, talking to Naomi. I *did* know her. I believed her that this was the only way she could be free. I trusted her.

And if I was being honest with myself, I didn't just want to do it out of friendship for Isabel. I wanted to do it for myself, for every woman he'd made feel powerless and every woman he had yet to meet whose life he'd shake off course and whose self-worth he'd demolish. I wondered, for a moment, if the drunk girl at the Milling Room bar had made it out unscathed.

I disappeared into my head for a minute and conjured my mom. I wondered what she would think of all this—of what I'd done, of what I was thinking of doing. I thought of how she'd always told me to trust my intuition.

And, crazily enough, my intuition seemed to be telling me I should help my friend murder her husband.

"God dammit," said Selena, finishing her wine and looking out toward the ocean.

I shivered as we exited the hot tub and walked back into the house. In the midst of everything going on, we'd forgotten to bring towels. But there was no way to know if I was shaking from the cold or because of what I was pretty sure we were going to agree to do.

Chapter Twenty-Seven

Friday, October 9

While the rest of our Montauk trip was hardly the restorative girls' get-away I'd envisioned, it was a relief to have everything out in the open, to know that Isabel was alive, and, for me personally, to know that I didn't have anything to do with her disappearance—at least not directly, not in the way that I had feared. And we knew that, in a matter of days, we'd be able to start putting all this behind us, because we all agreed that, if we were going to do this, we weren't going to waste any time.

We spent much of the rest of the night talking through the plans. We sat around the table and talked, and then when we couldn't sit any longer, we walked on the beach, occasionally grasping hands or elbows because it was so dark, the noise from the crashing ocean keeping our secrets safe. When we got back to the house, we went over every detail again. Doing everything we could to flush out every possible hiccup or surprise or misstep or unanticipated outcome. We took breaks to refill wine or when one of us needed to pump. We ordered pizza from a place called Best Pizza down Montauk Highway and ate every slice. We argued until we agreed. And then we were done. We went to bed very late and I slept like a rock, well into the morning.

When everyone was awake, we ate blueberry muffins that Vanessa had picked up from Round Swamp Market. For some reason, I was starving, and food tasted better to me than it had in months. It was like I was remembering my body's own likes and needs for the first time since Clara had been born. After we were full, we went for another walk on the beach, not even mentioning Connor, or what our return to the city and subsequent days would look like; we'd ironed all that out yesterday, as much as possible. Instead, we did what we always did: talked about our babies. How amazing and adorable and frustrating and all-consuming they were. How lucky we were. How tired we were. How beautiful and hard it was to be a mother. I knew Vanessa must have been thinking of Allison as we talked and how her sister wouldn't get to experience all that we were discussing.

That afternoon, the three of us—Selena, Kira, and I—took the train back to the city, leaving Vanessa and Isabel behind. Isabel's return had to be separate, obviously, and she couldn't risk being seen on a train. It felt strange leaving without her, but she assured us that she knew what she was doing and would see us soon.

As we neared the city, I started to itch to see Clara. Tim had been sending me All good texts and photos throughout my time away, and we'd FaceTimed briefly that morning. But I needed to feel her skin on mine, to hug her, to nurse her.

When I finally got home, Tim and Clara were on the couch. "I hear Mommy!" he said as I opened the door to our apartment. He was feeding her a bottle, and she was sucking it down contentedly, wrapped up in a fleece blanket. "How was it?" he asked enthusiastically.

I washed my hands quickly and rushed over to them on the couch, planting a dozen kisses on Clara's head, cheek, and neck as she drank. I kissed Tim, too. "It was good," I said, honestly. "I needed it." Even though I was petrified for what was to come, I was telling the truth.

"That's awesome. Well, feel free to go away anytime. This girl was an angel, and I think we had a lot of fun." He kissed Clara's head. "See, Daddy's awesome, right? I've been telling you," he said, shaking her hand in his. "Though I am ready to get some sleep tonight," he admitted, turning back toward me. "I'm exhausted. It's not easy, doing this"—he gestured toward Clara—"all night and day. I don't know how you do it." Tim put his arm around me. I nuzzled Clara's stomach with my nose. She looked at me and beamed. And I was grateful beyond measure for this one perfect moment before whatever would come my way days from now.

July 17

Dear Baby,

Last night you slept for nine hours straight. So did I. And I woke up this morning literally gasping for air, like I'd been underwater and I was finally surfacing. It was like the first time in so long that I could see things clearly. Things look very different after a good night's sleep.

I read what I wrote a few days ago, and I can't believe I wrote that. I know I did, but it wasn't *me*, if that makes sense. I may be a little crazy, but I've always been the good kind of crazy. Never that.

What happened with Connor—I'm ready to say his name, and I'll never call him your father again, because that's not what he is or what he'll ever be—it was traumatizing, humiliating, and brutal. But I *can* put it behind me. And I will, for you.

I wrote down the names of three therapists who specialize in postpartum depression and birth-related trauma. I'm going to call them today and start getting the help that I should have sought weeks ago.

In the meantime, though, your aunt thinks I've totally lost it. I hope she'll soon see that I'm trying and that I'm going to be okay. She's around all the time now, before and after work, weekends, checking on the both of us—which is good, I guess. It's nice to have the help, and she always brings Thai food. But I can tell that she's frustrated with me for being such a mess. The look she gives me when she asks me if I've done laundry yet and I say no . . .

I know it's all out of love and concern. She adores you and she's wonderful with you. I just wish she would stop mothering me and let *me* be the mother. But then, she's always treated me like I'm some irresponsible child. And sure, when I was thirteen and shoplifting earrings from Claire's every weekend, maybe I deserved that. But this isn't that. I'm a college-educated, gainfully employed, financially independent woman. I *am* responsible enough to be your mom, and I don't and will never regret my decision to keep you. I'm just having a hard time right now, which will pass. I only wish she could see that.

I'm taking some medication now, thanks to Aunt V, and that's helping me stay more even. I probably should have started taking something sooner. It makes me feel sort of numb, though, which I don't like. And my milk is drying up, so I'll have to start giving you formula soon. I wish I could have nursed you for longer.

All you need to know, for now, is that I'm on the mend. I'm on my way back to being the woman I was before you were born, the woman I want to be as your mother. You deserve a strong mom. You're going to get one.

I've been sinking lately, but I will learn to swim again. For you. For us. Thank you for inspiring me endlessly to be better, for giving me the best reason in the world to keep going.

I am so lucky that you are mine and I am yours.

Love you forever,

Mommy

Chapter Twenty-Eight

Sunday, October 11

In the late evening of the same day that the rest of us returned from Montauk, Friday the ninth, Isabel was found in the brambles by the Hudson River, all the way up near 168th Street, by a married couple completing one of their last long training runs before the NYC Marathon. Isabel was dehydrated, disoriented, and had lost several pounds. (She confided in us that she'd lost the weight by eating practically nothing but fish the whole time she'd been in Montauk, with the exception of our postdecision pizza. "It didn't even feel like a sacrifice," she'd said, laughing. "Montauk seafood is the best!")

She would tell the police that she'd cut her hand in the kitchen of their town house, and had cut it badly. She would tell them that she left the house to go to the hospital, sure she needed stitches. She hadn't wanted to wake Connor, who had just returned from a work trip and needed his sleep. Naomi was sleeping in their room. When the police asked why she brought the dog, she would say that she was so disoriented from the injury, she didn't even realize the dog had gotten out, but that she normally did walk him that time of night, so that's probably why he scampered along with her. When the police asked why there was no blood in the kitchen, she would say that she immediately put a towel on the wound, that she was used to being careful, keeping an immaculately clean house. (She'd cut her own hand as soon as she arrived in Montauk so that she'd have a healing wound to show: "Vanessa showed me how to do it cleanly, but it still hurt! Though, after pushing a baby out, cutting my hand was pretty much nothing," she'd added with a wry laugh.) When police asked why there was so much more blood on the sidewalk than could plausibly be produced by a cut hand, she simply shrugged, wide eyed, and said, "I don't know. It seemed like a lot of blood to me, though. It was a pretty bad cut, like I said."

She would tell police that she tried to hail a cab to take her to the hospital but she couldn't find one, so she kept walking west toward Riverside Park, hoping she'd have more luck on Broadway. But the streets were quiet that night. Not a lot of pedestrians to ask for help and no available taxis that she could find. She kept trying. (A car *had* picked her up that night, of course; Vanessa had driven her to Montauk and made it back for work on Friday morning. Phoebe had come along for the ride so that Vanessa didn't have to come up with an excuse for why she needed her nanny. It was simpler not to involve additional people, to avoid raising suspicion. Phoebe had slept for practically the entire ride, the angel.)

That's the last thing she remembered, she said. Searching for a ride to the hospital to have her hand stitched up. When she came to, she was being taken to Mount Sinai West in a taxi by the runners who'd found her by the river and carried her up to the street through the park. She had no idea how much time had elapsed but was shocked to learn she'd been missing for a week.

She supposed, she said, that a combination of chronic exhaustion, postpartum depression, and excessive blood loss from her cut hand— hence, the stains on the sidewalk, and the bloody rings, which she had apparently removed at some point in her delirium and was so happy to get back, by the way, because they were so special to her—had induced her into a catatonic state. To her knowledge, she'd just been essentially sleeping by the river for the past week, though maybe she'd walked around and forgotten. She couldn't remember eating, though that didn't necessarily mean she hadn't. She couldn't remember anything. She was just grateful to be alive, grateful to the runners who had found her, grateful to her mother for keeping faith and taking amazing care of her baby daughter while she'd been gone. She was grateful to her husband for keeping the media circus at bay in order to protect their family's safety and privacy, and allowing detectives to do their job unencumbered by the scrutiny or misinformation of the public. She was grateful to her friends who had offered their time and help to her family, and of course, she greatly appreciated the detectives' hard work in pursuing a variety of leads and possibilities. She was so happy to be back and was feeling much, much better.

It wasn't a particularly believable story—not in the least, actually. But what made it work was that people were usually willing to believe that a woman had been weak, crazy, had succumbed to some kind of psychotic episode. And that ultimately, she'd survived because of dumb luck. So maybe it was a story that everyone would be more than willing to believe, after all. *Thank God she's back*, people would say, brows furrowed in confusion as to what the hell she could have been doing by the river for the past week, but not venturing so far as to call her a liar. *What a miracle that she's going to be okay.*

The detectives would take notes on her story, asking predictable questions in incredulous tones. "I don't remember" became a mantra. But she was a victim, not a criminal. They didn't seem to suspect her of faking her own disappearance, or if they did, then they didn't see an interesting or malicious enough motive that would make it worth their while to go down that road. Easier to close the case. There was no crime, there were no dead bodies. The woman detective who had come to my apartment, Blaylock, turned out to be the mother of a one- and a three-year-old, which she disclosed when Isabel emphasized how happy she was to be reunited with Naomi. She would give her knowing glances throughout her recounting of how exhausted, how overwhelmed, how disoriented, how absolutely wrecked she'd been in the weeks following Naomi's birth.

Of course, the moms' group was thrilled to hear of Isabel's return. We sent her flowers to the hospital on Saturday, from the whole group, but didn't want to overwhelm her with a visit just yet. She needed to rest. We did a brief group FaceTime call on Sunday, though, and she assured us over the phone that she was feeling worlds better after spending the day at the hospital on a drip, eating egg sandwiches. She expected to be discharged later that day and would love to host us at her house as early as Monday, if we were available. Which we were.

Chapter Twenty-Nine

Monday, October 12

Whereas Connor may have been able to keep the media away when Isabel was missing, the story of a new mom who had entered some kind of a state of postpartum psychosis and gone missing and survived in the Hudson River brambles for a week without anyone finding her was a more compelling story than that of a woman who was simply missing, and there was nothing Connor or anyone could have done to keep the reporters away.

For twenty-four hours, there was a circus of reporters in front of their apartment. Eighty-Eighth Street was essentially blocked off to traffic. Headlines splashed throughout local and national news outlets alike.

EXHAUSTED NEW MOM SLEEPS BY RIVER WHILE FAMILY SEARCHES FOR HER

MISSING WOMAN FOUND BY RUNNERS, INJURED BUT ALIVE AFTER EIGHT DAYS ON THE HUDSON

Some were obviously skeptical of her story but still stopped short of making an accusation against her:

MISSING MOTHER FOUND ALIVE WITHOUT ANSWERS

And many articles were more nuanced, highlighting the postpartum depression angle:

MISSING MANHATTAN MOM SHINES A DARK LIGHT
ON POSTPARTUM REALITY

Fortunately for Isabel, two days after she was found, a man was caught masturbating in front of PS 9, so Upper West Siders seemed to lose interest in her. She was back. What more was there to discuss? Protecting the neighborhood, especially an elementary school, from sexual deviants was more pressing.

We'd be going to Isabel's that afternoon for our first moms' group meeting since her return, but in an effort to move the day along and distract myself from my own nerves about the *other* plans looming on the horizon, I took Clara to a baby music class in a kids' gym a few blocks from my apartment. I'd been meaning to take her to a class ever since learning from Facebook that this was something that apparently every other parent was doing with their baby.

There were three other babies in the class, one of them with a nanny, two with moms who had arrived together. When class started, we were instructed to put the babies on their stomachs and lay toys in front of them, to make them practice reaching and to strengthen their neck muscles. The teacher was a college-aged girl named Lisa, who played guitar and sang "Itsy-Bitsy Spider," "Wheels on the Bus," and "Head, Shoulders, Knees, and Toes," ending each song in a sweet but dramatic falsetto ripple. Lisa instructed us to tickle the babies' toes, massage their hamstrings, play peekaboo with scarves that she distributed. The grand finale was a parachute shake, and some bubbles, which Clara did seem to enjoy. Mostly, though, she drooled on the floor and glanced periodically at me with a look that said *What the hell are we doing here for forty-five dollars?* Even Lisa herself seemed slightly skeptical that we were willing to pay her for this.

As we packed up, I overheard the other two moms talking about Isabel.

"I can't believe she's allowed to get her baby back," one of them whispered. "At least not right away. I mean, she's obviously crazy. I hope she's being supervised."

"Oh my God, totally. Like, I've been tired, too, but if you're so tired that you're just lying by the river for a week, that's a whole other issue. What the hell? I've literally never heard anything so weird. She's lucky it was warm last week."

"Also, just, like, ask for help. She's rich. If you can't handle the baby, get a nanny. Duh."

"Totally! She's loaded! She could have five nannies! And if you're that depressed, see a doctor? I don't really get any of it. I'm jealous of how much weight she probably lost, though. Maybe I should do that, too."

"Ha, same! But really, it's so bizarre. Or listen, maybe she made up the whole thing. Maybe she was, like, off with her boyfriend for a week and created this whole thing as a cover."

"In that case, good for her!" They both laughed. "Do you want to get coffee on our way to the park?"

I shot them a death glare, which they didn't seem to notice, and walked out of the gym before they did. "Sorry about that, Clara," I murmured as we walked down the sidewalk, not totally sure what I was apologizing for but feeling that it was warranted nonetheless. She smiled up at me.

Her good mood didn't last, though; she started wailing as soon as we reached the corner. "Shh, shh," I begged. "It's okay. We'll be home soon."

A woman standing next to me as we waited to cross the street said dryly, "Oh man. Those newborn cries transport me right back. Hang in there. Mine are in school now, but I still remember those first few months." She shuddered in an exaggerated, funny way. "It gets better. You're doing great."

My eyes filled with tears, but I didn't feel embarrassed, as I would have merely weeks ago. I felt validated and genuinely appreciative. Empowered by the solidarity and strength of the mothers around me.

And grateful to have mom friends who would kill for one another.

Chapter Thirty

Monday, October 12

Later that afternoon, Kira met me outside my apartment, and we walked over to Isabel's together, single file up Eighty-Eighth Street with our strollers. The street was decorated extravagantly for Halloween: huge inflatable spiders on that fluffy white cotton that could be either a fake spiderweb or fake snow, depending on the holiday. Bats glued to windows. Massive pumpkins with elaborately carved, expressive faces. Upper West Siders go all out for Halloween.

Isabel answered the door. "Hi, girls! Come on in!" She seemed breezy and unbothered, loose cashmere sweater hanging over her thin frame, Naomi on her hip. Selena was already there, sitting barefoot on the floor while Miles gummed Naomi's shaker. She waved to us and smiled, but I could see the worry on her face.

There was a spread on Isabel's farm-style table of Orwashers' sandwiches cut into fourths, their amazing chocolate chip cookies, and of course, two bottles of cold rosé.

"It's so good to see you guys. I'm happy to be back," she said, with a wink. We'd wanted to have one last meeting so that we could see each other in person and make sure we were all feeling okay, or as okay as possible, leading up to tonight: essentially, to confirm that no one was backing out. To lead each other off our respective ledges and offer comfort, just as we always had in our group meetings; this time, it just happened to be about something other than our babies. But we'd also agreed to try not to discuss our plan openly again, even behind the closed doors of her home. We had gone over it in Montauk, and we knew what we were doing. It wasn't worth the risk of accidentally having any type of evidence on our phones or on her Nest cam or having anyone overhear anything at all. We were being careful.

"Vanessa's on her way," Isabel informed us, "and she has a surprise." At that point, I was a hard pass on any more surprises. But her lightness was reassuring.

I poured myself a generous glass of rosé. It would be my only one, though, I promised myself; it was going to be a long day. And night. I needed to stay clear for what was to come. But it was far enough away from nighttime that I thought one glass should be fine. My nerves certainly needed it. "Anyone else?" I asked. Everyone nodded emphatically.

"Connor's at work, I assume?" Selena asked.

"Of course. He's not thrilled with me for the media attention." She smirked. "He values his privacy, after all."

"Did he . . . buy it?" I ventured cautiously, mouthing the final two words of my sentence.

"I don't think so, but it doesn't really matter," Isabel said with a shrug. "And there's so much attention on us right now that he can't take his frustration out on me. He's on good behavior." She was right about it not mattering—any opinions Connor had about the true nature of her disappearance would be irrelevant in a matter of hours.

I glanced over to the mantel above their fireplace at a picture of Connor and Isabel dressed up at a party; he was holding her waist tightly, and she was smiling only slightly, her lips closed. I'd never have thought anything of it before, but now that I knew the truth about their marriage, I could see how uncomfortable she was with his grip on her, how his expression was more smug than happy. *Prick,* I thought silently.

As nervous as I was, I also felt an odd tinge of satisfaction knowing what was coming his way.

Vanessa let herself in, calling "Knock knock!" as she entered. "Hi, everyone!" she exclaimed, parking her stroller behind ours in Isabel's spacious entryway, unstrapping Phoebe, and kissing her several times as she lifted her out of it. "Sorry we're late."

"So what's the surprise?" Kira asked bluntly, wasting no time. "I'm not sure if I'm really too keen on another surprise, to be honest." We all laughed lightly; we were past politeness, past pretenses at this point. It was nice.

Vanessa set Phoebe down next to Miles on the play mat. She took a giant white box out of the bottom of her stroller. "Milk Bar cake! Have you guys had this? It's seriously the best. Cake. Ever."

We all stared at Vanessa blankly. *A murder cake?* I thought to myself. *Really, Vanessa?*

As if reading our minds, Vanessa said quickly, "I know, I know. This isn't exactly a party. But—well, sorry to be morbid, but today's Allison's birthday. I mean, obviously we don't have to sing or anything weird, but I want Phoebe to be able to celebrate her." Overcome with emotion, she suddenly flew a hand to her mouth. Her shoulders shook. We circled around her, each putting a hand on her.

"It's okay," she said. "I'm okay. I miss her so much. But I think she would be happy today. Because we're going to—" She stopped, remembering our rule about not uttering out loud any specifics. "We're going to do right by her," she finished. She nodded. "Thank you, guys. Thank you all."

We looked at each other, and it hit me then that at some point, we'd become actual friends. Not just mom friends. But real ones.

Vanessa disappeared into the kitchen for a moment, and when she came back, she was holding a cake knife. "Jenn, can you do the honors?" she asked. "I need to make up a bottle for this one." She gestured to Phoebe.

I started cutting slices. Vanessa looked up from the floor where she was feeding Phoebe and laughed. "Um, if you'd ever had this cake before, you'd know we need much bigger pieces than that! You're fired. Kira, take over please?" I laughed and put my hands up, surrender-style, and handed Kira the knife, relinquishing my duties.

As fun and shockingly normal as our meeting was that day, the goodbye felt heavy. The hugs were loaded; we knew they were the last we'd give as the women we were at this moment. Next time we dispersed from one another, only a few hours from now in the same place, we would all be changed forever—and our bond would truly be irrevocable, for better or for much, much worse.

Chapter Thirty-One

Monday, October 12

That night as I put Clara to sleep, the fears I'd been pushing out of my mind crept in. As much as I'd been trying to play it cool and stay the course, I could no longer deny that I was terrified. After tonight, I would be a murderer, or at least an accomplice to murder. To first-degree, premeditated murder. I was too scared to google the specific types of murder and their usual prison sentences, for fear of having an incriminating Google search history, but I was pretty sure the type of murder we were committing was the worst one. If we got caught, we'd go to jail forever, or at least what would surely feel like it.

And if we didn't get caught, would I be different after tonight? Because even though we were murdering someone who deserved it, it was still murder. Would I be traumatized, hardened, unable to be myself ever again?

There was an even worse potential outcome, too: that Connor would overpower us, hurt us, kill us.

I let Clara fall asleep nursing. *Stay as long as you want, sweet angel,* I thought. I had hours until I was expected at Isabel's. Clara was zipped up in her fleece sleep sack, so cozy, her cheeks so full and soft against my breast. I couldn't stop stroking her soft, fuzzy peach head. "I love you so much," I whispered again and again into her hair. "So much."

She'd been sleeping in my arms for nearly an hour when I finally put her in her bassinet and walked into the kitchen. Normally I'd pour myself a glass of wine at this moment, but I couldn't tonight. I needed to be totally clearheaded.

Like most nights, Tim and I watched TV after we ate the salmon burgers that he'd made while I was putting Clara down. We were watching one of the greatest episodes of *The Office* ever, when Michael and Jan host a torturous six-hour dinner party, but I couldn't focus on it at all. All I could think about was what I'd be doing merely hours from now. Was I making a huge mistake? How had I let myself be talked into killing some guy I barely knew, to help a woman who I also barely knew? What the hell was I thinking? I had a great life. And I was jeopardizing it all to help Isabel.

It wasn't just for Isabel, though. It was also for Allison, Vanessa's sister. It was for *me*, so that I could say goodbye to that awful night once and for all. It was for every woman who'd become entangled in a situation she couldn't safely or feasibly get out of. It was for Naomi, so that she wouldn't have to grow up with a dad who was in all likelihood incapable of love and kindness.

And I was pretty sure that these women would do something this big for me, if I needed it. Having that in my life felt good.

The plan, which we'd pored over painstakingly in Montauk, seemed straightforward enough. At first, Connor would think it was just a confrontation. An act of rebellion on Isabel's part that he'd later punish her for.

He'd pour himself a drink—something Isabel assured us he nearly always did when he came home, no matter how drunk he might already be, and would be *certain* to do tonight, given the crowd he'd be coming home to.

Apparently he used the same glass every night—a thick crystal tumbler, heavy as a cannonball and elaborately engraved with *CH*.

I've always hated monograms.

Unbeknownst to him, on this night, his special glass would be lightly doused with GHB, to slow him down and disorient him so that he wouldn't be inclined (or at least able) to lash out or fight back.

Then, at the right moment, when he was distracted or weak, Vanessa would inject him with a lethal amount of a drug called Trilaptin that would freeze his muscles, including his heart, and make it appear that he'd had a heart attack. Vanessa had access to all the medical supplies we needed through her job. After the fact, Isabel would tell medical examiners he'd been complaining of arm pain and shortness of breath, to corroborate the likelihood of a heart attack. Oh, he had *such* a high-stress job. The poor guy was always working. Heart problems ran in his family. Not to mention he'd just endured the stress of his wife's disappearance. A heart attack, even at his young age, seemed believable enough.

Officially, he would be alone in the house at the time of his death: just that afternoon, Isabel and Naomi and the dog would have gone to stay at her mom's in Tarrytown for a couple of nights, as her mom was helping her recuperate from her recent ordeal. Connor worked long hours, after all, and Isabel was still fragile. She needed her mom's help. So Connor likely wouldn't be discovered until the next morning, or even afternoon, after failing to show up to work.

And any evidence of *our* footprint there, the moms' group, would be easily explained by our meeting earlier that day, before Isabel left for Tarrytown. If it came up at all.

Of course, the Nest cameras would be offline, unfortunately. The town house frequently had Wi-Fi issues; it was surprising, considering how wealthy they were, that they hadn't addressed this problem earlier. Freaking cable company.

So Connor would die alone in his home of a heart attack. End of story.

And yet, a big part of me wondered whether we could pull this off. And I knew I wasn't in the right frame of mind to have made this huge decision. I hadn't slept properly in nearly four months. I'd drunk what seemed like hundreds of bottles of wine. I was always in a fog. It was just days ago that I had convinced myself that *I* had had something to do with Isabel's death. In some distant, imaginative corner of my mind, I'd even wondered if Tim could have been involved, after I'd seen his call log—if they'd been having an affair. It was so absurd, now, in retrospect. The fact was that it had been a while since I'd been at peace with myself, my thought processes, my rationale. And somehow, in this compromised state, I'd signed on to kill someone.

But it felt too late for hesitation. The choice had been made. I had to honor what I'd decided and trust myself. And the other moms.

Tim and I went to bed early, and I lay there beside him wide awake, waiting for it to be time for me to go. I wasn't remotely worried that I'd fall asleep; I couldn't have if my life had depended on it. Tim slept soundly beside me, snoring softly, though I could barely hear his snores over the drum of my own pounding heart. All these months I'd cursed him silently for being such a sound sleeper, but tonight I was relieved.

When the clock struck eleven, I got out of bed and picked up Clara to give her a quick "dream feed," filling her belly before my departure, buying myself a few all-but-certain hours. I hoped that if Tim woke up while I was gone, whether because of Clara or otherwise, and I wasn't there, he'd assume I went for another late walk, and that's exactly what I would tell him if necessary.

As Clara nursed, her eyes closed, I closed mine, too, and said a silent prayer, though I didn't really know who I was praying to, not being particularly religious. *Please let this be the right decision. Please let this be okay. Please let me come back to my daughter and husband.*

I put Clara back in her bassinet, still sleeping, and silently changed out of my pajamas into black leggings and a black Under Armour long-sleeved shirt. I crept out of our bedroom as quietly as possible, mouthing "I love you" one more time to both Tim and Clara as I left.

I hated how much it felt like a final goodbye.

Chapter Thirty-Two

Monday, October 12

It wasn't even midnight, but the quietness of the streets outside made it seem much later, and the fact that all the stores were closed rendered the neighborhood practically unrecognizable to me. I wasn't used to being out at this hour anymore. New York is supposed to be the city that never sleeps, but Upper West Siders didn't abide by that rule. There were a few people out, a few bodegas open, but I walked an entire block without passing a soul. I was reminded of Isabel's cover story about not finding a taxi, not being helped by anyone as she struggled along the street with her bleeding hand; maybe it had been more plausible than it had sounded.

As I neared Isabel's apartment, I saw Selena approaching from the other direction. She paused, waiting for me to catch up with her so we could walk in together. She was wearing all black, just like me, as we'd agreed. As I got closer, I saw that her eyes were puffy and her arms were wrapped tightly around herself.

"You okay?" I asked quietly, looking around. I didn't want us to be seen going into Isabel's. We had to be quick.

"I can't do this, Jenn," she whispered, her voice breaking.

My stomach dropped. I glanced around again, nervously. "We have to," I whispered back simply. *Who* are *you? Where is this steady voice coming from?* I liked it. I slipped my hand into hers and squeezed. "I've got you."

To my surprise, she closed her eyes and nodded, and we ascended the stairs grasping hands. I silently and fervently hoped that I wasn't steering her wrong.

Vanessa opened the door as we reached the top step. The slender door handle I'd once thought looked so stylish and inviting now appeared ominous and foreboding, like a weapon. We entered without a word and walked into the living room. Isabel and Kira were perched on the edge of the plush white sofa, like Daisy Buchanan and Jordan Baker, except, like me and Selena, they were also in all black. And the murder they would commit would be premeditated.

They looked grave as they nodded at us in greeting. Selena and I stood behind the couch. I squeezed her hand again.

"He should be back soon," Isabel said solemnly. He was at a work function, and it was unlikely to be one of his hunting nights. Especially with the recent media attention related to Isabel's disappearance. He was too smart for that.

As if on cue, we heard a key in the door.

He took off his coat and hung it on the rack without even noticing us, though the entryway was visible from the living room. Then he turned around and registered us, but his face didn't betray him, barely changing.

He looked at Isabel and said, coolly, "What is this?"

She stood up from the couch. Slowly. Calmly. "Connor, I believe you already know my friends, don't you?"

"Yeah, I guess," he said, eyes passing over us, vague recognition flashing across his eyes. But so far, I would've bet we were still just the moms' group members who'd brought food over. It hadn't yet hit him how he *really* knew us. "Kind of late for visitors, no?" he asked Isabel tightly, not bothering to address us.

"It's just easier," Isabel said, her voice lilting musically. "The babies are all sleeping, so we can all really talk, you know? No distractions." Isabel had sent Naomi to her mom's house, where, of course, she would claim to have been, too, when it was all over. Connor didn't know that, though. "So you *do* remember my friends, right?" She raised an eyebrow at Connor. As terrified as I was, I was pleased for Isabel. She was doing well. *You go,* I thought.

"Sure. Yes. They came here the other day. When you were *missing*." His voice dripped with sarcasm and disdain.

"Yes. But they should look familiar for other reasons, too. You know them personally," Isabel said, looking at him with exaggerated patience.

"Jesus Christ." His eyes flitted across each of our faces once more. My body felt cold as he looked at me. Finally, he understood, and his eyes surged with anger. "What are you doing, Isabel?"

"I'm doing what I should have done a long time ago."

"God, this is embarrassing."

"It should be. You're disgusting."

"I mean for *you*. Could you be any more dramatic? Staging some kind of a showcase? First the stunt you pulled with the disappearing act, and now this? You really are unhinged, aren't you?" I could see the anger brewing in his pulsing neck, though his eyes and voice remained calm.

"This isn't about me. It's about you."

"Okay. Fine. So? So yes, I'm with other women. A fact you've known for quite some time. So what's the goal here? What is it you hope to accomplish by parading them in front of me?" He looked at Isabel with such scorn, and suddenly it was easy to see how he'd succeeded in belittling her so these past ten years.

"It's not just about me and what I hope to accomplish. It's about all of us."

"Including Allison," Vanessa added icily.

Connor turned toward Vanessa and rubbed his temples, like all this amounted to no more than an irritating headache. "Allison?"

"Yes, Allison." Vanessa stood up from the couch, her face steely. "I wouldn't expect you to remember her. You met her in DC, about a year ago. She was just another girl in a bar, to you. But she was also my sister, and she gave birth to your child. Your actions have consequences, you know. Allison killed herself. Because of you. Because you don't care about the wreckage you leave behind. All you care about is yourself."

"Oh God." He wiped one palm hard down his forehead as though he were utterly exhausted. "Look," he said, his tone painfully condescending, "I can't place any Allison. And even if I could, I certainly can't be held responsible for decisions anyone makes about her own life. Do you have any proof at all that it was my kid? No, don't answer that. It doesn't even matter. It's not relevant. It's not my kid, not in any way. Maybe I had sex with her—let's say I did. Why not. But I sure as hell didn't force her to have a baby, and I certainly didn't make her kill herself. I'm sorry she died, but it has nothing whatsoever to do with me." He walked over to the bar table and picked up a glass to pour himself a drink, just like he was supposed to.

But the glass he was holding had no *CH* on it. It was a random unmonogrammed coupe glass that had been hanging on the stem rack. One that was certainly not treated with a drug. A drug that would protect us from Connor's wrath.

Who uses a coupe glass for whiskey? No. No. This was already falling apart. I was too scared to look at anyone's face, but I had no doubt that they were all wearing the same stricken expression that I was.

He peered at the glass in his hand. Then he held it up to the light and scowled. "This is *filthy*," he said to Isabel, glaring at her. And in one quick motion, he slammed the offending glass down on the table, picked up his ludicrously ostentatious *CH* tumbler, and filled it with whiskey.

All a show. A chance to criticize Isabel's housekeeping.

While insignificant on his long list of offenses, this little display set me aflame with rage and renewed my commitment to what we'd signed on to do.

He took a sip of whiskey—*we're back on track, asshole*—and continued. "I can't and won't be blamed for someone else's weakness," he said smugly. I could tell that he really, really believed what he was saying.

He took another drink, more a slug this time, and then put his glass down on the bar table. He turned back toward Isabel and said, "So, is that it? That's the whole show?"

"No," Isabel said, and offered nothing more. He rolled his eyes at her cruelly.

He picked up his drink again and turned back toward Vanessa with another shrug. "I'm sorry your sister is dead. I really am. But you can't possibly want to pin that on me." He turned away from Vanessa as if that settled it. He was absolved, as far as he was concerned. Case closed.

He walked to Isabel then, stood no more than six inches from her, towering over her. His movement around the room seemed strategic, like he was trying to take up as much space as possible. "So, what now—you're gonna ask me for a divorce again? That's the grand plan? And you needed an audience so that you wouldn't lose your nerve, as you always do? Well, let me remind you: You've never worked. You don't have any money of your own. You have no skills. Acting doesn't count, and you aren't a good actor, anyway. God, I remember having to sit through your plays when we were in college—what a joke." Isabel was trying hard to keep her poker face, but she winced ever so slightly at that. "And I'll insist on joint custody, which I'll get, so you'll only be with Naomi a few days a week. You'll be the one who has to shuttle her to and from whatever hellhole you live in. You know, I might even get sole custody, now that I think of it—after you all but publicly declared yourself unfit by disappearing for an entire week and leaving your newborn baby behind. It wouldn't be difficult at all to convince a judge that you're totally unstable. I could afford a great nanny, or a couple of them, and my life would pretty much continue just as it is. Except that I wouldn't have to see your annoying mom anymore. That would be that. You'd get supervised visitation, probably. If you're lucky."

He treated himself to a deep, self-satisfied, another-job-well-done breath after this monologue, then took another drink, licked his lips, and peered down at her. "So, Isabel, is that what you want? Do you have any *idea* how much I take care of that you don't even know about? Have you ever paid a bill? Filed taxes? Would you have health insurance without me? I know you don't appreciate any of it, and you'd rather just play the victim, but I do *everything* for you. You really aren't good for much around here besides folding laundry. You'd find out pretty quickly if you left me that you don't know shit about shit. There's no way you could live alone, or take care of a baby by yourself. You need me and you need my money."

I could see how Connor had convinced her to stay in the past. This litany of threats felt as real to me as it undoubtedly always had to Isabel. He said everything so evenly, as if he were stating facts as undebatable and objective as state capitals.

Isabel answered in kind, though. "Oh, I'm not going to leave you," she told him. She smiled sympathetically, playing his game to perfection.

"So what's the plan here, then, honey? You've gathered your new friends together as, what—an intervention? To get me to stop? To hear me apologize? To make me understand the error of my ways?" He laughed at his own sarcasm, turning away from Isabel and toward us, addressing us finally. "You ladies might not get your money's worth if that's the case. Sorry to disappoint."

Isabel pressed on. "Just humor us, will you? Why don't you tell us why you do it, for starters."

"Why I sleep with women? I like them. I like sex. Is that simple enough for you?" He laughed at his own cleverness, and I could taste acid in my throat, remembering how it felt to be touched by him. Kira and Selena wore similar repulsed expressions, and I saw Kira squeeze Selena's arm in solidarity.

Isabel shook her head, not accepting his answer. "What you're doing—it's not about sex. That much is clear to me. I think it's clear to all of us." Isabel gestured toward us.

Connor narrowed his eyes at her. "What is it about, then, Isabel? If you're such an expert, if you want to play therapist—go ahead. Why don't you present your thesis about why I do what I do?"

Without missing a beat, Isabel said, "I think you crave the power you didn't have as a child. I think you measure your worth in bowling pins—deals at work, women—because it allows you to convince yourself that you're winning the game, in control of everything and everyone. I think it's a distraction, too—from the fact that you're a bad person and the world would be better off without you."

Connor popped his eyes wide. "*Fascinating* diagnosis, Isabel. But you know what *I* think it is?" He turned to all of us with a flourish. "I can sniff out spineless, pathetic women who will let me do whatever I want. Women who know they're worthless and want someone to confirm it for them."

He smirked, well pleased with himself, and took a long drink while we all stared at him. Then he grinned. "You want me to go even deeper here? I'm game. This is therapeutic as shit. Here you go: I think it's because my mom just let my dad hit her and never did a damn thing about it. He'd crack her in the face and she'd be serving his dinner fifteen minutes later. She disgusted me. If she'd had any balls—or, whatever—she would have left and taken me with her. It's not like I wasn't taking a beating myself.

"You know, I don't know if I ever told you this one, Isabel. But this one time—I was heading into my freshman year and was, you know, not huge yet, but relatively jacked from summer lifting and doing two-a-days before football kicked in—I did get around to fighting back. And I knocked him out. I still remember the surprise on his face before he lost consciousness. And, you know, all conquering hero, I turned to my mother and said, 'Mom, let's go. Let's get the hell out of here.' And she just shook her head and told me to go to my room, that she knew I hadn't meant to hurt him and that we weren't going anywhere. The next morning he beat me senseless while she made breakfast. I guess I have to thank him, though—he gave me all the motivation I needed to get into a good college and get a great job so that I never, ever had to go back to that hellhole. And I haven't been back since leaving, not once. What I've figured out is that she *wanted* to be hit. If she didn't, she would have figured out a way not to get hit anymore." He took another swig of his drink, his jaw hard with the pain of these remembrances.

"It's messed up, admittedly, but I think the women I find out there tend to remind me of her, in some ways. I mean, you sure as hell do, dear wife. I've told you before. Dependent. Needy. You're lucky, though, because I'm not a deadbeat like my dad. I can actually provide for you, give you this life." He gestured to their house.

"But maybe, in some ways, I'm teaching you, *all* of you, an important lesson. Don't ask for something if you don't want it. Know your own desires. That's why I've been so successful in business: I know what I want and what I don't, and I make sure everyone around me knows it, too. And look, all of you came on to me as much as I came on to you. So if you regret it now, or feel like it was wrong in some way, then that's on you." I was reminded of what he'd said about Allison's demise, that it had "nothing to do with him." His ability to claim no responsibility for his actions was astounding.

"So this is a service you're providing?" Isabel asked. "A lesson you're imparting to all the unsuspecting women who are unfortunate enough to fall into your line of sight?"

"Ha. Not exactly. But the bottom line is, if you don't want something, don't go sniffing around for it. How hard is it to be sure of what you want? Besides, it's just sex. Let's not make it a bigger deal than it is."

"It's not sex," Selena said, staring at him from behind the couch, her voice quiet but clear.

"Excuse me?" Connor said, whirling a bit to find the new speaker.

"It's not sex. It's rape," she said, and with that word, I felt the strangest, biggest rush of relief wash over me. Finally. The word.

Why had it been so difficult for me to see it that way? Perhaps it was that women in my generation hadn't been taught all the nuances of consent that the younger generations were learning: that consent must be enthusiastic, stated out loud, continuous, given soberly. That it can be taken back at any time. The only reason I knew any of that was because I worked at a high school, where these understandings were part of the new health curriculum. Yes, when I was young, we'd all been given the generic "no means no" talk. But at the same time, the boys were being whispered to that a girl's *no* might be because she's just shy or coy and should actually be taken as an invitation to keep pursuing with renewed zeal. And we girls were being told that we shouldn't dress "provocatively," because if we did, well, then we couldn't very well expect the boys to control themselves. So I'd viewed my encounter with Connor as entirely my fault. Something I'd brought upon myself.

Rape. It's what it was. Connor sought out women who were drunk and alone, always, always alone, got them drunker, or gave them something, as he had with Selena, had rough and hurried and painful intercourse with them, and sent them—no, not them, *us*—on our way, wondering what the *hell* had just happened.

Well now I had an answer: it was rape.

"I have never raped anyone," Connor said, studying Selena's face curiously. "Why would I need to? Women are very receptive to me, trust me. You included—I remember you. All dressed up at the High Line bar, right? To be honest, I thought you were a prostitute at first."

If looks could kill, he would have already been dead because of the one Selena gave him. He raised his glass to her, then took another drink.

"I think we're done here," he said. His speech was starting to slur, whether from the booze or GHB, or both. "I hope this was everything you dreamed it would be, Isabel." He turned to the rest of us. "Can all of you go home now, please? I'd like to get some sleep." Then he looked back at Isabel with something that could almost have been mistaken for fondness. "I honestly don't know what I'm going to do with you at this point." He shook his head.

"It's not about what you're going to do with me, Connor. It's about what we're going to do with you." Isabel's voice was quiet but steady. "You asked me what the plan is. The plan is that tonight will be your last. We've all had enough of you. So enjoy the rest of that drink."

"Ha!" His laugh came from deep within his belly. He looked genuinely amused and not the least bit scared. "Oh my God. That's amazing. It's actually . . . seriously, it's almost cute. You're ridiculous. Are you being serious? You can't possibly be."

"Connor," Isabel said, as if she were speaking to a toddler, "I don't think you understand. At this point, it would be irresponsible of us to allow you to stay alive. We are protecting other women from meeting you. We can't follow you around all the time, and this is just more efficient. Not to mention, I obviously can't permit you to stay in Naomi's life, in any capacity. You've had many chances to be a decent human being, and you've taken none of them. So, enough is enough."

Connor was starting to look mildly concerned, but only mildly. His expression was more perplexed than worried. But we had his attention, at least. "Izzy, you and your pals don't have the balls, and there's no chance in hell you'd get away with it. Have you thought about that? Going to prison? No, I don't think any of you would enjoy prison. They don't serve oat lattes and chardonnay, you know." He laughed at his own joke.

"Well, I disagree," said Isabel thoughtfully. "I think we *can* get away with it. We're actually pretty smart women. I know that's probably a surprise to you, but it's true. We've got a pretty damn good plan, and it doesn't involve us going to jail." She waved her hand dismissively. "But let us worry about the logistics. You simply worry about—well, nothing, actually."

A few discernible beads of sweat appeared on the chest of Connor's crisp white shirt, and his eyes were unfocused. He was swaying slightly as he tried, with difficulty, to settle on Isabel's face. The GHB had definitely kicked in.

"You're not going to kill me," he insisted, but his tongue was thick as he said it, and I had to admit to myself that I was enjoying seeing him unravel. I was also shaking with fear at what I knew was coming.

"We are, though," said Vanessa.

"Stay the fuck out of this," he snapped at Vanessa. "Izzy, please—"

"Stop calling me that. I hate being called Izzy. No one calls me that."

Isabel looked at Vanessa and nodded. Her face showed no emotion.

Connor started to lunge, unsteadily, toward Isabel, his hands outstretched, reaching for her neck. With that, Vanessa grabbed a huge knife that I hadn't noticed on the coffee table behind her and unceremoniously plunged it into his neck, inches from my own face.

Chapter Thirty-Three

Tuesday, October 13

Blood spurted out of Connor's neck and splashed onto my shirt. It poured out of him like lava, immediately soaking the carpet a shade of dark crimson, like spilled cabernet. His eyes went blank, and then he collapsed, falling onto the couch first, and then the floor. His body convulsed. And then he was still. So, so still.

He was dead, or appeared to be. That part we'd agreed to. But *this* was not what we had discussed.

"What the *fuck*, Vanessa!" Isabel cried out. "What about the injection?"

My body felt numb. *This was not the plan. Fuck. Fuck. Fuck.*

Kira's hand was to her mouth. Selena just kept saying, "No. No. No." We went over and stood with Isabel, who had turned completely white.

Vanessa's back was to us. She was still holding the knife, unmoving. She didn't respond to Isabel's question.

"Vanessa!" Isabel screamed.

She turned around slowly and moved a strand of hair off her face with the back of her bloody wrist, looking at all of us with disdain. "God, you guys are so gullible. There was never a magical heart attack shot. Give me a break. This isn't *Breaking Bad*. Honestly, it's unbelievable—you guys agreed to a murder and you didn't even bother to, like, I don't know, google the feasibility of the proposed plan? Dermatological surgeons don't just have access to lethal drugs that make a crime look like a cardiac arrest. Especially when those drugs are completely *fictional*. For God's sake. Do your due diligence. You guys are as helpless and unprepared as Allison!" She scoffed, a cruel laugh that almost reminded me of Connor's, who was still lying at our feet, his lifeless body continuing to pump blood onto the rug.

"What do you mean?" Isabel asked, frantic. "Why did you lie to us? What are we supposed to do now, with this mess?"

Selena sank to sit down on the armrest, head in her hands. "Our lives are over."

Vanessa rolled her eyes at the two of them. "I didn't tell you, Isabel, because he really did deserve to die, and none of you would have agreed to do it if you thought there was any chance of getting caught." She turned to face the rest of us. "If Isabel's disappearing act proved anything, it's that you all only care about your own asses. If you'd come forward as Isabel had hoped—which I highly doubted would happen, by the way—I could have left you out of this next part. But you *are* needed for this plan. There is still a plan, after all. It's just not the one you thought."

"And what is the actual plan?" Isabel asked, tears welling in her eyes.

The bloodstain on the carpet was getting bigger and bigger.

"To punish *everyone* who deserves it. Not just Connor," Vanessa murmured, too calmly. My body was tingling with panic. This was going terribly, terribly wrong.

"Meaning what?" Kira choked out.

"Meaning you're to blame here, too, Isabel. I'm sorry, but you are. You claim you had no idea what he was really out there doing to women, but please—you knew who he was and what he was capable of. And if you really didn't know, which I find hard to believe, it's only because you didn't *want* to. No one who's halfway normal about sex keeps a list of conquests. Plus, Allison tried to tell you, and you practically hung up on her."

"Vanessa, there was nothing I could have done! You know that. I was trapped." Isabel's blue eyes were wide with panic and confusion.

"You were a doormat. So complacent. So defeated and self-pitying. Until I came to your rescue, handed you an escape plan on a silver platter. Even then, you totally just let me do the heavy lifting, figuring out every detail. What kind of a daughter are you going to raise? The way I see it, people like you really don't deserve to be mothers," Vanessa mused.

"What the hell does that mean?" Isabel's anger at Vanessa's comment seemed to have eclipsed her fear, for the moment.

"None of you do, actually. I hate to agree with Connor on anything, but you're all *so* pathetic. Do you not realize that? God, there's nothing I hate more than a weak woman. You have these amazing gifts, these beautiful children—all of whom were conceived with no difficulty whatsoever, of course—and all you do is complain about how tired you are. How *hard* it is. Give me a break. Do you know how lucky you are? There are so many women who'd love to be mothers and can't be, and they'd probably do a much better job of it than you, too, because they—we—wouldn't take it for granted."

We stared at her, each of us unable to say anything, unsure and terrified of where this was going.

She continued, her voice filled with a quiet anger. "Years ago, I miscarried a baby boy at twenty-eight weeks. I was devastated. I had to deliver him." Her eyes got glassy and she looked to the ceiling. "I thought that holding my blue, lifeless little boy was the lowest moment of my life. But it turned out to be hours later, when they told me that my uterus was basically destroyed and that I'd never be able to have another child." She shook off her tears and looked back at us again. "To add insult to all of it, my fiancé at the time wasn't really into the idea of being with someone who couldn't give him kids. Someone who reminded him only of sadness and loss. So that was the end of that, too." She took a deep breath. "Do you know how frustrating it is to listen to you gripe about unpredictable naps and green poops and clueless husbands and pumping when I would give anything, *anything*, to have my baby boy with me today? To have a family? Do you know how infuriating it is that my sister got pregnant from one time with a stranger, while on the pill, and just, you know, on a lark, figured she'd be a mom? Do you *know* what that did to me?" My stomach dropped.

"Vanessa," Kira said in a voice just above a whisper, "that's awful about your son. Awful. But you realize that we aren't responsible for what happened to you, right?"

"Yes, thanks, Kira, I get that." Vanessa rolled her eyes. "But you're all squandering what you have. Not appreciating it. Not making enough effort. And you should be ashamed of yourselves. Especially you, Isabel—girls need strong role models. And you're the furthest thing from that, letting Connor just do whatever he wants to you and whoever else."

"I didn't *let* him—" Isabel began, but Vanessa held up a hand to silence her.

"So what is it you plan to do?" Selena was stone faced, just as she'd been when we first found Isabel in Montauk. My stomach dropped when I remembered how I'd ushered her into Isabel's house tonight, assured her that it would be okay. *If only I'd known how wrong I was.*

"What do *we* plan to do, you mean. It's still *our* plan, girls. You're all in on it, whether you like it or not. Well, not you." She looked at Isabel with sarcastic sympathy. Then she looked back at the rest of us. "The plan is that this"—she gestured toward Connor's now-lifeless body—"will be a murder-suicide. Isabel killed Connor, then herself."

After a ringing moment of silence in which every jaw but Vanessa's (and Connor's) hung open, Isabel finally spoke up. "What are you talking about?" she sobbed, trembling. "I'm not killing myself."

"Okay, I'll spell it out for you, sweetheart." Vanessa slowed her speech as though addressing someone exceptionally unintelligent. "I am going to kill you and make it look like you killed Connor and then yourself. It would be the most believable thing in the world, given your now well-documented history with postpartum psychosis and exhaustion. It will look like you simply couldn't handle it anymore. You snapped. You'll be like a cautionary tale: *Don't let it get to this point!*"

"Isabel is innocent, Vanessa." I was surprised that my voice even worked. "You have a lot to be angry about, with your son, and what Connor did to your sister, but Isabel isn't responsible for any of it. She was a victim, too."

"Well, that's where I have to disagree with you. Her complicity makes her responsible."

"You'll never get away with it," Kira said, though she didn't sound convinced herself.

Selena agreed: "Cops can always sniff out staged suicides. There are always clues."

"Well," Vanessa said, "lucky for all of us, between my medical degree and my experience staging suicides, I don't think it'll be a problem."

Once again, we all settled back into gaping at her.

"I guess there's no harm in telling you," she said. "There are no secrets between us, at this point. I loved my sister dearly, but it became very clear to me that Allison was simply not up to the task of being Phoebe's mom. She was always immature and impulsive—even her decision to keep the baby was so rash, so uninformed. Who does that? Especially after essentially getting assaulted? And who gets pregnant from one time, *while on the pill?* My sister, that's who. Things always just *happen* to her. And then, what—she's going to raise the baby on her own in her studio apartment?" Vanessa shook her head with exasperation and then looked at us like she expected us to agree. When we showed no reaction, she continued. "She was always like that, even as a kid. Making these reckless decisions that I had to help her undo after the fact. I couldn't talk her out of keeping the baby, but it didn't take long for her to prove me right—she fell apart quickly after Phoebe was born. She was hopeless at changing diapers, constantly falling asleep holding Phoebe. She could have rolled over and suffocated her! She had no idea how to soothe her. She couldn't figure out a feeding schedule for anything. She barely left the house to take her for walks and fresh air. She just moped around all day. I had to do something."

"So you killed your sister?" I couldn't breathe as I spoke.

Vanessa bobbed her head from side to side, considering my question. "I don't really look at it that way. I simply nudged her toward what she'd probably eventually have done herself anyway. She was heading down a dark path, trust me. I saved her some unnecessary pain by expediting the process for her—giving her some medications that, as it turns out, aren't supposed to be mixed." She shrugged as if it had all been an unfortunate accident.

"But look," she continued, "I'm not a monster. I did it so that her daughter wouldn't have to deal with the pain of having a weak, incompetent mother. In truth, I did it for Allison, because I knew deep down that she loved Phoebe and would want her to have the best life possible. And that's with me, not with her." Vanessa sighed. "It killed me to do it. It really did. I loved my sister. I mean, look at what I'm doing for her—killing the guy, the couple, who messed up her life. If that doesn't prove sisterly love, I don't know what does. And I'll always miss her. But Phoebe deserved—deserves—a stronger mom than Allison.

"And this was a familiar road for me. I knew how this would end. Allison came by it honestly. Our mom died by suicide when we were young." I remembered Vanessa mentioning her mom had passed away when she was young. She hadn't said how, though, and I hadn't asked. For the briefest moment, what I thought was grief clouded her eyes, but as quickly as it appeared, it was replaced by resentment, and she refocused herself. "Allison was too young to remember her, but I wasn't. And it was easier for Allison that way. So I wanted to do the same for Phoebe. Because Allison was bound to follow in her footsteps, eventually. Allison's always been like her."

We all just sat with this for a few long moments. It was too much to process.

So Vanessa had killed her sister, taken her baby, killed Connor, and planned to kill Isabel, and now we were stuck in this situation, in this house, with her. *How could you let yourself get here?* I asked myself. *How could you have messed everything up so badly?*

I begged myself to speak again, but no words came. Finally, Selena said all I'd have said anyway. "Vanessa, it sounds like your sister had postpartum depression. That doesn't mean she was going to commit suicide or would 'approve' of you *murdering* her. Postpartum is rough for practically everyone. She would have gotten better. You're insane and delusional." Selena was remarkably clear eyed as she spoke.

Kira chimed in quickly. "And we're not going to let you kill Isabel. We're just not." Selena and I nodded in agreement. Isabel looked at us gratefully, tears streaming down her face.

I finally found my voice again. "Vanessa, none of us are perfect. But how can you blame Isabel for what Connor did? He was an abuser and a predator. And like Selena said, we're not going to stand by and watch you kill Isabel."

Vanessa turned to face me. "Then you're going to find yourself in a tough spot, Jenn. Because your fingerprints are all over the murder weapon."

"What are you talking about? I didn't touch that knife. I didn't even know it was there until—"

"You did, in fact. Earlier today, when you were cutting Allison's birthday cake? Today really is her birthday, by the way. Go figure. Your fingerprints are there, too, Kira. Remember, the pieces Jenn was cutting were too small, so I had you take over? I put the knife right back in the knife stand without washing the handle. And then I moved it to the living room when I arrived here tonight so I'd have easy access when the time came. I've been wearing gloves this whole time, by the way." She held up her hand and wiggled her fingers, and sure enough, there was a tight plastic glove covering it. "So if any of you refuse to go along with this, you're going to have to come up with a really good explanation as to why your prints and Connor's blood are all over this knife. You've also all got a motive, obviously, what with your storied pasts with the victim. Hate for all that to come out, too." Her eyes were wide with false sympathy. "But that's not all. Not only are your fingerprints on the weapon, I also have you on a voice memo from Montauk saying that you want to kill Connor. It's a very choice segment. Something about, 'He's a bad person. He deserves to die.' Selena, I think that might have been you. Sounds familiar, right? Unlike you guys, I actually *do* cover my bases." She looked so pleased with herself. "So, if you help me finish this and stage it, we can all leave together, and then it's like we were never here. If not . . ." She paused ominously. "Then there's a good chance that one, or all, of you will be on the hook for Connor's murder." She shrugged. "And knowing how selfish all of you are, I'm guessing that's not a chance you're willing to take."

The three of us were silent. Shamefully silent. Deadly silent.

Isabel was sobbing and could barely speak. "What about Naomi? Think about her. You care so much about Phoebe. Enough to murder your own sister. But Naomi is an innocent baby, too. Just like her. And you'd be leaving her without a mother."

"Thought you'd never ask. Finally, you think of your daughter. Took you long enough." She shook her head reproachfully at Isabel. "Of course I've considered Naomi. She does deserve a family, and she'll have one. She has a sister, who she should be with. I'll come forward with Phoebe's paternity and offer to raise both girls. It'll be the right thing, an amazing opportunity for them to grow up together as sisters. I'm a fit parent, a friend of the family—I see no reason anyone will object." She practically glowed with excitement. "It's so wild—I thought I would never have even one baby. And now I'm going to be the mom of two beautiful girls." Her smile made me nauseated.

Tears streamed down Isabel's face. "Maybe you're right. Maybe I'm not the best mother, or the strongest person. Maybe Naomi could do better than me. But you're not a good mother, either. You're a manipulator and a liar. And a judgmental bitch. And a *murderer*."

"In other words, I'm a strong woman who knows my own mind and goes after what I want." *She sounds just like Connor,* I thought. "I'll take it. I've been called worse. And I'll raise those two girls to be tenacious women, too. Which is more than you could ever do."

Kira spoke again, desperation seeping into her voice. "Vanessa, we'll tell the police what you did. We're all witnesses to what's really going down here. You won't get away with it. You'll go to jail."

Vanessa laughed mirthlessly. "And where will you be if you tell, Kira? The cell next to mine!"

Selena said, bravely, "We would just tell the truth. Their prints are on the knife because they cut a cake at our group meeting. There's no reason that police and a jury wouldn't believe that, because it's actually what happened."

Vanessa looked at her with raised eyebrows. "Well, sure, you're the lawyer, so I guess you know best. But that's really a risk you want to take? It's a pretty thin alibi, and when you combine it with the voice memo and the fact that you did all have your own personal motives to kill Connor, it won't be enough. You don't really have a choice, do you? You get that, right? I'm talking you through all this as a courtesy, but the only way out for you here is to adapt to the new plan. Isabel killed Connor and then herself. That's our story." She turned to Isabel. "Look, I'll make it painless. I know exactly where on your wrists to cut to make it all go really fast. Just like I helped you with the cut on your hand. Remember? I know what I'm doing. Trust me."

Vanessa had us. Our only way back to our children and our lives was to let her have her way. But I knew that I couldn't continue with my life knowing that I had stood by and let an innocent woman be murdered.

Isabel gave herself over to begging for her life. "Vanessa, please. Please don't do this. Don't do this to my daughter. I know I'm not perfect, but—you've helped me so much. You've taught me so much about standing up for myself. I'll be better. Just please let me stay. I don't want to leave. Please. I need to be with her."

Selena had been silent for several moments but had not taken her eyes off Vanessa. I saw out of the corner of my eye that she was holding a wine bottle opener that presumably she'd taken from the bar cart. I had no idea when she'd grabbed it. She saw me register it, and our split-second eye contact communicated all we needed it to. As Vanessa slowly approached Isabel, Selena inched toward Vanessa while her back was turned. She started to raise the wine opener.

"Enough talk!" Vanessa said. "This is happening."

"No, it's not," we heard from a new, but familiar, voice. "No." Louise, Isabel's mother, had descended the stairs without any of us hearing a thing. She took a small silver pistol out of her leopard fanny pack and aimed it at Vanessa.

"Huh?" Vanessa's face failed to conceal her shock.

"Mom!" Isabel cried out, a mixture of relief and horror flooding her voice. "You're supposed to be with Naomi! What are you doing here?"

"She's at your aunt Joan's for the night. Don't worry, she's fine. I wanted to be available for *my* daughter tonight, but I knew you'd never let me, so I didn't ask. I've waited as long as I could, to try to let you girls sort this out on your own. As a mom, it can be hard to know when to let live and when to intervene. I regret standing back for as long as I did with Connor, Isabel. And I wasn't going to do that again." She glanced our way. "Get out, ladies. I'll handle this. Just leave. Now, please, girls. That includes you, Isabel. Vanessa, stay just where you are."

I felt like a high schooler being kicked out of a party by parents who'd returned earlier than expected. It was the unique sense of being both busted and rescued, both ashamed and relieved.

The four of us ran out the front door and down the stairs, not looking back, though I thought I heard Isabel whisper, "Thank you, Mom."

Chapter Thirty-Four

Tuesday, October 13

We each speed walked in different directions when we exited Isabel's house. We knew implicitly that we couldn't risk convening, being seen as a group by any witnesses.

I had no idea where to go. I was spinning out. I had Connor's blood on me. My walk turned into a half jog, if only for a way to direct the frenetic energy that was swirling around my body. The streets were still basically empty, and I hoped that to anyone who did happen to be looking, I appeared to be midworkout. It was after 1:00 a.m., but fortunately, in Manhattan, there is no weird time to go for a run.

I jogged over to Riverside Park and all the way down to the Hudson River footpath. There were even a few other runners on the path, which gave me hope that what I was doing appeared normal.

The irony of wandering around the exact spot where Isabel had supposedly gone missing was not lost on me. *How did I get here?* was what I kept circling back to. I was sure that the same question had dominated Isabel's thoughts many times over the past week, and probably years—about her situation with Connor, the arrangements she'd made with Vanessa, and of course, now, after everything that had transpired tonight. *How did I get here?* It wasn't a new question to me, either. I'd pondered it in bed holding Clara after my encounter with Connor—no, after he raped me—tears running down my face.

Connor, who was now dead and draining blood on the floor of his living room.

I peeled off my sweatshirt and dumped it in the river, leaving me wearing only my tank top. It was warm for October, just under sixty degrees, but I was shaking with chills. I splashed some of the water over my arms to rinse the blood off them. I'd never touched Hudson River water before, always kind of skeeved out by it, thinking of the possibility of dead bodies floating beneath its surface. And here I was, confirming my own suspicions about it as I disposed of my bloody clothes.

Eventually, I had no choice but to walk home. Clara would be bound to wake up soon, if she hadn't already; I'd been gone for nearly three hours. I fervently hoped that she was still asleep so that I wouldn't have to concoct some story about a late-night walk to Tim, as I'd planned to if needed.

When I got home around two—terrified I'd see someone else in my elevator, and relieved beyond measure when I didn't—I yanked off the rest of my clothes and put them straight into the washing machine, which was conveniently right by our door. I walked naked down the hall and into the bathroom and turned the shower on as hot as it would go. I took a "real" shower: I shampooed my hair, scrubbed my body all over, and shaved my legs and underarms for the first time in at least a week, cutting myself several times because my hands wouldn't stop shaking. But I wanted every trace of Connor's blood, and what I'd participated in, off my body. I have no idea how long I stayed in there, but my skin was practically purple with heat when I finally got out. I couldn't help but think of the fact that the night that I met Connor and the night that I participated in his murder ended pretty much exactly the same way: scalding myself in a shower, wondering how I would face my family and my life in the light of day.

I fumbled in the dark for sweatpants that I knew would be on the floor and pulled them on, walking over to Clara's bassinet to check on her. She was fast asleep, as was Tim in the bed a few feet away. I couldn't touch her. I felt like there was still blood on my hands, even though I'd probably never been cleaner, physically.

I crawled into bed, but as bone tired as I was, I doubted I'd be able to sleep without knowing what had happened with Louise and Vanessa. And police could be discovering Connor's body at that very moment. A neighbor could have heard something and called it in. I was sure that any minute, I'd hear pounding at our door and it would be the police, knowing exactly what I'd taken part in, ready to cuff me and take me away from my family and to jail forever. And Clara would grow up with a mom who was in prison. But perhaps Clara would be better off without me. Tim would be a great dad to her. He'd probably get remarried to someone sweet and fun, someone normal. They'd have another baby, or two, and his new wife would handle early motherhood with ease, laughing off the exhaustion and enjoying the long days of sweet cuddles. And she'd be the kind of woman to make sure to treat Clara like her own daughter. This was the kind of wife Tim should be with. Uncomplicated and good. He shouldn't have been saddled with a woman like me, an absolute mess who'd kept the truth from him and was now entangled in a murder. Whatever consequences awaited me, I deserved them.

Tim stirred as I tried to get settled in bed and shake away these thoughts. "Did you just shower?" he mumbled.

"Yeah. I couldn't sleep. Thought it might help."

"Clara doing okay?" He really was dead to the world, including our daughter, when he slept. I was so grateful that my absence hadn't even been discovered—one less lie I'd have to tell. It was too long a list, at this point. *Thank you, Clara, for not making me have to lie again,* I thought.

"Yeah. She's good." At that exact moment she let out a desolate, desperate-sounding wail. We both sighed. "Can you please give her a bottle?" I asked Tim. "I'm too tired." Really, I couldn't face her; I didn't deserve to hold something so pure and sweet. I might ruin her.

"Okay." He sounded surprised but completely willing. "We'll do it in the living room so that you can sleep." He got back out of bed, walked over to her bassinet. "Hi, baby girl. Hungry?"

I closed my eyes and thought I would never fall asleep, but when I opened them again, light was filtering through our window. Clara was asleep on the DockATot beside me, grunting blissfully, occasionally pursing her lips in a sucking motion as she slept, one hand out of her swaddle with her finger pointing at me as if accusing me of something.

I got up quietly to dress. I knew Clara would likely be awake in a minute or two, stirred by my movements and noises, and ready to eat. My plan was to feed her quickly and get out the door right away to walk over to Isabel's and see what was going on. I had no idea what to expect—police cars and ambulances, probably—but I needed to see for myself. I knew that returning to the scene of the crime was never advisable, but I lived only a couple of blocks away, after all, so my presence shouldn't have been that suspicious.

Clara woke and I fed her, grateful for the physical relief of draining my breasts and the emotional unburdening of actually doing something *good* for someone else. I put Clara's fleece suit on over her pajamas and poked my head back into the bedroom to tell Tim we were going out for a walk. I asked him if he wanted us to get him a coffee, to make it seem like that was the purpose of the outing. He was sitting up in bed scrolling through his phone and said he was impressed that we were getting out so early. I put Clara in the stroller, covering her with a thick blanket to protect her from the morning chill.

The walk to Isabel's was so short that I saw the police lights less than a minute after leaving my apartment. Her street was lined with squad cars. Isabel was standing at the top of the stairs of her town house holding Naomi, while her mom was being escorted into a police car. My heart leaped into my throat—Louise was under arrest. *Please, no.*

Then I noticed that she wasn't cuffed, which I thought—hoped, prayed—was a good sign. I didn't think I could handle seeing Louise in handcuffs, knowing the truth, what she'd done for us. Her face was stoic. She didn't see me and was in the back of the police car within seconds of me and Clara arriving.

Isabel did see me, though, and locked eyes with me from her stairs. I could tell she was crying. She nodded at me, ever so slightly. Then she turned her gaze across the street. There were Kira and Selena, looking solemn, each with their babies in carriers on their chests, standing about thirty feet apart from each other. Kira started to walk away, and then Selena followed at a distance. I could see her turn the opposite direction from Kira when they got to the corner.

I, too, turned around, and walked home slowly, never taking my eyes off Clara, terrified of the reckoning that I was sure was coming my way.

Epilogue

"Come back here, baby girl!" I call. Clara is clomping around the apartment like a maniac—her signature (and brand-new) Frankenstein walk. I wriggle into black jeans and a silky white top while simultaneously attempting to chase her down the hall. I know full well that the white top will end up covered in avocado and hummus at some point today, but I don't care. It's my favorite shirt, and it's a special day. Strange, yes, but special.

After I've wrangled her, she sits on the bathroom floor and plays with my makeup brushes, one of her favorite activities, while I put on some eyeliner and mascara and my gold hoops. When she's bored of the makeup brushes, she moves on to the roll of toilet paper, unraveling the whole thing, and then finds a box of Band-Aids under the sink and dumps it on the floor. I smile wryly at her path of destruction and pat on some lip gloss to finish up. I am significantly more made up than I normally would be on a Saturday; these days, weekends are strictly reserved for leggings and sneakers and no makeup and the playground. But today is different. Today the moms' group is reuniting for the first time since—well. Since all of it.

I haven't seen Isabel much this year. I gather she's spent some time in Tarrytown, at her mom's place. I've run into Kira and Selena at the playground a handful of times, and it's surprisingly easy between us, though we never actually make plans to see each other. We speak through the babies: "Clara, go say hi to your friend Miles! Do you guys want to go on the seesaw together? Hold on tight!" And they toddle or crawl around in each other's vicinity, a one-year-old's version of friendship, while we make the smallest of small talk: weather, work, which Netflix shows we're watching. Usually, the presence of other adults in our conversations helps us maintain these barriers we've set for ourselves. We've pretty much never spoken out loud of that night with each other, except in an unavoidable "neighborhood gossip" kind of way, when we've been forced to endure being pumped for information by acquaintances in the park: *Didn't you know her? What is she like? How's she doing? Did you ever meet the husband?* But we've never *actually* spoken about that night. It's an unspoken concession we allow each other, not forcing each other to revisit it.

I know today will change that.

We all know the official story, of course, as does everyone else on the Upper West Side. Vanessa broke into the town house and killed Connor to avenge her sister, not realizing that Louise was in the house. Louise's story was that she'd been retrieving some clothes for Isabel, who was staying at her house with the baby while she recuperated from her recent ordeal. When it got late, Louise had decided to stay the night at Isabel and Connor's town house and return to Tarrytown in the morning. She'd woken up to the sound of fighting and was scared. She knew Isabel and Connor kept a gun, for protection, high up in their bedroom closet. She acted out of fear and instinct and immediately called the police after it was done, which helped her case immensely. (She'd actually waited about thirty minutes, to allow Isabel to return to Tarrytown in a taxi she paid for with cash, so that she'd be there when police arrived at the town house and called her back to the city, already showered and changed and at the home of her aunt Joan, who was like a second mother to her.) Besides, Louise was a white grandma, which, as I'd overheard a few women at the park pointing out, made her any lawyer's ideal client. The "facts" presented themselves in a surprisingly clean fashion, given that they weren't the real facts at all: Vanessa had intruded into their home and killed Connor. Louise interrupted them, too late to save Connor but with no choice but to kill Vanessa in self-defense, after what she had witnessed. It was completely unpremeditated. It was a legal, registered firearm. (I could only guess at the various ways Connor had used the presence of the gun to frighten and manipulate Isabel.)

Of course, the detectives talked to us during their investigation, but any traces of us in the town house could be easily explained away by our meeting earlier that day—as we'd planned, in the plan we thought we were agreeing to—so we weren't suspected of anything. If there were multiple prints on the murder weapon, the police never mentioned it to us. We claimed ignorance on nearly all fronts: we had no idea Vanessa was connected in any way to Connor; we had no idea about her sister; we'd only been meeting for a bit more than a month and didn't really know her that well at all, in fact. The last part, as it turned out, was completely true. We never really knew her.

It was all over the news. Every part of the story was salacious. The hedge fund exec by day / sexual predator by night, the marital abuse, the (alleged) suicide of a young DC mother, the sister's quest for revenge, the hero grandma. It was irresistible to journalists and consumers alike and resulted in headlines like:

GRANDMA INTERRUPTS UWS MURDER—TOO LATE TO
SAVE PHILANDERING SON-IN-LAW

KILLER GRANDMA SLAYS SON-IN-LAW'S MISTRESS

Of course, Vanessa had never been anything close to Connor's "mistress," and what a word, truly, but it was a much easier headline if she was, and the *Post* usually went for ease.

HEDGE FUND MILLIONAIRE KILLED IN QUEST FOR
REVENGE

PREDATOR INVESTOR BLUDGEONED TO DEATH: AND,
AFTER LEARNING THE TRUTH, IS ANYONE SURPRISED?

WOMAN VOWS REVENGE ON DEAD SISTER'S BABY'S
FATHER (YES, YOU READ THAT RIGHT): UWS MURDERS
ENSUE

The headlines varied widely depending on who they'd decided was the most interesting player: The quick-thinking grandma? The rich, abusive husband? The vengeful, beautiful doctor? The traumatized, entrapped wife? But all of them got it at least partly wrong because none of them ever found out what only we knew: that Vanessa had killed her sister, that she wasn't really the honor-seeking avenger that even she thought she was, in her twisted logic. But in spite of myself, in spite of everything she'd put us through, I felt sorry for her. She'd experienced so much loss in her life, and her way of dealing with it was to be ruthless. To condemn and destroy any shred of perceived weakness in herself and in those she loved. Although I could never condone or even understand the things she'd done, I could also imagine the depths of her pain after losing her mother as a child, and her baby as an adult.

There would have been no way for us to safely reveal the truth anyway, and there was no reason to. For the time being, at least. When Phoebe was older, that would have to change. We would have to find a way to make sure she knew that Allison didn't kill herself—that she had wanted to be here with her, and that the opportunity to be her mom was stolen from her. But how and when we would do this could be shelved, for now. Phoebe was still just a baby. I had heard from Selena, in a brief playground conversation, that Phoebe was with Allison and Vanessa's dad and stepmom in California, but only while they figured out something permanent, because they were quite old. I vowed to myself to keep track of her, from a distance, so we could somehow find a way to reach out when she was old enough to know the truth.

Ironically, Isabel's original vision came to life after Connor was killed. Woman after woman came forward in the news, sharing their ill-fated stories of meeting Connor in a dark bar. Isabel herself never commented publicly, no doubt wanting to disappear from the headlines as quickly as possible, but I like to think she felt validated by the stories that emerged. Even if they were far too late for "plan A."

Upper West Side Moms on Facebook ate it all up, too. Everyone had an opinion about the case that they were more than happy to share.

> **Iris Chandler:** Did everyone see this? (link attached) How could this have happened in our neighborhood? I thought this was a safe family neighborhood. Sad how much the UWS has changed in the past few years.

> **Nora Howell:** Keep your husbands close and your babies closer, that's all I can say.

> **Geri Hershon:** No wonder this woman was losing her mind to the point of disappearing—she was living with a sociopathic predator.

> **Sarah Tassel:** Thoughts and prayers to everyone involved. Except the husband, who, from what it sounds like, deserves what he got.

> **Wendy Cudell:** Louise Wahrer was the attendance secretary at my high school. She wasn't to be messed with then, either. What a gem. God bless her.

Maggie Cox: What's happening with that poor baby??? She's lost two mothers now. I saw them at Starbucks once and the aunt or whatever appeared to be very loving. This is a tragic story all around.

Gina Heinz: My question is how did the wife not do anything herself about her cheating husband. Like how do you not know? I know what my husband eats for every meal and how long after eating it he takes a shit. Sorry if TMI (and maybe we need more privacy in our marriage lol) but this sounds like a case of willful ignorance to me.

Alyssa Aron: Isabel, enjoy his money honey. You earned it.

Becca Leigh: Is anyone else appalled that this family had a gun? This is Manhattan, not Texas! Do people have guns around here?! This concerns me. I always wanted to raise my daughter in the city but maybe it's time to have eyes on the burbs, after all. I mean, trigger-happy much? This Louise woman could have called the cops before just shooting people. Good grief.

Danielle Luft: I worked with Connor, back in the day. He was an asshole, to be sure, but it's always sad when someone is killed, especially since he was a dad. RIP.

Alexis Brandt: @Danielle Luft I also worked with Connor and believe me when I say that he deserves what he got. Big difference between a father and a dad, know what I mean? That guy never would have been a real dad. RIP and all, sure, but frankly, good riddance.

Emily Brown: Holy Shit. I had sex with him. Or rather, he had sex with me. I don't want to speak ill of the dead but he was NOT a nice person.

Elise Cordero: @Emily Brown OMG SAME. I wasn't gonna say anything but so glad you did. DM me please. Let's talk.

I spent way too much time reading these comments. I was tempted to reply to some, like the ones that criticized Isabel or Louise, to set them straight without revealing any privileged knowledge, but I exercised some self-control and stopped myself every time I came close.

I was caught off guard when Isabel reached out to the three of us to get together. Our unspoken agreement seemed to be to keep our distance. I have no idea what she wants, but strangely, I'm looking forward to seeing her. Seeing all of them. Just being together again. I'm surprised by my own feelings.

Equally surprising to me is that I haven't tried to bury and suppress my memories of that night, as is my usual tendency. On the contrary, I think about that night all the time. I'm traumatized by it, yes, but it's a trauma I want to own, to squish in my hands like a stress ball, to explore and make sense of.

Clara toddles ahead of me from the bedroom to the living room, surprisingly (and dangerously) quickly. She's only been walking for about two weeks, and our apartment is a whole new world to her now. Within seconds, she bounces off our coffee table and spills the last of my coffee onto a pile of student papers that I was attempting to read earlier this morning while Tim, at the gym now, took Clara out for bagels (Clara squealing with excitement and saying "Dada! Dada!" as he lifted her into the carrier for their weekly Daddy and Clara Bear-a breakfast date). I had no business leaving coffee on such a low table, but luckily there was only a sip or so left, so the spill isn't disastrous. And though it is early in the school year, my students are already used to getting their papers back a bit weathered. They're good sports about it.

This assignment was to write a response to Lady Macbeth's ruthless speech in act 1, scene 7 of *Macbeth*, when she tells her husband, "I have given suck, and know / How tender 'tis to love the babe that milks me: / I would, while it was smiling in my face, / Have pluck'd my nipple from his boneless gums, / And dash'd the brains out, had I so sworn as you / Have done to this." She's trying to make a point to Macbeth about the importance of keeping one's word, in an effort to make him keep his promise to kill King Duncan. The illustrative analogy she uses about killing her own child always appalls readers, and I know that one of the only ways to get high schoolers interested in Shakespeare is to sell its shock value. "What do we learn about both Lady Macbeth and Macbeth in this scene?" I had asked, leaving the question as open as possible to see what students homed in on. The responses were insightful if generally one note: "Lady Macbeth is manipulative and wants the throne even more than Macbeth does," one student wrote. Another put it more candidly: "Lady Macbeth is #girlpowergoals but she's also completely crazy." "Macbeth is insecure about his masculinity, and she knows it, so she uses it to get what she wants," someone astutely pointed out.

But I was most struck by a student who noticed something no one else had made much of: "Macbeth and Lady Macbeth are grieving." I sat up on the couch at that. "Lady M doesn't pose this analogy about hurting a baby as a hypothetical. She says she knows how sweet it is to love and nurse a baby. But they don't have a baby anymore. So the baby probably died, and they're mourning. And grief can make you do insane stuff. Especially losing a baby, probably. Anyway, I think her ruthlessness comes from the fact that she *was* a mother, but she's not anymore, and she doesn't know how to deal with that. Maybe she feels like she has nothing left to lose, so why not risk it all and try for the throne? She probably figures being queen will help give her purpose and ease the pain she's feeling. Unfortunately, she's probably wrong, because grief doesn't work that way." My arms were covered in goose bumps. Why were teenagers so much smarter than adults? I couldn't help but think of Vanessa—her mother's suicide, her awful miscarriage. Of course, it didn't justify what she'd done, but I felt that what I'd witnessed and heard from her that night a year ago had been nothing if not a public display of the depths of her pain.

Clara and I leave for Isabel's just before 11:00 a.m. I know Isabel will probably have an elaborate spread of food prepared for us, but I bring some bagels and lox from Barney Greengrass anyway, for good measure. As we walk, Clara smiles broadly at strangers and waves at doormen, who delight in her. I do, too, asking her more than once during our short walk, "Are you the cutest and sweetest lady in town?" It's a rhetorical question, but I like to think she knows that the answer is unequivocally *yes. Yes, she is.* She replies by saying "Mama, Mama" over and over again, and it never ceases to amaze me that I get to be the one she calls *Mama, Mommy, Mom,* or even, later, probably, *my annoying mom,* for the rest of our lives. All of it feels too good to be true, and sometimes I am tempted to pinch myself to make sure it's real—that I am hers and she is mine.

I haul Clara in her stroller up Isabel's stairs, which for whatever reason, Clara finds hilarious. The long silver door handle has been replaced by a regular old knob, and while I'd admired the elegance of the former one, I can't deny that the new knob makes the place look more homey, more approachable.

Isabel appears at the door before I can ring, smiling cautiously but warmly. Her hair is much shorter now, an artsy asymmetrical chop, almost ice blonde. It's a statement haircut and she wears it well. "Hi, Jenn," she says sweetly. "Oh my gosh, Clara, you are a big girl now. Come on in."

She leads us inside, and after parking our stroller in her entryway, we enter her living room, which looks starkly different. For starters, there is a new rug, hunter green; still, when I look at it, I can see the white rug that once lay in its place, soaked with red. The white couch has likewise been replaced with a warm taupe-colored one, which goes nicely with the new carpet. White furniture makes no sense with a toddler, anyway. There is no bar cart anymore. The coffee table that the knife lay on before Vanessa disappeared it into Connor's neck has been replaced by a cushioned ottoman. There are houseplants all over the place. Lots of toys scattering the floor.

The room looks cluttered, in a good way. Lived in. Comfortable.

The other difference that I notice is that there are no pictures of Connor anywhere. The ultrasound picture I'd admired, though, is still on display—the first picture of Isabel and Naomi together, Naomi growing inside Isabel along with her strength and resolve to escape from her husband once and for all.

Kira and Caleb and Selena and Miles are already there. Caleb is holding and shaking an enormous plant; Kira gets to her feet from the floor and hustles over to intervene in his mayhem. Miles is stuffing his mouth with a scone, getting crumbs everywhere, which Selena is admirably trying to pick up as they fall. Naomi is on the floor with them, crawling around and looking with curiosity at the comings and goings of her guests. We all exchange a too-loud, too-enthusiastic, nervous "Hiii!"

I move toward the dining table to add my bagels to the already-plentiful selection of food. A woman with her back to me is arranging muffins on a tray. For a second, I think that Isabel has hired a caterer. But then I see a leopard fanny pack on her hip. Louise.

She turns around. "Hello, dear," she says. "It's good to see you. You look wonderful." She touches my shoulder lightly, perhaps unsure if a hug might be too much, though it wouldn't be.

We all get some food and sit on the floor in the living room. I ignore the bottle of prosecco on the table and pour myself sparkling water instead. The four babies are digging into a few different toy bins, pulling out stacking blocks and an Elmo doctor kit and a tiny ukulele. They are busy and self-contained for the moment.

"It really is good to see all of you," Isabel says. "I'm sure it's been . . . a hard year, after everything. For everyone. And I never got to properly thank you. For being willing to risk everything to help me flee a marriage there wasn't any other way out of. I can never repay you. And I'm sorry. For putting you in that position, and for how it all went down. I am so sorry."

We all nod appreciatively, silent for a moment.

"It wasn't your fault," says Kira.

Selena and I nod our agreement. "And thank you, Louise," Selena adds. "We would be—well, who knows where we'd all be if you hadn't been there. You saved us. All of us."

"Not all," says Louise sadly.

"She was going to kill your daughter, though," Kira says quickly and quietly, while deftly avoiding saying Vanessa's name. "You did the only thing you could." She also doesn't say what none of us have ever said, which is that while Louise did save us that night—from digging ourselves an even deeper hole, from being arrested, from having our lives completely upended—Isabel wouldn't have died even if she hadn't been there. We wouldn't have let that happen. If it hadn't been Selena with the wine opener, we would have found another way to save her. Or we would have died trying. But we wouldn't have abandoned her. Of that I'm sure. I realize that's easy for me to say now, but it's also true.

Louise sighs. "I just wish—well, I wish it had unfolded differently, that's all. She was so turned around," she says wisely, generously.

"Thank you," I reiterate. "I can't imagine not being here for—" I look at Clara, who is trying to bury Caleb in multicolored sheer scarves. I can't find the words to describe what I'm trying to say. Louise looks at me knowingly. "Just—thank you."

"Everyone needs a mom's help sometimes," she says, reaching over to pat my hand. "Even if it's not your own mom." My eyes fill with grateful tears.

There's a knock at the door. *Please. Not another surprise.*

"Speaking of moms!" Isabel says, jumping up and running to the door.

When she returns, she's holding the arm of a thin older woman in a wool cardigan, who is holding a one-year-old.

It takes me a minute to realize that it's not just any one-year-old.

It's Phoebe. Vanessa's Phoebe. No. Allison's Phoebe.

"Everyone, this is Lucy, Connor's mom. And you obviously remember Phoebe!" Isabel confirms her identity with undeniable joy.

Lucy nods shyly at all of us. "Hi," she says.

"We got in touch after Connor passed and I asked if she wanted to be in our lives," Isabel explains. "She's staying in the city for a few days. She's been coming down from the Cape every couple months." She turns to Lucy. "How was the park?"

"Oh, it was great. I've never seen anyone who loves squirrels as much as this one does." She laughs and turns to us. "It's so wonderful being a grandmother," Lucy says, putting Phoebe down. Phoebe toddles over unsteadily to join the other babies at the toys. "I didn't think I'd ever get to."

Lucy settles into a chair and regards us all for a long moment. It's clear she has something to say, and after taking a deep breath, she says it. "I don't know how well all of you knew my son, but . . . he was angry with me. And he had every right to be. I wasn't the mother to him that I wanted to be. I regret it enormously. But this"—she looks at Isabel with appreciation—"this feels like a second chance."

Just then Naomi toddles over to her for a hug. "Lala. Lala," she says, over and over. Lucy hugs her close, closing her eyes, breathing her in for a moment, until Naomi wants to be freed to go play.

"And Phoebe . . . Phoebe lives with me and Naomi now," Isabel tells us. "That's why I wanted to have you all over today. To tell you. Because you ladies were such a big part of . . . getting us here. It's been a long process over this past year, getting everyone to agree—Allison's dad and stepmom, family court. It's an odd solution. I know that. But it also makes sense. There weren't any family members who could realistically take her long term. She could have been adopted, but the fact is that she and Naomi *are* sisters. If there's a way for them to be together, they should be. And it's not just that. I *want* her. I think I can be the mom that she deserves. She's already experienced a lot of loss in her first year of life. And I'm going to do everything I can to make sure her next years are filled with joy. I think I can do right by Allison. I'll certainly try to. And she'll have her grandparents in her life, too. *All* of them. We'll visit California twice a year to see Allison's dad and stepmom, and my mom will be around all the time helping, and Lucy will visit, too." Lucy beams with gratitude, and Louise pats her on the shoulder. Lucy reaches up and squeezes her hand, the two grandmothers clearly becoming fast friends. Isabel lifts Phoebe from the ground and kisses her cheek. Phoebe buries her head in Isabel's neck.

I look around the room with watery eyes. Kira is greeting Phoebe, still in Isabel's arms, kissing her little hands like she's a queen. Selena is chatting with Louise while also trying to clean blueberry residue off Miles's face. "Oh, Clara, you're a mess, too—I've got you," Selena says, and she reaches out to gently wipe my girl's cheeks for me.

ACKNOWLEDGMENTS

Thank you so much to YOU for reading this book! When there are so many enticing books in the world, I am grateful and thrilled beyond measure that you chose to spend some of your time with this one. I hope it gave you what you were craving. Thank you, thank you, thank you.

Thank you to my absolutely wonderful agent, Kathy Green, for seeing potential in this book from the beginning, giving me crucial and wise notes, and making me feel like I belonged in the world of writing. I could not have asked for a kinder and more encouraging agent to guide me along. I am so very lucky to be working with you, and I hope this is just the beginning!

Thank you to Jodi Warshaw for believing in this book and in me, and for making my dreams come true! Words can't describe my debt of gratitude to you. The entire Lake Union team has been a joy to work with and has made the process both organized and fun; thank you, Danielle, Erin, Jen, Gabe, and everyone who has been involved in publication, for giving my book such a warm home.

I can't sing loudly enough the praises of David Downing, my developmental editor. David, your notes were careful, insightful, elevating, funny, and just . . . right. Always right. I knew from the first page that we got each other, and because of you, the editing process was more enjoyable, addicting, and gratifying than I ever could have imagined.

And you were so nice to me . . . even when what I had written was nonsensical. Or when it was yet another f-bomb. Or when I asked inane questions about Track Changes. Thank you. You're the best.

Thank you so much to Haley, Kellie, and Sarah, for their brilliant copyediting and proofreading. Editors are wizards! Really patient ones. You'd think as an English teacher I would know when to use *whom* or where to place a modifier, but nope! As it turns out, I absolutely do not! Thank you for your extraordinarily careful eyes and consideration of the intent, and for turning this into a real, actual book.

And Eileen Carey designed a cover that I just can't stop staring at (and sometimes petting in the manner of Dr. Evil). I love it so much. Thank you, Eileen.

Thank you to my parents for making me an enthusiastic and critical reader from a very young age. I'm grateful that you weren't above occasionally bribing me to read a book, ha! Ultimately, you showed me that a love of reading means rarely being bored or lonely. Thank you, moreover, for your unconditional love and steadfast cheering on throughout my life. I hit the parent jackpot. And an additional thanks to my mom, who frequently babysat my girls while I chipped away at this book. Your devotion to your granddaughters is a bright spot in all our lives.

Thank you to my sister Ellen, beta reader extraordinaire and the best twist predictor in the game (known to finish a thriller and say "I saw that coming from the second paragraph"). If you weren't my sister, I would *definitely* want to be friends with you. (Kevin: same goes for you—you're pretty cool, too.)

A big shout-out to all my former Beacon English students: I thought I loved reading when I became an English teacher, but you all made me love it a million times more, by consistently drawing my attention to interesting details I hadn't noticed myself. I never would have attempted to write a novel had it not been for the time we spent together considering what went into them. Even on its worst day, being an English teacher was a job I loved, and that was entirely because of you. Thank you.

To the collective Magidson/Frankel/Bennett families: Thank you for your love and support, and your excitement about this book. I only wish I could have included Adam's quote on the back cover: "That's a lot of pages!" You guys are the best.

I am so lucky to have the loveliest "mom friends" (an earlier title of this book!), old and new, near and far. I'm inspired daily by your resilience, compassion, creativity, grace, and humor. Even moms I don't know always offer to help carry a stroller up or down stairs, when their own hands are full, and it just blows my mind. I hope the implicit sisterhood that I feel so strongly with all of you came through in these pages. And to the very few I told I was working on a book: thank you for rooting for me every step of the way. Lauren Quinn, I'm pretty sure I wrote this book only because you told me I should and could (and thanks for letting me borrow Clara's name). And Chrissy Daemi, thank you for reading a very early and unpolished draft, and for being so generous with your enthusiasm and time.

Thank you, Eric, for cheering me on and believing in me the whole way through. Thank you for the author photo and title help and tech support. (Microsoft Word is challenging for some people, okay?!) Thank you for resisting the urge to talk to me while I was writing (most of the time). You're the best partner to me, and the best dad to our girls. It doesn't get said enough . . . I like you! And I also love you. (No, Will Hubbard, none of the husband characters are based on Eric. Saving that for book two. Kidding!)

Lastly, thank you to my incredible girls, Zoey and Margo, for filling my life with joy and renewed purpose. I'm so grateful that I get to be your mom and frankly not sure how I got so lucky. You two are magical. *Love* doesn't even feel like a strong enough word when it comes to how I feel about the two of you, but it'll have to do: I love you, and always will.

ABOUT THE AUTHOR

Kathleen M. Willett taught English at Beacon High School for ten years. She lives on the Upper West Side of Manhattan with her husband and two young daughters. This is her first novel.